Book #1

To Lorrie from
Deron Rennick.

24/Feb/2019

The Staff of The Demon Chaser

The Staff of The Demon Chaser

Written By

Deron Rennick

Order this book online at www.trafford.com
or email orders@trafford.com

Most Trafford titles are also available at major online book retailers.

Printed in the United States of America.

ISBN: 978-1-4269-4870-1 (sc)
ISBN: 978-1-4269-4871-8 (hc)

Library of Congress Control Number: 2010917311

Trafford rev.12/07/2010

www.trafford.com

North America & international
toll-free: 1 888 232 4444 (USA & Canada)
phone: 250 383 6864 • fax: 812 355 4082

Dedication

To my friend and fellow writer, Peg Ainsley, who continued to believe in me even when I no longer believed in myself. Your screenplay has made this story even better. Also to my friend Jeanette Blackwell, who put so much love into bringing our bullybeasts to life on my book covers. Just looking at them and thinking of you makes me feel all nice and warm inside. I so love both of you ladies. Nice noogies.

Table Of Contents

TALETELLER

"Well, hello, hello, hello, hi. It is truly a pleasure to make your acquaintance. That is, assuming we have never met before. After all, this is by no means my first trip to your beautiful blue globe. Oh no. No. No. Uh-uh. Nope. But constant travel across both space and time can really sauté one's senses. Can so. Can too. So please don't have a flaming asteroid if I should know you, but do not.

"Oh, my. I've neglected to formally introduce myself. Tsk. Tsk. This certainly will not do. Will not do at all. Nope.

"Ahem. INTRODUCING THE WELL AGED, WELL TRAVELLED, INVISIBLE, INTELLIGENT AND MOST LEARNED, THE ONE, THE ONLY, (Psst – notice I left out humble), TALETELLER OF THIS BOOK!

"Actually, my full name is Me. And, of course, if I am Me, then that makes you, You. Together we're just Me and You. Ha! Hmmm. You know, if I had a chin, I'd rub it. For certain. For sure.

So. So. So. So. So. So. Just what in the name of creepy constellations is a Taleteller doing roaming about Earth, you ask. What? You didn't ask? WELL PRETEND YA DID!! Sheeesh.

I'll have you know I skipped out on this millennia's Convention of the Disorder of Galactic Gossips to be here with you in this one brightsphere solar system! The convention is taking place half of forever away and only occurs once in every thousand cycles. Now personally, I'm not at all interested in hearing tell of who actually got lost in a charted galaxy or singed themselves by flying too close to a skytwinkler. BORING. I'd much rather taletell to you. So please don't close the book on Me. Ha!

"Ah, thank you, You. Now, where was I? Oh, yes. There are actually two reasons why I'm here. One, whenever I'm feeling a little cooped up in the cosmos and fancy a good giggle, I often lighten up by traveling here to watch you earth types manage your planet. In fact, amongst aliens, Earthling jokes are really quite popular at comet-rides and other such functions. For example, have you heard about the new Earthling dolls? Wind them up and they foolishly waste irreplaceable resources! Ha! Ha! Ha! Hmmmm. Guess you have to be an alien to get that one?

"But alas, I'm also here to entertain and intrigue you. Am too. Am so. Am. Am. Besides, what I now observe going down on your planet somehow just doesn't seem really all that funny anymore. In fact, in the future I think I'll only venture here in the past. But enough about Earth. Let us get on with the tale!

"Our tale mostly takes place in the Land Of Ranidae, which lies downaway and across The Saline Sea from the Divided Continent. Or, as it is more commonly called, just The Continent. If we have met before, I may have taletelled of past events there. And if not, no matter. All you need to know to enjoy this tale is that The Continent does indeed exist and that it sustains The Fluorescent Forest, where an aged plantimal named Rimp dwells.

"But, more about it later. What really matters most if you are to understand this tale is that you should know the legend of the Demon Chaser.

"You see, millions of zillions of kawahillions of....well, a very long time ago, anyway, even before your own planet was created, a pair of wicked Demons roamed about the skytwinklers. Sworn enemies of Destiny, they set out to undo all the beauty forged over eternity. None know for certain why, although one theory has it that they were in fact jealous of Destiny's superior powers. As well as envious of both Morgue and Seed, who need answer only unto Destiny.

"Together, the resentful Demons began wreaking total havoc across both time and space, using their combined, evil might to un-anchor globes from their proper routes, thus causing them to collide with skytwinklers.

"According to legend, Destiny became enraged and created a Demon Chaser to seek out and destroy the pair. To properly carry out its task, the Demon Chaser was granted a staff. Not just any old staff, though. Oh no. Not at all, at all.

"Created by Destiny and forged of the purest of white gold, this staff grants its bearer the powers of a sixth sense. Also, at the bearer's will it hurls beams of hot light, which can actually melt stone. And, of course, slay demons. Apparently, the staff's powers can only be unpowered in the depths of any Saline Sea. Destiny made it so because the sly demons were known to lurk well beneath the whitecapped wetrollers. Thus, should they somehow defeat the Demon Chaser in morgual combat and seize the staff, eventually and inadvertently they would destroy it themselves.

"Still, should the staff ever fall into other wrong hands, all nearby creatures would suddenly find themselves in a right fine mess indeed. For certain. For sure.

"Anyway, the Demon Chaser eventually found the wicked pair sneaking amongst some fluffy, white skysheep off the rocky coast of the Land Of Ranidae, high above the Isle of Countless Caverns, to be more precise. And that is exactly where they engaged in battle for an entire Bright, until Black once more won a temporary victory in their never-ending struggle to rule the skies.

"Finally, the Demon Chaser, aided by the staff, was able to slay both Demons. However, the price paid proved to be its own being. Morgually wounded, it plummeted downward until its fall was finally broken by the Isle's rocky skin, where it met Morgue.

"But not before it managed to drag its own broken form deep into one of the countless caverns. Where it sealed the lone entranceway with molten granite, thus securing the staff for all eternity – or so it intended.

"Why then, is the staff still unfound? Excellent question. Most, most excellent.

"Three reasons come to mind. First, legend also dictates that whoever bears the staff shall grow increasingly mad over time. Only the Demon Chaser, for whom it was originally forged, was immune to such side effects.

"Secondly, the Isle Of Countless Caverns is most aptly named, with each cave appearing exactly as all the others.

"Finally, I give you the third and perhaps most important reason. Hardly a creature, mortal or otherwise, actually believes in the legend of the staff. And of those very few who do, virtually none would ever dare to seek it out.

"That is, virtually none but one…"

(pronounced - Chebek)

Xebec peered thataway from the tower of his pinkish coral castle, which squatted atop a steep plateau at the extreme thisaway end of his island.

A dim sorcerer by choice, Xebec's appearance can only be described as glumdreary, with the most-wickedest grin and the most sinister stare that there has ever been. Or ever will be.

Patience had never been one of his few assets, and this bright would prove to be no exception to this rule. He paced back and forth across the tower balcony, pausing at long intervals to view across the marshy terrain, as far thataway as his sights could see. He viewed beyond the Bay of Seabeasts to the distant coastline.

Vapors of mouthmist smoked from his silent lips. His mind, as per usual, was absorbed with a single thought. As it had been for many cycles, since he first switched from white magic to dim sorcery. He was drawn to his choice by an unquenchable thirst for power, like a famished finner unto bait. Unable to alter course, even if he so desired, he was a virtual prisoner of his own greedy ambitions.

He often remained awake during black. Pacing, always pacing. Deeply engrossed in thought, until the break of bright shattered the spell and his mind moved to other matters. Yet, the primary thought never really went away. It simply napped, awakening often to once again menace his mind. He was truly obsessed.

BOOM! BOOM! BOOM!

The pounding upon his chamber door annoyed him. But then, everything annoyed him. He entered the relaxing realm of napvisions annoyed and returned to the realm of reality equally annoyed. Skywater certainly annoyed him. The sphereshine also annoyed him. Bright and Black equally annoyed him. Skysheep. Wetrollers. Wind. Calm. Napvisions. They all annoyed him. In fact, even he annoyed him.

BOOM! BOOM!

"Enter!" Xebec shrilled.

Slowly, the door creaked open, exposing one of the multitudes of bullybeasts that served and feared Xebec. Burly characters with skinny legs, huge hairy torsos and thick arms that dangle to the ground, they propel themselves upon their hard knuckles, and whatever advantages they lack in intellect are well compensated by their sheer strength and numbers.

Smart like sticks, their superior ignorance is only surpassed by that of their senseless sidekicks, the Cruel Critters: which are only called cruel because of their swampy stench. Scaly-skinned creatures with enormous jowls and long, slurpy lickers which roll from between filthy fangs, they have webbed digits for swamp dwelling, as well as transparent lids that can cover their piercing yellow peepers. YUCK!!

"What!" Xebec snapped. "Why have you disturbed my thoughts?"

"Mastoor Xebec…" The bullybeast donned a look of utter denseness. "Sez comes from Isle. Duh – dooz find meld thing."

"The melted wall? Braindolt, are you certain?"

"Duh - ????" The bully was baffled.

"Are you sure?"

"Duh – beez sure." Braindolt replied with a nod.

Sparks ignited in Xebec's seers. "Could it be true?" he wondered. He must go and find out for himself – at once.

"Braindolt, have my Griffin readied for flight. Now!"

"Me dooz, Mastoor Xebec." The bullybeast turned and knuckled from the chamber, neglecting, as usual, to shut the door behind him.

For once, Xebec was undaunted. "Can it be?" he muttered aloud, snatching his black cloak and skullcap from wallpegs. "Have they really found it at long last? Is it possible?"

Next he scooped a black sack from the coral floor, slung it over his shoulder, and likewise exited the chamber, also neglecting to close the heavy sinkwood door.

With youthful haste, the old sorcerer bounded down a spiraled stairwell before passing through a narrow archway and slippersliding on into a wide coral antechamber. Then he strided with purpose down the long, winding corridor that descended in stages to the courtyard; indifferent to its many grim wall paintings, the meanings of which are known only to magicians and sorcerers. Others dare not ask.

His loyal griffin eagerly awaited him in the beautiful courtyard. It was a magnificent beast, with the silver body of a mature saber-tooth, and pure gold wings and the head of an eagle. Xebec had forged it himself and breathed it into being by way of dim sorcery. Many attempts had failed before he finally met with success. Subsequent efforts to produce a mate had always met with more failure. Yet, the sorcerer was still somewhat satisfied, having under his control a metallic beast capable of streaking across the above with him upon its back.

Avoiding speech, he motioned two bullybeasts to armswing aside. Paying them no further mind, he seized the flying beast's reins with one wrinkled hand, while stroking its neck with the other. With the agility of a folk half his cycles, Xebec threw a leg across the griffin's back and drew himself upright. Then he heeled it into flight.

Even at streak speed, almost a full rotation of the palesphere would elapse before they reached the Isle of Countless Caverns, which loomed atop the whitecapped wetrollers off the thataway tip of Xebec's Island.

Xebec grinned sinister as they passed over the thin ribbon of white, which separated the marshy land from the green wetrollers of the Bay of Sea Beasts. Below, several enormous spouters rolled through the wet, spitting geysers into the wind.

"Soon," Xebec muttered, "even your kind shall obey me."

Black came and retreated and came and retreated before they reached the far shore, yet they rested not. Beasts forged of precious metal were quite immune to fatigue, and its creator was himself accustomed to napping only half of his own body at any one time during long flights. Thus one wary seer could keep constant vigil for the other, whilst one hand always gripped the reins.

No, there would be no stops on this trip, at least not until they reached the Isle. Even if such required rising well above any angry black skysheep to avoid a drenching.

Eventually the marshylands gave way to Fern Forest. Covering fully one third of Xebec's Island, it sprawled in all directions like a rolling carpet. Its emerald and blue form was only broken by shinesilver aquaveins and its inner body crawled with creatures, both big and small.

Xebec muttered, "Soon, all below shall serve only me."

Bright and Black fought many pitched battles before the griffin cleared the far edge of Fern Forest. Again passing over marshyland, it straddled the upaway rim of The Baobabs, where the treefolk grow so large you can get lost in their trunks. Entire communities of chirpers nest upon every bough. Sphereshine seldom strikes soil. The Baobabs were indeed a most dark and mysterious place where peepers peek from the shadows and scary sounds shiver your skin.

Xebec himself had never dared venture into that place. Nor would he, unless he possessed the staff. Even then, conquest in the Land Of Ranidae had priority.

Finally, after what to the impatient sorcerer seemed like forever, they at last cleared the last ribbon of sand which divided soil from sea and veered due thataway.

Not far distant loomed the bleak outline of the Isle of Countless Caverns, its grey peaks stabbing holes in the body of soupmist, which always choked its base. Always. Be it Bright or Black, warm semicycle or cool, be there sphereshine or skyshowers, skytwinklers or naught, the thick soupmist never waned. It steamed one's skin and boiled one's bones.

Even though the metallic griffin would itself be unphased by the soupmist, it nevertheless rose well above the scalding spray. Many past visits had conditioned it so Xebec needn't utter commands. The loyal beast simply avoided the hothazard by instinct and flew directly for the highest peak.

Scald Summit, with her flowing orange ooze cooking in her bowled apex. The mountain, who, when awrathed, spat glowing cinders at the sky and spilled white, molten magma over her rim. And often caused the entire isle to tremble.

Like the lingering soupmist, Scald Summit never waned. Always, she hissed and crackled, and breathed smoke – an ominous warning to intruders. **"CHALLENGE ME NOT!!"**

Xebec wondered if the staff could tame her?

But for now, the griffin heeded her warning' maintaining a safe distance from her apex, and flapping towards that of her slightly smaller sister, Slumber Summit, whose bowled apex was cooled, bumpy and hard. She never uttered a sound, not even a gaseous yawn.

Several bullybeasts stood stooped within Slumber's bowl, supporting their huge, hairy torsos upon their hard knuckles.

Near them lazed some cruel critters, their long, slurpy lickers licking the ground. YUCK!

As the griffin touched solid, the biggest bullybeast knuckled up to Xebec. "Mastoor Xebec, we dooz find meld thing."

"Show me!" Xebec demanded. "And have my griffin wetsponged and polished."

The big bullybeast frantically motioned with his huge, hairy hands and all others took to the task. Except for the cruel critters, of course; they being much too tardy of wit to risk attempting such tricky chores.

Xebec glanced about the bowl. "Where?"

"Dooz go blue path…"

"Don't tell me!" Xebec snapped. "Show me!"

The big bully turned and knuckled his way across the bowl's bumpy surface, declining further comment, lest he be scolded. Or worse…

Slightly shy of the bowlsides, the big bullybeast and Xebec entered a yellowish cage, which was weaved of strong hollow chutes. A thick vine was knotted to a metal ring on the roof, from which it stretched straight upward until it reached the sturdy boom of a huge overhead hoist; which jutted well out past the upper lip. Many beastly faces peered down at them.

Somewhere beyond the lip, unseen hands commenced cranking a creaky winch and the cage began to rise. It swayed and spun slightly as the vine slowly slid through the grooved rims of sinkwood pulleys, enroute to the spindle. Only the wind answered the winch.

Xebec stewed in serious silence. Could they have truly found the melted wall? Was it possible after all these cycles of seeking? Or did he once again travel the breadth of his island for – FAILURE?

The very word caused him to gnash his biters. It reddened his cheeks. Quickly, he erased the vile thought from his mind and patted the black sack. Could its contents burst through the wall? Could anything?

"I shall succeed," he muttered as the boom swung about and cleared the bowl lip. "I shall. I shall. I shall."

Xebec stepped from the cage without acknowledging the presence of others. His serious stare stayed all speech, save for his own. "Make haste."

The big bullybeast nodded, then turned and knuckled his way over to a huge slab of stone. A blue arrow was dyed on the side of it. Aiming down the steep and rugged incline, it pointed precisely at a boulder far below. A second blue arrow on the boulder indicated a slight change of direction, guiding whosoever obeyed it to yet another arrow. And so on. And so forth. All quite necessary to keep one from becoming hopelessly lost in the terranean maze of crevices, craters, chasms, cliffs and corners, each of which appeared much like the last. Even so, a good many bullybeasts had vanished trying to find Xebec's prize.

Plus there were the caves – more than a hundred scholars could count in a hundred cycles. Home to silkspinners and blackwings, they served as black mouths for the tunnels that led down into a labyrinth of countless caverns and catacombs. Where green stoneswirls twisted from ceiling to floor and drips echoed like skybangers. It was an eerie, awful place where the dampness chilled breath and shivered skin – a place where no breeze had ever blown.

This was the mythical dwelling den of the Chimera, a ferocious, hoofed monster with a maned head and a dragon's tail; which only awakened to the smell of fresh flesh.

Together, Xebec and the big bullybeast zigged and zagged their way down from the summit, guided by the blue arrows. They struggled with great difficulty to maintain their balance whenever the pitch of the hazardous trail dropped down too steep, or narrowed to a squeeze. As it most often did.

Occasionally, they were forced by circumstance to straddle bottomless rifts, or tippydigit along narrow ledges to avoid an abyss.

Being accustomed to armswinging, the big bullybeast in particular found such moment's breathbating at best. Always mindful that one errant step of his unskilled foots could mean an early meeting with Morgue, he was also wary of the obsessed sorcerer at his back. So, with many a gulp, he pressed on.

Eventually, their tricky trek led them to the gaping mouth of a tunnel. A pair of bullybeasts and a cruel critter stooped sentry outside whilst an unattended torch flickered within. Secure in its metal bracket, the torch bent light in silent rhythm for a troop of dancing wallshadows.

Xebec ignored all gestures of greeting and stomped directly for the torch. Snatching it into one wrinkled hand, he then nodded for the big bullybeast to lead on.

Despite the torch flame, a chilldamp breeze nipped at their nostrils and hearers. Nip. Nip. Nip. Like frosty breath rolling across ice.

At least until they rounded the first bend. Then the wind slept and all was still. Still and silent and cold. Very, very cold. Blue crystals coated the walls.

"Lead on," Xebec prodded, seemingly indifferent to the temp.

As the pair descended deeper and deeper into the Isle's innards, the stillness and silence grew. And grew. AND GREW. Until they could hear themselves shiver in sync with their chattering biters.

Yet Xebec refused rest. Drawing fresh torch sticks from strategically placed supply barrels, he pressed onward. Down and around and down again, until suddenly the temp began to climb – rapidly.

Finally the big bully braved a question. "Mastoor Xebec, dooz beez so hot?"

"We have passed into Scald Summit's belly. Molten magma flows through her veins."

"Huh? Dooz ye sez?"

Xebec was annoyed, yet simplified his explanation. "The mountain's belly is so hot that it melts stone. See how the wall crystals are melting."

It was true. Little blue droplets glistened upon the tunnel walls and ceiling. The surface became slippery as dew upon ice. Breath ceased spouting in vapors and hearers burned from a thawing. Yet the silent stillness stayed. The pair could almost hear each other's thoughts.

Soon the tunnel surface became patched by slushpuddles, but planks had been placed across the deeper ones, and the pair's progress was unhindered.

Eventually they rounded a bend and sighted an orange brightbeam far in the distance, beyond a steep incline.

Xebec quickened his pace as the brightbeam shone nearer. His breath grew labored and skindew soaked his garments. Both legs stretched and pained as he hastened to exit the now sweltering tunnel. He could feel its walls closing in about him. Squeezing him. Trying to trap him like the insides of a serpent.

Suddenly he was free. Huffing and puffing, he stood on the narrow licker beyond the tunnel's inner mouth, grinning and gawking at the strange spectacle before him.

He had entered a cavern unlike anything he'd ever imagined. Bigger! Beautiful! Brilliant!

Its concave walls were highly luminous. Sparkling orange and clear crystals provided plenty of rosy light. Blushing pink stoneswirls twisted upward to support a refulgent red ceiling, which was likewise decored with colorful clusters of crystal. A green, mossy mat covered the flat floor and effervescent pools shone like turquoise gleamglass.

Freakish flowers grew near the pools, with stems not unlike limbs and flushed petals about emerald peepers. They blinked up at the intruders, and Xebec was certain some moved.

“There,” Xebec stated, pointing at some flowers. “One must have just submerged itself in that pool. See how the surface is now rippled.”

“Beez bad thing lurks in pool.” the bullybeast said.

“Like what?” Xebec inquired.

The big bullybeast merely shrugged his broad shoulders.

Xebec would have pressed the issue, except just then he spied the upper rungs of a vine and floatwood ladder, which had been spiked to the wall adjacent the ledge. Grabbing hold of the ladder, he carefully stepped out onto the first rung and eagerly began his descent.

“Wait until I am clear!” he ordered, already concerned about his clumsy guide slipping and then snagging him along for the crunch.

Numerous nods elapsed before Xebec felt the solid surface beneath his soles. Releasing his hold on the vines, he beckoned for the big bullybeast to follow. Then he turned to once again inspect the immense cavern, and gasped in gawk. The freakish flowers had vanished, yet all the pools were smooth of surface!

"OOOOPZ!"

Xebec reacted just in the bat of a blink to avoid being squashed beneath fifty stones worth of falling bullybeast.

However, Destiny smiled upon the big clutz. His thick skull absorbed all of the initial impact. Therefore, although dazed and dizzy, the tough bullybeast avoided any serious injury.

Xebec glared in disgust at the clumsy oaf, who had somehow managed to press himself aknuckle and smile. Briefly. Before both blank seers spun back into his swelling brow and he pitched forward to enter the relaxing realm of napvisions.

"Dung!" Xebec cussed, "Now how shall I find the others?"

He slowly scanned the luminous cavern, which twinkled and shined all about him, noting that the luminous walls were broken by a multitude of recesses and caves. Yet no other bullybeasts were about.

"Hmmppff," he grumbled, dipping a wrinkled hand into his cloak.

Retrieving a tiny glass vial from the inner pocket, he quickly removed the cork. Quick as a blink, a ghostly haze spewed forth from captivity and swirled about the sorcerer.

Xebec raised both arms high as he chanted:

"OH, DIM SORCERY – ABET WITH THIS SPELL…

INSPIRE THIS HOUNDHAZE TO SERVE ME QUITE WELL…

MY GUIDE IS WITH NAPVISIONS, FROM THE LADDER HE FELL…

LET IT SNIFF OUT THE SPOT WHERE MY BULLYBEASTS DWELL…"

The hazy apparition ceased swirling and began to drift across the mossy mat. Gently. Effortlessly. As if drawn by a strong draft - yet the cavern's aura was still?

Only its subtle sniffing broke the silence as it floated mere digits atop the mossy mat, tracking a scent. "Snff – Snff – Snff," ever increasing its speed.

Xebec panted and cussed as his aging limbs struggled to keep the houndhaze in sight. For what seemed like forever, he chased after it. Along brilliant corridors and around hidden corners, winding in and out of pink stoneswirls, about pools, beneath arches and hanging pointy things, across moss and rough crystal it went.

He worried his breathers might burst. Then, just when he could chase it no further, the houndhaze vanished, its adept task fulfilled. It was at last free to hide and haunt.

Using each other as pillows, about a dozen bullybeasts snoozed atop the moss in one large pile of lumpy fur that breathed up and down in unison. There were some cruel critters nearby, too, but Xebec's stare was not upon them. He saw only that section of wall directly behind the snoring sentries.

Unlike the rest of the cavern, there the wall was clear and smooth, like it had been poured as a liquid and then cooled with care. Although much too thick to sight through, one could certainly feel the source of vibrant energy emanating from deep within. And the circular section glowed not unlike a full palesphere.

Still panting and fully fatigued, Xebec staggered up to the melted wall and pressed both palms against its smooth surface. Vibrant warmth rushed up his arms and into his weary body. At long last he had found what he sought. Too fatigued to cheer, he merely smiled and pressed his cheeks tight against the warm surface.

"Mastoor Xebec…?"

The sorcerer turned about to encounter many burly shapes stirring about him.

"Bullies dooz good thing – huh?" one asked.

"Tools!" Xebec demanded. "Have you the boring tools?"

"Dooz got," several voices responded in unison.

"And buckets?"

"Got," replied the burly bunch, each nodding as he spoke.

"Then fill them with water from the ponds whilst I mark out the wall for drilling."

All seers gawked at him.

"Well, what are you all waiting for?"

"Beez monster lurks in pool," replied one of the bullybeasts.

"A monster?" Xebec inquired skeptically.

"We dooz heerd roar," informed another.

"Oh you did, did you?" Xebec's tone revealed much cynicism.

Every bullybeast wided seers and nodded its head.

Xebec smirked sarcastic. "And exactly where is this monster?"

His question was met with lowered seers and shrugging shoulders. The cruel critters skulked away, determined to avoid Xebec's wrath.

"Well?" Xebec pressed.

An abnormally thin bullybeast dared step forward to speak. "We heerd hooves clopping."

"Ooooooh – hooves clopping?" Now Xebec's tone was beyond taunting.

"A – And a splash…"

"Oooooohh – and a splash?"

"Uh – huh," replied the bullybeasts.

"Phooey!" Xebec scoffed, reaching inside his sack. "The only monster you'll encounter this bright is Me! Now fetch what I ask...MOVE!!"

Panic erupted as the bullybeasts scrambled to do the sorcerer's bidding. All feared the monster, but they doubly feared him. None amongst them wanted to risk a scolding. Or worse...

Xebec scowled and produced a sinkwood peg from the sack. His plan to break through the wall was quite simple, yet ingenious.

The pegs were to be soaked in water. Meanwhile, he would keep the bullybeasts busy boring holes into a portion of the wall. Trial and error on granite faces had proved it best not to space the pegs beyond two hands apart. Therefore, he himself would mark out the points of drilling, knowing all too well the mathematics skills of his hairy servants.

Then, once all necessary holes had been drilled, the saturated pegs were to be pounded into them like plugs. Prior experiments had proved that sinkwood does indeed shrink when wetted. Plus, it expands when dried. Xebec's gamble was that the heat and energy from the wall would dry out the pegs quite quickly, and that the ensuing pressure produced from such rapid expansion would split the smooth surface of the wall. This, he reasoned, should enable the powerful bullybeasts to break out chunks with weighty iron swingbashers and stonesplitters. All that would be required was a hole just big enough for him to slip through. Then the staff would be his!

Prodding digits into his cloak, Xebec produced a white stick of chalk. Next, employing his own hand to gauge spacing, he marked out the wall, carefully plotting each X into its exact proper place.

Eventually, the bullybeasts returned with full buckets.

"What, not eaten by monsters?" Xebec teased as he spilled the sack's contents into the wooden pails. "Good. Now you can all share in the work. And do put your backs into it. I want to hear those boring bits hum. We shan't neither nap nor nourish until our deed is done."

Several bullybeasts fetched some heavy metal augers from a battered old box and immediately set to work armcranking the steel bits aspin.

Boring into the clear stone proved to be a most arduous task indeed, and soon every bullybeast was puffing amoist. Beads of skindew danced atop their thick 'skulz'. Backs ached with each twist and forearms were numbed. A fine, clear dust stung into their seers and moved them to sneeze.

Yet they slogged on and on, even making a game of their labors. They competed to see which team could bore out a hole to the desired depth first, with the winners of each heat being rewarded with a vigorous round of knuckle-noogies upon their thick skulls. Awarding knuckle-noogies was a strange and confusing ritual, which never ceased to puzzle Xebec, yet seemed to be very serious stuff to the bullybeasts.

Xebec thought, at least it keeps them working.

After ample drilling, they finally managed to bore out enough holes that Xebec instructed two of them to begin pounding in pegs, and the dullhollow crack of mallet meeting sinkwood echoed off the luminous walls.

Save for the knuckle-noogie rituals, the bullybeast's toil continued uninterrupted until all the necessary pegs were pounded into place. Only then did Xebec permit the dusty bunch to nourish on fruit and nuts – and, of course, desserts. While he commenced with a chant.

"MAGICAL SINKWOOD, BACKWARDS YOU ARE…

WHEN WET YOU SHRINK UP, THEN DRY LARGER BY FAR…

THE BULLYBEASTS WILL DRILL, THEN IN YOU WILL GO…

WE WILL REST WHILE YOU DRY, THEN THIS ROCK WALL WILL…

BLOW!!"

Once they'd all greedily stuffed their mouths and bellies full, and finished with the mandatory round of post-meal noogies, the bullybeasts all quickly armswung over to a corner of the cavern, where they commenced to use each other as pillows and cuddled into a pile of lumpy fur which breathed up and down in unison.

Shortly thereafter, the pegs began to dry out and expand. Soon one tiny wee crack, thin as a thread, started to slowly sneak across the smooth surface. Zigging and zagging. Seeking.

Another appeared, followed by yet another. Then another one still, until an entire network of fine, thread thin cracks crisscrossed the surface like a silkspinner's net. Next, the crackling of rock became so loud that it awakened the breathing pile of fur.

Xebec was beside himself with uncharacteristic joy. Perplexed bullybeasts exchanged quizzical glances as the smiling sorcerer swaggered over to the battered old toolbox and attempted to retrieve one of several weighty, iron swingbashers. However, it proved to be much too heavy for his frail frame to even budge.

Gloating with glee and in a cheery tone, he requested, "Could some of you fine bullybeasts perhaps assist me?"

More quizzical glances were exchanged. Somebody whispered, "Me thinks Mastoor Xebec beez boink?"

"I'm waiting." The tide of uncharacteristic joy was already ebbing from Xebec's tone, plus the smile was slipping back into a scowl. "And you all know it is most impolite to keep a sorcerer – WAITING!"

At once, the bullybeasts leapt aknuckle and armswung over to the toolbox. After retrieving the swingbashers and some iron stonesplitters, they hurried back to the wall and began bashing the stonesplitters into the cracks, exactly where Xebec indicated.

Large chunks of clear stone were gradually loosened, then removed with heavy swingspikes. It was a slow and fatiguing feat, which required much puffing and skindew.

Yet, the obedient bullybeasts simply wiped their wet palms upon their loincloths, gritted their chompers, and continued with their task. Relentless. Determined. Eager to please the sorcerer and avoid a scolding. Or worse…

On and on and on and on they slugged, with neither rest nor complaint, swinging bashers and spikes.

Until eventually, just when Xebec considered granting them a brief rest to replenish, it happened. One of the swingspikes pierced a tiny peephole through the clear surface. A blue streak of hot light beamed forth from within.

Xebec tried to peek inside, but the brilliance stung into his seers. "Work!" he shrilled. "Swing harder! Faster!"

Now every swing seemed to remove a chunk, each blow widening the gap until it was large enough for a thick serpent to slip through. Or even a thin sorcerer.

"Enough!" Xebec commanded, waving the bullybeasts aside. "Push me through the opening. Now!"

Yet, try as they might, the bullybeasts simply could not force the irate sorcerer through. They stared, confused, as his feet and legs flailed wildly at the air.

"Me noze!" one of the bullybeasts suddenly piped up, looking very smug. "Me rams Mastoor Xebec through with thick skull!"

All the other bullybeasts cheered as one of their number lined up the sorcerer's squirming buttocks, then lowered his thick skull and armswung full speed into his target.

"Eeeyyeeow!!"

"Hoorray!" cheered the bullybeasts as the hole became dislodged. Then they became too engrossed in granting one of their own a required round of congratulatory noogies to take note of the screaming and cursing pouring forth from the other side of the glowing wall.

Xebec crashed to the floor, bruising his back and grabbing his cramping buttock with one hand. Sealing his lids, he tried to arm-shield his face from the brightness. The searing heat within scratched at his flesh. His throat became parched, and his breathers puffed and pained. Skindew drenched his garments and they became heavy. Saline drops trickled between his lips, and stinged under his lids.

Finally, the determined sorcerer pressed astand. With one outstretched hand, he stumbled toward the unseen source of heat. The floor was cluttered with hard objects that rolled beneath his soles, and he knew at once that they were bones.

"M-M-Must h-hurry," he panted, "B-Before flesh blisters."

His nostrils nabbed the biting stench of singed chinhair. "M-Must find staff. M-Mustn't meet Morgue…"

He could feel his exposed skin glowing. In sheer desperation, he began groping with his free hand.

"Yeeoww!" he screamed as the searing wall scorched his digits. His hide slippers were beginning to smolder.

"Where?" he shrilled in a panic. "Where?"

Then he was answered. His palm slapped about a solid shaft. Smooth. Hard. Warm, yet not uncomfortably so. And instantly the brightness dimmed into a dull glow -whilst the heat ceased its rage.

"Yes!" he screamed, lifting his lids and brandishing the gold staff in triumph. "At long last, I finally have my prize! IT…IS… MIIIIIIIIIINE!!"

Silence followed the sorcerer's outburst. Not just within the cave, but everywhere. Across the Isle of Countless Caverns and beyond, all beings of breath could sense that something was suddenly very wrong. Back at Xebec's castle, Braindolt shuddered as if from the cold at the exact same instant that the sorcerer gripped the staff. In Ezu, sheebullies with knots of ribbon-tied hair in the center of their thick 'skulz' stopped drawing wet from a well and looked to the above for the source of the odd feeling they'd just experienced. All along The Sweet River, entire villages of Cyclops farmers ceased their toil to sense the danger in the air.

On The Sweet Sea, humanfolk dropped their nets and huddled together for comfort. In the Swallow Mountains, a lone ladfolk with a long tie-tail of black hair gazed upwards at the skysheep. And even as far away as The Divided Continent, Lizarme soldiers and Black Apes stopped in mid-battle to fill their nostrils with the smell of fear pervading the entire Universe. Almost as if all creatures could sense an impending doom – yet knew not why, nor from what?

Firmly gripping the staff with both hands, Xebec pointed the tip at the melted wall. Then donning an exaggerated smirk of satisfaction, he commanded the glowing object, "Staff, do my bidding!"

Instantly, a beam of hot light bolted forth and struck the wall, cutting through the clear stone like a blushing blade through churned cream.

Xebec skillfully directed the beam, tracing out a circle pattern large enough to step through, then he oscillated the staff tip until the center melted away.

Bones crunched beneath his hot soles as Xebec stomped towards the opening, barking commands at the bullybeasts.

But the terrified bunch had already scattered and hid, refusing to heed his calls.

He cared not, however, for at last he had his prize. He sensed that it would lead him out of the caverns.

Across rough crystal and moss, beneath hanging pointy things and stone arches, about still pools, winding out and in of pink stoneswirls, around hidden corners and along brilliant corridors he went.

Somehow, he just knew the way without concentration or memory, and somehow he sensed that something was watching his every move. There was something unheard and unseen lurking nearby, stalking him as prey.

Only Xebec was well aware of its presence, and its intentions. Tightening his grip about the shaft, he nervously muttered an inaudible challenge, daring danger to expose itself.

"EEEEEEEEEEEEEEEEEEEE!!!" wailed a scream of attack.

Shimmering liquid splashed across Xebec's garments as a hoofed monster emerged from the depths of an effervescent pool and pounced upon the mossy bank; mere strides from its intended quarry. Foam frothed from its fanged mouth and its thick, dragon's tail whipsnapped the air. Its forked licker flickered in and out, and Morgue glared from its crimson peepers.

Initially frozen with fear, Xebec narrowly averted being struck by his assailant's lethal tail. He stumbled backwards and fell upon his back.

"EEEEEEEEEEEEEEEEEEEEE!!" The creature once again whipsnapped its tail, nearly dispatching its victim to meet Morgue.

The breeze blowing upon Xebec's brow thawed his thoughts. He pointed the staff. "Do my bidding!"

Instantly, a beam of hot light bolted forth from the tip and, in the bat of a blink, the ferocious Chimera was burned into swirling dust. Then gone!

Although still somewhat shaken, Xebec managed a wicked grin. "It seems my prize is most precious indeed."

Springing afoot, he turned and sprinted for the tunnel's inner mouth. Newfound strength gushed through his aging limbs. His senses told him to make haste as he scaled the vine ladder like a nuteater up sinkwood. Then he hopped onto the licker.

Upon entering the sweltering tunnel, he could again feel its stone walls squeezing in about him, trying to trap him. He could feel it pulsing as it constricted and he knew he must hurry.

Scald Summit would not surrender the staff so easily. It had been her treasure for far too long and no mere mortal was going to snatch it from her belly without a fight! **NEVER!!**

Even before the enraged mountain trembled, Xebec braced for the jolt. Battering blasts of wet wind slammed him repeatedly against the tunnel walls. Without pity.

"NEVER!!" howled each blast**. "NEVER!!"**

"Staff – fare us well!" Xebec shrieked, as Scald Summit's hot breath pinned him as her prisoner. The staff vibrated violently before unleashing a shield of light. More newfound strength invigorated Xebec's limbs. The staff had been his obsession for far too long, and no mere mountain was going to snatch it from his grasp without a fight. "Never! Never! Never!" he screamed.

"NEVER!! NEVER!! NEVER!!" Howled each blast of breath. Searing, melted stone turned a bright crimson and started to flow through Scald Summit's veins.

"Staff!" Xebec shrilled, as the searing crimson of the mountain pumped and splashed its way around a distant curve and sizzling cinders slapped off the protective shield. "STAFF!!"

The staff jerked and twisted so that much effort was needed to keep it in his grip. It quickly weaved a bubble of protective light about its new bearer, completely encasing both itself and him.

Xebec pumped his burning thighs forward with vigor well beyond any mortal's limit, sourced fully from the staff. Slowly the bubble began rolling atop the searing crimson liquid, which attempted with molten vengeance to bite through its contoured armor of light.

Sizzling white cinders continued to slap at the spherical shield while Scald's hot breath hurled debris at it. Ugly, black smoke sought to strangle it. The tunnel walls tried harder than ever to squeeze it.

Yet onward and upward it rolled. Faster and faster. Across the raging river of hissing embers and boiling liquid it went, bouncing off the numerous jagged chutes that sought to crush its shell!

All the while, it protected the staff-bearer within. It even melted into flaming fluid those boulders which tumbled to block its path and prevent their escape.

In desperation, Scald Summit tried every possible means to stop the spinning sphere. She shook! She smoked! She split, spat and spewed! Until finally she awakened her sister from her eternal slumber.

Together, they spoiled the above. Their black, tumbling breath blocked out the brightsphere. The entire Isle trembled beneath them. Tall geysers of gas and steam burst through their crust. Boulders bounded down their barren bodies as they spilled their peaks and flexed their combined muscles of magma. Their lesser brethren slid into the boiling sea, which hungrily swallowed them whole!

But the staff, too, possessed incredible power. The bubble seared a swath through Scald's fossiled flesh, spinning increasingly quicker until, like a charging skytwinkler, it split open her stony shell and bounced down her back to her base.

For several long, terrifying nods, the dizzy sorcerer struggled to re-focus. Everything swirled around him, and he was unable to stand. Still, he clenched tight his prize.

Eventually, his blurry vision did clear and he sighted through the transparent orb, and then gasped. A mighty morass of molten wrath was flowing down to engulf them!

"Staff – into the sea!"

Without hesitation, the bubble rolled across Scald Summit's base and spun over a cliff.

Xebec could feel his innards coil as they plummeted towards the steaming cauldron below. Down…down…down…down… down……..

"SPLASH!!"

They plunged deep below the wetrollers, to where bubbles seldom go, then shot swiftly back upwards to break the choppy surface. Still dry and aglow, they bobbed and spun amongst the splashcraters.

Xebec squeezed the staff firm against his torso. He felt ill and uncertain. Already, the protective bubble was dissolving and losing its protective powers. If one drop of wet should touch the staff, then his prize would be lost forever. What to do?

Then the silver claws of a saber-tooth plucked the bubble from the foam and spray. And the gold wings of an eagle whisked Xebec and his prize off to safety.

TALETELLER

"Wow! Whew! Wow! Whew! Wow! Wow! So! So! So! Top that for a tumtwisting escape! Whooaa! I'm dizzy from just telling you about it!

"And check out the power of that staff! Awesome! Awesome! Aw-Aw-Awesome! Imagine taking that to class for show and tell. Straight A's from then on. HA! Hmmmm?

"But alas, there is a most serious side to these events. Oh yes, yes. For the staff is now in the wrong hands. Very wrong hands. And many creatures of breath have suddenly found themselves in a right fine mess indeed. For certain. For sure.

"Xebec never even returned to his coral castle for more than two cycles. Uh-uh. Noper.

Instead, the dim sorcerer had his loyal griffin swoop downaway over The Baobabs and on across the channel to Ezu, City of the Bullybeasts. Of course, the bullybeasts and sheebullies were already so frightened of him that there was no reason to remind them who was boss. Yet Xebec torched the city core anyway. Just for laughs!

"Next, Xebec began flying about Ranidae, exerting his authority over many creatures – great and small.

The staff itself was simply more powerful than all the armies in all the kingdoms in all of all. Was so. Was too. For certain. For sure. And the normally passive inhabitants needed few demonstrations of its awesome power to encourage their surrender. Although some chose to flee into the forest rather than succumb to the sorcerer's wicked will.

"Cycity fell next when Xebec melted its defensive wall. Upon witnessing the golden weapon's fierce force, the Cyclops King sued for peace and thus spared his beloved city from complete annihilation. Then he reluctantly ordered his subjects to obey all the sorcerer's new decrees, including the one demanding absolute obedience to him.

"However, a few Cyclops disobeyed their own ruler and sneaked out of the city under cover of black, determined to maintain their freedom. Did too. Did so. Did. Did. Did.

"From Cycity, Xebec flew upriver to Folkton, where the humanfolk dwell. He, of course, made certain to wreak havoc in each hamlet along the way.

"Again, the terrified inhabitants surrendered without a fight. Although some fled into the forest, where they joined with their large neighbors in a united struggle to remain free.

"Finally, after two cycles of relentless seeking, Xebec discovered the whereabouts of The Hidden City.

"The Hidden City. Home to the Mighty Mugwumps. Beefy, blue beasts with big feet and nasty dispositions. A most mysterious species, which greatly prizes its privacy.

"But unlike the other victims of Xebec's evil ambitions, all of the mighty mugwumps simply refused to become his servants. Under cover of black, they sneaked away from their ancient city and stole upthataway. Every single last one of them. They did. They did.

"In orderly file, they stomped all the way to the right bank of the Deep River, where the fiendish finners lurk: the fiendish finners being malicious little biters that in great numbers can quickly strip a burly beast to bone in bits! Chomp! Chomp! Chomp! Eeeeeeee…

"After dropping thick sinkwood planks over the murky waters, the mugwump column cautiously filed across and vanished into the darkest depths of the Dismal Jungle. Where they still dwell to this very bright, greatly prizing their privacy.

"Xebec was furious! He'd wanted their might and nasty dispositions to help keep the other beings in line. Plus he'd wanted them to hunt down all the deserters who'd fled into the forest, and he would have granted the blue beasts some degree of autonomy in exchange for such loyalty.

"So, in retaliation for their defiance, the entire Hidden City was melted into molten mush. In fact, virtually everything in it was so thoroughly destroyed that the former inhabitants could never return even if they wanted to.

"Then, in a huff, Xebec finally returned to his pinkish coral castle to plot his future conquest of the Divided Continent and to oversee the new order of things in Ranidae. His order. And he began learning the distinct loco-laugh of one going mad.

"So-so-so then. Of what more can I tell? Oh, do not close the book on me yet, You. Ha! Hmmmm? For there remains much more to be told. Much, much, much more.

"We shall now pick up on our tale in a distant land. The Divided Continent, which lies far upaway beyond The Saline Sea.

"More specifically, our tale continues in the tall graingrass that grows in golden abundance all along the inland fringe of the Fluorescent Forest, which itself lies as far downthisaway as one can travel on The Continent.

"There, a young galfolk named Shoenia is being hotly pursued by a Lizarme military unit, against whom her kind and their ape allies are at war..."

Shoenia

The young galfolk's golden skin blended well with the tall graingrass all about her. Long, straight hair, white and shiny-fine, draped about her neck and shoulders. Her alert, emerald seers scanned between the stalks in search of movement, and her hearers sought to snag sound. Breath alone passed between her full, cherry lips.

No stranger to combat, her firm yet slender frame bore the scars of many past scraps. Yet her beauty was unique beyond compare. She bore slimsolid limbs and possessed a strong, ladfolk's grip; the result of much warrior training. Plus she had keen wits to match.

She was clad in a soiled hangtop and pouched skirt, each woven of tough cloth and dyed rust. Her nimble feet were concealed by well-worn slipperboots. A hefty hurling blade was asheath to one calf. In her dirty digits she gripped a sinkwood scrapstick.

Bellybees buzzed about her knotted-up guts as she crouched low to avoid detection. Her knees near knocked and her pumper pounded her heaving chest. Painful cramps bit at her thighs and back, yet she dared not move.

Her thoughts reflected back. It had been a most costly battle for both sides. She wondered if any other humanfolk had sneaked free?

Three brights past, her unit had been ambushed by a much larger enemy contingent, which was accompanied by a pack of those vicious canine lizards with twin tails and fluorescent fangs. Rexids! Just thinking of them shivered her spine.

Somehow, she had managed to slip undetected through the Lizarme ranks and flee into the tall graingrass. Since then, she had somehow managed to keep herself hidden and upwind of the enemy, while constantly on the move and often praying of Destiny to keep her concealed from the winged phantoms seeking from above and their scaly Lizarme riders.

Thus far, Destiny had complied, and the young galfolk's position was not betrayed.

For two long and napless brights, she had stolen due thisaway in a vain search for more humanfolk, until her trek had brought her near the Fluorescent Forest, from which none who dare enter ever return.

She had then straddled the forest fringe for another full bright, hoping to encounter more folk, yet always mindful to avoid straying too close to the dancing curtain of blue beams which completely shielded the inner forest from view.

Then her hearers snagged sound. Faintly, at first, but unmistakably the constant crunch of feet stomping through graingrass, and blades hacking it down.

Next, she'd caught the sound of hoarse voices. Foreign voices, speaking unknown words. At once, she'd known they were Lizarme. Many Lizarme, and they were stomping straight towards her!

Thus, she now found herself crouched low amongst tall graingrass, with buzzing bellybees and a pounding pumper. Skindew stuck hair to her brow and fear bated her breath. Her habitually keen mind was suddenly amush with near panic. She sought in futile desperation to still her trembling limbs. Frightpimples crawled beneath her flesh.

The Lizarme had her encircled on three sides, with the Fluorescent Forest at her back!

"Oh, destiny…" she whispered, "Guide my thoughts, for I cannot."

The hoarse voices were getting quite close now, growing ever louder – and meaner. Suddenly they were joined by the chilling squeal of a rexid as it snorted a new scent. A humanfolk scent! Her scent!!

Shouting and squealing erupted from all directions as more of the canine lizards began picking up her scent.

There was no more time for thought. “Destiny, deliver me!” she shrieked, realizing what she must do.

Spinning about, she sprang afoot and sprinted towards the curtain of blue beams, intent on charging through. But, to her surprise, the beams parted to admit her entry, and she tripped and fell upon her knees. As they closed behind her, she became aware that the shouting had ceased. There was no breeze.

Pressing astand, she absorbed the incredible spectacle before her. Virtually everything glowed. Everything! In slackjawed awe, she gawked about, her mind already cleansed of thoughts of the Lizarme and their squealing rexids.

It was apparent that she had just entered the realm of the most mysterious. Strange, fleshy flowers stemmed about her. Their flushed petals glowed like a red palesphere and brash beams bolted from yellow buttons in their centers.

The curious galfolk reached to pet one of the flowers, but it drew away from her.

“Don't!” a saucy voice objected.

“Wh – Who are you?” she asked, trying not to look scared.

“I'm a flowa, stupid!”

Shoenia took a step backwards. “B – But flowers can't talk?”

“But flowas caint tak. But flowas caint tak.” the saucy plant mimicked. “Whatsamatta, Strangeling? Ain't ya never heerd no flowa tak before? Ya lid a shilted existence or something?”

"Well no, but...?"

"Go on! Beat it! Scram! Shoo! Git lost!" The rude blossom tilted so its beam stung into the stupefied galfolk's seers.

"Sorry," Shoenia apologized; arm-shielding her face and backing even further away from her saucy tormentor. Giggles were erupting all about her. She pondered her own sense. Had she gone *'round the twist'*?

The trees of the forest were equally strange. Their pinkish skin glowed in such a weird way that it seemed one's digits bended upon touching it. It felt cool, yet smooth like glazed clay. And every single tree bore only two limbs, both jointed in the middle and tipped with twigs that wiggled.

Plus there were equally eerie bushes. Each was supported by a pair of jointed stalks with knobby knots, and clothed in fleshy leaves, which faded and brillianced in breathe.

Aside from the vegetation, much else about the place was also peculiar. Although Shoenia attempted to step faster, it felt, and indeed looked, as though her movements were somehow slowed. Also, the forest air carried a meaty odor, yet it revealed no creatures, nor clues of creatures. And instead of spherical, the sky above the forest was convex like a slack canopy. It was like peering up from within a glowing breather, only there wasn't quite enough breath to blow out the sagging surface.

Shoenia strolled about the foliage, enchanted. And some new species of vegetation began to approach her.

The new trees were tall as towers, and very thin. As with the pink trees, their silvery skin also felt like glazed clay. Long vines drooped from their tops, sweeping the forest floor. Their limbs were clothed with lappy leaves, which constantly licked one another. Even though the forest bore no breeze, these trees swayed to an inaudible beat.

Soon Shoenia came upon a new type of flower. She never noticed them at first because their stems were reclined upon the ground and their multi-hued petals were wrapped tightly into buds. However, as she unwarily trod past them, the stems suddenly stretched upright and the blossoms bloomed like an awakening. The orange petals blushed like hot embers. Blue peepers blinked and batted their stamen lashes as the blossoms traced the strangeling's movements with the utmost suspicion.

Eventually, the weary galfolk chanced upon a narrow, black crick. It's gooey liquid flowed slowly like thick muck. Surface bubbles puffed, then popped with a splatter.

Shoenia opted to rest a short spell, lounging on some spongy soil in a small clearing beside the crick. With weighted lids, she looked about.

Enormous, naked trees with coiled trunks and groping limbs ringed the clearing. Their twiggy digits raked at the void.

Peeking out from behind the coiltrees were some bashful flirtflowers. They giggled and blushed and batted their petals.

There were also pink smoochers, with transparent stems. Each smoocher had two juicy petals, which smacked at the others, and red pistils wagged between their petals like lickers between lips.

Shoenia's lids grew heavier by the nod, and her head teetered and tottered in its battle against fatigue. "Need nap," she muttered, yielding to a yaaawwnn."

Suddenly something pricked her leg. Then it pricked her again. And again.

With much effort, she raised her lids and struggled to focus.

"Ouch!" she yelped. "Ouch! Ouch!"

Unbelievable! Bold blades of nasty grass were actually jousting her with their pointy tips!

"Ouch!" she yelped again. "Stop it! Stop or I'll stand and stomp you! Ouch!"

"BOOM!! BOOM!! BOOM!! BOOM!!" The forest floor rolled and quaked beneath her, tripping up all efforts to stand! In shock and horror, she watched with wided seers as the trees with the coiled trunks springpounced across the clearing towards her!

"STOMP!! STOMP!! STOMP!!" they bellowed.

"BOOM!! BOOM!! BOOM!!" echoed the forest floor as the coiltrees springpounced ever closer. **"BOOM!! BOOM!! BOOM!! BOOM!!"**

In sheer desperation, the frightened galfolk somehow struggled astand. Both legs trembled in the battle for balance. With great difficulty, she stumbled to escape the towering titans that sought to trample her.

"C L A C K I T Y - C L A C K - C L A C K ! CLACKITY-CLACK-CLACK!"

Now she froze, terrorstunned! Almost the entire forest was attacking her, led by a hopping batch of beastly bushes with hairy stems and pincered petals. "CLACKITY-CLACK-CLACK-CLACK!"

"Ouch!" she yelped, somewhat regaining her senses. She swatted at some grass that jousted her ankles.

"STOMP!! STOMP!! STOMP!!" bellowed the coiltrees as they springpounced ever closer.

"**BOOM!! BOOM!! BOOM!!"** echoed the forest floor as it bounced her about.

"CLACKITY-CLACK-CLACK!" sounded the pincer petals.

"Staaawwpp!" whined some wimpweeds along the crick bank. "Staaawwpp thaaat."

And the bold blades of grass relentlessly wriggled after her, squeakchanthing, "Jab-jab-jab-jab…"

Instinctively clenching tight her scrapstick, the frantic galfolk stumbled for the crick.

"Staaawwpp thaaat," whined the wimpweeds.

"**AW – SHADDUP!!!**" the entire forest retorted in unison - including Shoenia.

Next, some tuffy thornthistles arrived and took to tumbling down the crickbank to block the strangeling's only route of escape. Brandishing their spiraled scythes, they dared her to challenge them. Even double dared!

But Shoenia's wit and agility foiled their ploy. When next the forest floor quaked to bounce her, she seized upon the rhythm of its roll. She keenly engaged her scrapstick to vault over the thornthistles and then hurdle the crick, before sprinting down a sort of spoor.

"Ow!" she yelled, as a root snagged her ankle and slammed her to the dirt.

"**STOMP!! STOMP!! STOMP!! STOMP!!**"

"BOOM!! BOOM!! BOOM!! BOOM!!"

"CLACKITY-CLACK-CLACK-CLACK!"

"Jab-jab-jab-jab-jab-jab-jab…"

Wet seeped from her seerducts as Shoenia surrendered the struggle. It was of no use. The roots and some slithervines held her in vice, keeping her prisoner for their cousins to prick, pinch and stomp!

“BOOM!! BOOM!! BOOM!!” The forest floor rattled her bones.

“CLACKITY-CLACK-CLACK-CLACK!”

Now Shoenia could see the beastly bushes. With no lack of courage, she prepared to meet Morgue. She thanked Seed for the precious gift of being and asked Destiny to care for the other folk, plus their ape allies. Then she sealed her lids and bravely awaited the beyond.

“**STOMP!! STOMP!! STOMP!! STOMP!!”** shouted the springpouncing coiltrees.

“BOOM!! BOOM!! BOOM!! BOOM!!” echoed the forest floor.

“CLACKITY-CLACK-CLACK-CLACK-CLACK!” sounded the pincer petals.

“Jab-jab-jab-jab-jab-jab-jab…” squeakchanted the bold blades of grass.

The gallant galfolk refused to unlock her sealed lids, trying in vain to ignore the climbing crescendo, which now surpassed the wrath of even the most tormented skybangers. “N-Not long n-now,” she gasped with great difficulty. “Destiny, let it all end in a blink.”

“STOMP!! STOMP!! STOMP!! STOMP!!”

“BOOM!! BOOM!! BOOM!! BOOM!!”

"CLACKITY-CLACK-CLACK-CLACK!"

"Jab-jab-jab-jab-jab-jab-jab…"

They were very near now. Almost near enough to feel. Shoenia winced in prep for the final pounce.

"STOMP!! STOMP! STO…"

"BOOM!! BOOM!! BOO…"

"CLACKITY-CLACK-CL…"

"Jab-jab-ja…"

Silence…beautiful… peaceful… silence.

"Is it done?" she wondered aloud, not daring to look. Her mind groped for a clear thought. "No, I still feel the vines about me."

Suddenly the forest erupted again!

"STOMP!! STOMP! ST…"

"BOOM!! BOOM!! BOO…"

"CLACKITY-CLACK-CLA…"

"Jab-jab-ja…"

"Wait," Shoenia thought. "They're all going away?"

It was true. As the roar faded back into silence, the rolling vibrations also stilled.

Next, the slithervines began to unwind, freeing her torso and limbs.

Only the root held firm, binding her ankles.

Unlocking her lids, Shoenia cautiously drew her torso asit. She was most puzzled? All of her tormentors had vanished, save for the pesky root.

"Leggo!" she commanded, twisting her feet about and beating the root with her scrapstick. She glared daggers at her last remaining tormentor. "I said release me! Now! Do so or I'll bash you!"

Yet the root kept its grip. No matter how hard its captive beat it and regardless of her screams, it simply refused to yield.

So the galfolk opted for pleading. "Oh, please, Mister Root. Please let me go."

But the root simply ignored her.

Next, she tried flattery. "My, you certainly are a fine looking root. Won't you please release me?"

Again, the root simply ignored her.

So, back to threats and insults, once again glaring daggers at her tormentor. "I'm partial to boiled root stew, you tacky tuber! And I have a blade!"

The root twitched nervously, yet refused to slacken its grip.

Skindew drenched the galfolk's garments as she continued to beg, bribe, threaten, beat, hack and struggle. Until, in exhausted defeat, she flopped down on the forest floor and began to weep, with the wet pasting her locks to her trembling cheeks.

"Ahem…"

"What?" Instinctively, Shoenia tried to spring astand, but the root yanked her feet from under her, slamming her back down: hard. The heavy impact punched wind from her breathers and pained her bonecage and limbs. All her strength was instantly drained.

Unable to move or speak, she stared, dropjawed, at the source of the voice, hoping the creature meant her no harm.

Its shinesilver skin was rough like old bark. Gray grass grew in clumps atop its crown. Nutshells served as hearers, and it possessed a knurled sniffer. Twin, purple peepers were set deep within puffy hollows, above which grew strips of white moss. Its thick mossy beard was broken only by a black hole, out of which wagged a reedy red licker.

Stooped at its middle, the aged creature was supported by stumpy trunks with knotted knees. Two stubby branches were tipped with twiggy digits, in which it clenched a sturdy rush stem. It seemed to need the stem for balance while making slow, shuffling steps towards the snagged strangeling.

Upon reaching her, it gently tapped the rush but once upon her stubborn captor and the root instantly relaxed its grip enough for her to wriggle free.

The creature's voice seemed soothing and sincere. "Are your limbs free of breaks, Humanfolk?"

Shoenia was still too awed to answer.

Sensing her fright and distrust, the creature spoke to comfort her. "I do so hope that you are all right. You are actually most fortunate. So seldom do I venture into this section of the forest. The plants here about are especially nasty. Had you come any other time, I expect…"

"Wh-Who are you?" the galfolk interrupted. "I – I mean, what are you? I mean…"

The creature raised a twiggy hand to calm her. "Relax, my young guest. I shan't harm you. It is well outside my nature to do so."

"B-But…the trees?"

"Perhaps I can quell your curiosity. My name is Rimp. I am a plantimal. Actually, a well aged plantimal I must admit." The creature smiled, exposing one ivory biter. "And I am the keeper of this Fluorescent Forest. All plants here obey me."

"This Fluorescent Forest?" The galfolk was noticeably perplexed. "You mean there are others?"

"Oi. In fact, too many to even count. They're scattered in distant parts all about the skytwinklers. But I only dwell here. Just one keeper to each fluorescent forest; that is the law."

"Whose law?" the galfolk pressed.

"Why, Destiny's law, of course. You do have faith in destiny?"

"Oh yes, I most certainly do."

"Splendid," responded Rimp. "Now, perhaps you shall share with us your name?"

"Us?"

"Oi. I came with two smuzzles."

"Smuzzles?"

Rimp pointed a twiggy digit at the soil near her feet.

"Ooooo," Shoenia squeaked in pleasant surprise.

A pair of cuddly cuties blinked up at her. Their reddish, furry bodies were bloated at the bellies, and their bushy tails bore rings of blue. Four fat legs with wee paws supported their bodies. Long, silky whiskers twitched at the tips of their short snouts. One bore blue, mask-like facial markings, while the other had a blue patch about one of its seers. Both sniffed at her scent and wiggled their perky hearers.

Disregarding all caution, the smuzzles scampered up to the strangeling and embraced her legs, chattering to each other as they patted her exposed flesh.

The galfolk reached to pet one, and it fondly licked her digits.

But when its jealous mate nose-nudged under Shoenia's digits, a most heated spatachat erupted, followed at once by a tight tumbletussle across a mossy mat.

"Why, they're simply adorable!" She exclaimed, giggling with glee.

"Oi." Agreed the plantimal. "Although they do tend to compete for attention. Now, I assume you are in need of nap and nourishment, hmmm?"

"Uh – yes, er – oi?" she replied, suddenly suffering a ferocious belly growl. She offered her host a shinewhite smile.

"Very well, then. Now, perhaps you might share with us your name? And from whence you have wandered."

The galfolk blushed. "Oh, I'm terribly sorry. My name is Shoenia…and I, uh, well…I sort of opted to enter your forest."

"Opted? My, you are an unusual humanfolk. None ever opt to enter this place." Rimp offered her a stubby branch. "Shall we?"

Shoenia nodded and took hold. "Oi."

"Oi." Replied the plantimal. "Now, do speak more of yourself."

But before Shoenia could utter a sound, the smuzzles scampered up and embraced her legs again. She released Rimp's branch and scooped them both up into her arms. "Do – ha – do they – hee, hee – have names?" she managed, while they licked dirt from her neck.

"They do," Rimp said. "The rascal with the masked features is called Sneek, and the rogue with the blue patch is called Peek."

"Mmmm. Sneek and Peek."

"Oi. Come, we shall all retreat to my roost."

"Roost?" Shoenia placed the smuzzles back down.

"Oi," Rimp replied, again extending a branch. It pointed with its rush. "And do mind that slinky snapdragon. They are most devious and undisciplined, forever causing me grief." Rimp sighed. "Always eating my smuzzles."

Shoenia glanced askance at the peculiar plant that giggled and wriggled alongside them. A solitary, fanged flower grew on the tip of its thorny stem. It smacked its fat lips as it watched the fuzzy snacks.

Shoenia shivered and pressed tight to Rimp, nothing that Sneek and Peek now clung tightly to the plantimal's rough back.

"Relax, my furry friends," Rimp said, "That one is not mature enough to swallow you."

"Y – You mean they grow bigger?"

"Oi. Much, much bigger."

The wary galfolk gulped and squeezed tight to Rimp's branch.

It smiled and patted her hand. "Do not feast on fear, Shoenia, you are most safe in my presence."

She smiled back in silence, knowing her rescuer spoke the truth.

Often, Shoenia's steps were stilled by the shining splendor of the forest. She watched waltzing weeds, which whirled about to a symphony of songsaplings. Bouncing beets provided the bass, while a choir of tenortrees kept rhythm and pace. With pitchplants providing the peaks, and fluteflowers feeding the flow. Even some fiddlesticks joined in the chorus, whistling a melody while stroking stretched vibevines. And all to the clap of the palms.

There seemed to be no end to the splendor. Diving dazzledills somersaulted into clear pools, to the annoyance of lounging lazelillies. Buttercups melted into yellow puddles of pollen. Thorn trees scratched bite burs from their bark. Sadwillows wept and wimpweeds whined, while happyhusks hopped and hooted and had a grand time.

Humblehops festooned most graciously before their keeper. Stemmed seers batted their blinkbuds. Helmeted hopstools did drill in tight ranks, whilst stepping-stones stomped past in pairs.

Now there were strange critters, too. Colorful crawlers with wide, crooked grins. Plus climbers and creepers, and tree dwellers with big peepers. There were bold bugs with biters, and bugs that just buzzed. Hairy bugs. Scaly bugs. And winged bugs that sparked.

Some bugs jumped, others just crept, most were up and about, yet spotted lazybugs slept. And the pools were filled with floatfinners that glowed.

Eventually they came upon a huge herd of titantrees, which were all entwined at the limbs. They seemed to bow as their keeper approached.

And the titantrees were home to a host of furry tenants. An odd assortment of curious smuzzles blinked down from their stick and bark boughcanies.

"It's not far now, Shoenia," Rimp assured her. "We'll pass through the root canals."

"Their roots grow big enough to trek through?" Shoenia was shocked.

"Actually, drift through. On my reed flatfloater. Soon you can take nourishment. Titanroot sap is thick with nutrients. Tastes not so bad, either. It has sustained myself for far too many centicycles to count. And see for yourself the result." Rimp slowly spun about and parted branches. "Ta-da!"

"But I am not made like you," Shoenia noted.

Rimp sighed. "All beings are alike in some manner, Shoenia. We are bound together by Destiny's breath."

Shoenia blushed and hoped she hadn't hurt her host's feelings.

Rimp brought her to a dark archway in the base of a titantree stump. Nothing her hesitation, he spoke to reassure her. "Do not worry, Shoenia. Shinebulbs have been strung all throughout the root canals. They shall respond to our presence."

True to Rimp's word, no sooner had the four entered the archway, than a pale light began to shine. It reflected off the smooth surface of the sap down below. A bark ramp of sorts wound down and around the inner wall of the titantrunk, gradually leveling out to form a crude dock.

As the group descended, many more Shinebulbs were awakened to their presence. Their pale light exposed a square flatfloater, which was vined to the dock. Two tiny push poles were lying atop its deck.

"Sneek and Peek like to propel it," Rimp explained. "Smuzzles are actually quite strong for their size. Quick to learn, too."

The vine obediently released the craft upon Rimp's command, and all four stepped aboard. Then the eager smuzzles shoved off.

It was quiet and cool within the root canals, yet comfortably so. Shinebulbs dangled in great abundance from the ceilings and walls.

"Mmmmmm," Shoenia remarked, licking rich sap from her digits. "It's so savory and sweet."

"Savory?" Rimp inquired.

Shoenia flashed her shinewhite smile. "That means it is very tasty."

"Oi. It is that. And most nutritious, too. Indulge."

"I certainly shall. Mmmmmm."

Shoenia had not the slightest idea how long they spent drifting through the canals. Each appeared much as the others. Although she and her host were sometimes forced to duck to avoid a skull bonk, and, on occasion, the canals would converge into a titantrunk. Yet the capable smuzzles knew exactly which new tuber to follow.

Finally, they drifted majestically into an exceptionally massive titantrunk. Much larger than all the others, it spanned many strides in breadth. A bark dock wound about the trunk wall, gradually rising into a sturdy ramp. Many Shinebulbs lighted the way, and intricate wallcarvings depicted scenes from lost legends.

"Welcome to Rimp's Roost," the proud plantimal offered, as the smuzzles gently guided the flatfloater alongside the dock. Then Rimp swept the rush in a gesture to disembark.

"Why thank you," Shoenia remarked, stepping onto the dock. She then extended a helping hand to her aged host.

Well that she did, too. For the plantimal teetered for a moment and seemed to draw no breath.

"Are you ill?" Shoenia asked in a panic.

Regaining both balance and breathe, Rimp patted her gently on the back. "Just a slight case of old age," he replied. Then noticing her concern, he smiled and added, "I'm dandy. It's simply been a very long bright. But thank you for your assistance. You are too kind."

"One can never be too kind," Shoenia noted with a smile.

"Ha! We have a case of youth learning to mentor," Rimp responded in a most cheery tone. "It is clear that I must watch my words around you. Come. Let us climb."

Together, the four friends ascended the ramp. Up and around and up and around.

More than just a few times, the intrigued galfolk asked the puffing plantimal to pause and explain the many wallcarvings. And her polite host would always stop and learn to her the legends.

At last they came upon a closed door. Rimp smiled and spun the latch about, then rushtipped the door aswing. He gestured for Shoenia to enter.

She smiled politely and stepped through the arch, then stood stunned into silence.

Rimp's roost was truly a spectacle to behold! A rug of red reeds unrolled to greet them. Wallcarvings shouted out their welcome. Butterbells jingled and boysenbells bonged. Tiered shinebulb chandeliers spinned and beaconed. Even a tiny band of buzzing bugle bees belted out, "Hi ya, Honey, tis so sweet ta have ya hive!"

There were benches that bowed, and a crooning couch that curtsied. In a far cranny, there crouched four helmeted plopstools. They supported a thin slat of napwood, upon which lazed a striped mattress of mistbow moss.

Three busy maid moths fluttered about, dustin' and sweepin' and shooin' dirt out. And a huge tails-clad buttlerbug took charge of Rimp's rush.

Thank you, Mister Roach."

The butler bug simply nodded its reply, glanced briefly at Shoenia, and then scurried away down a crooked corridor.

"WOW!" Shoenia was unable to contain herself. She waltzed about the roost, meeting many new friends. "Hello. How are you? Hello. So pleased to make your acquaintance, Ms. Portrait."

Suddenly, a fantabulous mural snagged her sights. Gleambeams and shinestones had been painstakingly inlayed into one wall, depicting a pair of wicked, winged phantoms doing battle with a staff-wielding angelbeast.

"What legend is this?" she inquired.

"Ah!" Rimp exclaimed. "That is my favorite. It is the Legend Of The Demon Chaser. And what makes this legend so special, is that it is entirely true."

"Oh, do learn this legend to me," she pleaded.

"Shoenia, should you not nap first?" Rimp suggested.

"I shall nap later, but first learn me this legend. Please, Rimp. Please." She kissed her host's rough cheek.

Rimp smiled. The plantimal had never been kissed in all of its many centicycles, and the galfolk's affectionate act made it feel all nice and warm inside. "Oi. Very well, then, we shall share of this special legend out on the boughcany. I'll have Mr. Roach prepare us some crunchcones and cream."

Once they had gotten their delicious treats, Rimp began learning Shoenia the Legend Of The Demon Chaser.

Shoenia listened and licked as the plantimal began learning her of events zillions of kawahillions of kilocycles past. It told of a time when a pair of wicked demons roamed about the skytwinklers, seeking to undo all of the beauty that Destiny had forged over all of eternity. Her seers wided as Rimp described the havoc they wreaked, combining their power to hurl globes form their proper routes and even causing the collision of skytwinklers.

Next Rimp learned her of Destiny's ire, and how Destiny had created a Demon Chaser to seek out and destroy the wicked pair. It told her of how the Chaser was granted a staff of white gold, which can actually melt stone, noting that it can only be unpowered in the depths of a saline sea.

The crunchcones were long gobbled by the time Rimp learned her of the trio's brightlong battle, which took place high atop the Isle Of Countless Caverns. In conclusion, her host revealed to her how the Demon Chaser, victorious yet Morgually wounded, sealed both itself and the staff inside one of the countless caverns, for which the isle was named; lest the powerful weapon should ever fall into the wrong hands, for it would quickly make the bearer mad.

"...then all creatures would surely find themselves in a right fine mess indeed." Rimp smiled to expose his lone biter and indicate that his tale was complete.

A lengthy silence prevailed before Shoenia spoke. "But if this staff makes its bearer mad, whoever would want to seek it?"

Rimp raised its mossy brows and its tone sank sullen. "Perhaps one who is already almost there?"

Another long silence prevailed before the plantimal spoke again. This time in a much cheerier tone. Anyway, your weighted lids speak of your need to nap. As do mine. Not near so young as I once was. Come. Mr. Roach has fixed you a comfy mattress of mistbow moss. He's also warned it not to tickle you, so you should nap well."

Shoenia gulped, then nervously followed her host in from the boughcany.

Rimp guided his guest over to a striped mattress beneath the fabulous mosaic. "If I should be out and about when you unnap, Mr. Roach shall tend to your every need. Nap well, my young humanfolk friend."

"Rimp?" Shoenia called as her host shuffled towards its own mattress.

"Oi?"

"I'm most happy we met."

Rimp turned and nodded. "Oi."

Then the weary galfolk flopped down upon the mistbow moss, and entered the relaxing realm of napvisions. There she saw diving dazzledills and stepping-stones and crawlers with grins and wallcarving that spoke and…

…gradually, the groggy galfolk became aware of voices drifting in from the boughcany. They appeared to be arguing. Knuckling napsand from her bleary seers, she slowly drew her torso asit.

Only one of the voices was familiar. The strange voice was most flat and unfeeling, and she could not understand its words.

"Fine bright to you," greeted part of the mosaic.

"Uh – fine bright to you, too," Shoenia replied, exchanging smiles with the Demon Chaser and ignoring its two scowling adversaries.

"Destiny has need of you, Shoenia," said the Demon Chaser.

"Huh? H-How do you know my name?"

"Don't listen to that one!" growled one demon.

"Listen to us!" snapped the other.

"To Morgue with you both!" shouted the Demon Chaser, brandishing its weapon.

Suddenly the three eternal enemies engaged in battle.

Frightened free of her wits, Shoenia fled for the boughcany. "Rimp! Rimp!"

"What is it, Shoenia?" The plantimal's purple peepers were brimmed with alarm.

"Rimp…" she gasped. "The – The mosaic is doing battle. The d-d-demons…"

"Shoenia! Shoenia!" Rimp interrupted, that is its very purpose, to portray their battle."

"B-But it spoke to me. All three of them…."

Rimp sighed and gently cupped her trembling hands in his twiggy digits. "Be still, my young humanfolk friend. Often they do such things, but their power to harm you is nil. Now tell us, what words did they speak?"

Shoenia filled both of her breathers to the brim and blew wind through her lips before replying. "Well, the Demon Chaser said that Destiny has need of me. And the demons said that I should listen to them. Then they started fighting..."

"Hmmmm?" Rimp sighted into the roost. "Strange, they've never spoken anything like that before? But then, Destiny has need of all creatures. And demons do seek to control all they meet. There, look, the mosaic has returned to its proper form."

Shoenia stared back at the mosaic, which had indeed reverted back to its original scene. Although she would swear the Demon Chaser blinked.

Rimp guided her the rest of the way out onto the boughcany. "Come, I want you to meet my most learned student. Though not near so learned as myself – hee, hee." Rimp smiled and winked at her.

A tall, lanky grandfolk offered her a curt nod. His pale flesh was wrinkled with wisdom. His hearers and his pug sniffer bore a frosted tinge, despite the warm temp. Thick, chillcreamed hair and a bleached beard both waved well past his thin waist, and thick, bushy brows topped his odd seers. Odd in that one was colored dull green and the other bright blue. Yet both seemed to equally chillgaze right through her.

His attire affirmed that he was a magician of sorts. He donned a high, pointy cap with blue streamers dangling from its peak. And he wore a blue robe, patterned with red crescent spheres. Laceless sandals padded the soles of his much-traveled feet. Strong, wrinkled digits clenched firmly a wand of pink crystal.

Shoenia mutely returned the nod. The moody magician's serious scowl proved to be most unsettling.

Rimp tactfully intervened to alter the tense atmosphere. "Shoenia, do you recall the last legend I learned you?"

The magician moved to interject, but Rimp motioned him to hush.

"You mean the one from the mosaic that spoke to me?"

"Oi, that's it. The one about the Demon Chaser."

"Yes – er – oi… I remember. Its power came from its staff."

"Oi. You remember details well." Rimp landed the moody magician a smugproud smile.

"Why?" Shoenia inquired. "Is it…"

The moody magician's tone was curt and uncourteous. "My mystic mist has revealed to me a most disturbing illusion. I have come to confer privately with my mentor."

Shoenia glared daggers at the pushy grandfolk. Rudeness had long been her prize peeve. She sniped, "One should at least give One's name before interrupting."

Her rebuke caught the magician entirely unawares. In awkward silence, he glanced at Rimp.

The plantimal landed him a second smugproud smile. "I warned you, this young galfolk certainly doesn't lack for spunk."

The magician's flat tone was respectful, yet firm. "But mentor, I have great need of your wisdom and magic."

"And I have already told you, I am much too aged to go and would only hinder your progress. And time works not in our favor. But Shoenia is youthful and fit and blessed with keen wits."

Rimp and Shoenia exchanged smiles.

"Indubitably." The magician toned cynical and rolled his odd seers. "But she wields no magic?"

Rimp's normally soothing voice became laced with a tinge of annoyance. "Zebu, who learned you your magic?"

"You did, of course. But…"

"Yet now you doubt my wisdom?"

"No, Mentor. I would never…"

"Splendid," Rimp cut him short. "Then there is no more cause for debate. Shoenia shall become your apprentice and aid in your quest. Together, you both shall voyage downthisaway to this Xebec's Island and…"

"Whoa!" Shoenia cut in. "Apprentice? Quest? Island? Xebec? Rimp, of what do you both speak?"

Rimp and the moody magician exchanged awkward glances before the plantimal offered her a smile.

"Well?" Shoenia demanded, folding her arms across her chest.

Rimp sighed. Its tone became somber. "Shoenia, sit with us on the plopstools."

All three were seated before Rimp carried on. "Shoenia, we have great need of your help." The plantimal paused and shot Zebu a warning glare. "We now face a colossal crisis. Perhaps the biggest crisis the Universe has seen since the demonic pair themselves roamed the skytwinklers before they were slain by The Demon Chaser."

Shoenia glanced at the moody magician.

Zebu glared back in obvious contempt.

Now Rimp's tone bore great concern. "Zebu's magic cauldron recently boiled over, and the mystic mist clearly revealed some distressing illusions."

Rimp paused and sighed heavily.

"What types of illusions?" Shoenia pressed.

"Perhaps," Rimp suggested, "it is best your new mentor explain."

Zebu spied Rimp with nil gratitude. "Uh – yes, perhaps it would be best," he grumbled.

"Explain what?" Shoenia asked.

"Patience," Rimp cautioned, twigging her arm. "Carry on, Zebu."

The moody magician made a face. "Oh, very well then. As the mystic mist cooled, it revealed to me the whereabouts of the Demon Chaser's staff. No longer entombed, it has indeed fallen into the wrongest of hands."

"Whose hands?"

"Patience, Shoenia," Rimp again cautioned, smugsmiling at her annoyed mentor. "Your lack of patience does so remind me of a certain former apprentice of mine. Hmmmm – Zebu?"

Zebu frowned, yet kept on. "The staff is now the prize of the most evil of dim sorcerers – Xebec Of Ranidae. He was once a white magician, such as us." He pointed to indicate both Rimp and himself. "And he was apprentice to the master magician, Spidey Smeals."

"Spidey.....Smeals? Ha! That's funny."

Both magicians ignored her flippant licker.

Zebu carried on. "Although a master magician of the highest order, Spidey Smeals is also a very poor judge of character. It was he who taught Xebec the art of white magic. Of course, Spidey had no way of knowing that his sly apprentice thought not at all like he spoke. Until, on the blackest of Blacks, while Spidey swinged in trance, Xebec skulked into his lair and stole off with the Sealed Tubes, in which were encased the Webscrolls Of Dim Sorcery."

"The Webs of what?" Shoenia asked.

"The Webscrolls Of Dim Sorcery," Rimp put in.

Zebu paused for breath before he continued. "When Spidey finally untranced and saw he'd been duped by his most senior apprentice, he immediately ordered his lesser apprentices to seek out the thief. But Xebec was by far the most learned of the lot, and armed with traditional knowledge from the scrolls, he easily dissolved into putrid moo-pies all of his pursuers, who proved to be no match for the art of Dim Sorcery. Then he fled to an island."

"But why didn't this Spidey Smeals chase after him, too? Wasn't he the master magician?"

Zebu gloatgrinned at Rimp. "Because, my dear apprentice, even we master magicians have our limitations. You see, Spidey Smeals is also an albino arachnid."

"Albino arachnid?"

"Which means he is a silkspinner who must always avoid the warm rays of the brightsphere," Zebu explained, "lest he melt and meet Morgue."

"Thus he dwells only in his subsurface lair," Rimp added.

"Which explains why this sorcerer, Xebec, fled to an island," Shoenia put in.

Zebu glanced at the plantimal and actually almost grinned. "She may have some potential after all?"

"Indubitably." Rimp rolled its purple peepers and toned cynical. "But what would this master magician know? After all, I do have my limitations."

"So what of this quest?" Shoenia inquired.

"Xebec is unworthy to wield even a pebble of power," Zebu explained. "He must be relieved of the staff."

Rimp suddenly viewed Zebu with grave concern. "The staff must be tossed into The Saline Sea. None are worthy to wield it. None."

"Of course, Mentor," Zebu said, bowing his head as if in shame.

Rimp looked to the galfolk. "Will you not help us, Shoenia? Zebu shall teach you the chants of white magic."

Shoenia's mind balked at the mere thought of voyaging anywhere with the moody magician, whom she truly disliked at best. And what of her own folk still fighting the Lizarme? Surely she should return to help them? Or at least bid farewell?

Yet she realized that the staff must be unpowered, lest all would be lost anyway. Besides, Rimp had spared her a sure meeting with Morgue. How could she refuse her new friend's request now?

Finally, she made her choice. "Rimp, I owe you a debt. I shall do as you ask."

Rimp slowly shook his head. "True friendship avoids such binds, Shoenia. You owe me nothing. This choice must be made of your own free will – because you truly believe it to be just. I am not a factor."

Shoenia briefly reconsidered her choice. Then spoke from feeling. "Rimp, I do want to help you. I still opt to go."

"Splendid! Splendid!" Rimp embraced her.

"Splendid," Zebu mocksneered beneath his breath. "Simply splendid."

"Now," Rimp continued, "there's not a nod to waste. I've already instructed my smuzzles to gather their tools. They really are quite handy, you know. We shall set trek for the coast at once, where my most skilled of smuzzles shall construct a sturdy sea craft from a boulder pea pod. We'll use dandytower stalks for masts, and tidypalm leaves for sails. It shall be steered by a fanlilly rudder and a chute tiller."

Rimp wagged a twiggy pointdigit at the sagging above. "Skytwinklers will guide you and Destiny shall guard you. Come, let us be off at once!"

So the three of them ventured forth for the coast, along with a passle of tool-toting smuzzles.

In the Fluorescent Forest, one can never be certain how many Brights have passed. Or even if it was Bright or Black who currently ruled atop the sagging canopy above. However, numerous naps were needed during their long trek for the coast.

They threaded through tight thickets of slashthorns, and about brush budded with bows. Passed by silly trees with hooped hearers, and a vainvine with a schnobb nose. There were big trees, who hopped by on footstumps. As well as mossy midgets, who crept about on root digits.

There appeared bushes that bowed, and bushes which balked. Round bushes who rolled, and others who walked. Plants made of fiber, and plants made of rubber. Disgusting flowers that belched goop, plus bouncing puffballs packed with blubber. They saw weeds that wiggled, then mushreeds which wagged, heard some cheery trees giggle, and saw sadwillows who sagged.

Once they were even amused by a trio of tapsticks, who just loved to show off. Plus cacti with shinesharp needles, who bellowed bass tunes through conk horns. You see, in the Fluorescent Forest, not one plant fits in with the norm.

Stepping-stones stomped flat flowers, who sprang back up filled with much ire. Leading Shoenia to ponder, do the plants here expire?

Multifaced silkspinners dangled from boughs. There were luverpents with fat lips, who slithered and hissed, plus made smoochsmackin sounds whenever they kissed. In fact, it seemed the whole forest was just teeming with pests.

On and on the group trekked, through thicket and thatch, topping up growling bellies from each chowveggie patch. Though munching down only those eggplants that Rimp said could not hatch. And they nibbled on wheyfigs from feedferns, and downed berries by the batch.

They gulped sweet cream from hairy bonkerbeans, and slurped sweet sap by the pail. Once all was considered, they fared really quite well.

Then, at long last, they passed through the parted curtain of blue beams and out from under the sagging surface of the slack canopy. Finally, they had broken free from the forest and arrived at the coast. Bended tidypalms rimmed the shore in greeting, and hairy bonkerbeans littered the beach. Dandytowers loomed over the tallest of palms.

Monster wetrollers crashed in from the deep, curling to splashbash the beach. Surf spat foam at the wind, and the retreating tides sucked silt out into the gray and chilly depths. But boulder pea pods held their sand, well anchored by subsurface stems.

Early next bright, the skilled smuzzles commenced construction of a sturdy sea craft. They labored without rest, racing against both Black's next attack upon Bright, and the ensuing assault of the tides.

They cut the hull from an enormous boulder pea pod, and fitted it with two dandytower stems. Tidypalm leaves were stitched together for sails. A thick fanlilly was found and fashioned into a rudder, to be steered by a chute tiller.

Bright still ruled when the craft was completed. Then the smuzzles began loading supplies as the first advance tides came creepscouting ashore in preparation for their post-bright charge, which never failed to come.

While Zebu oversaw the final stocktaking, Rimp took Shoenia aside so they could chat free of unwanted hearers.

"I have some items to aid with your quest, Shoenia," Rimp explained, slinging a stalkhollow about her slender neck. "Titanroot sap also helps heal hurts."

Next, the nervous plantimal tied a snoozing shinebulb to her scrapstick. Then, it glanced warily about before pressing some hard objects into her palm. "Hide these objects in your skirt pouch, and mention them to absolutely nobody. Not ever."

Shoenia opened her palm, exposing a stone flint and a striker, plus an empty glass vial, plugged with a cork. "Why are they so secret?" she inquired, dropping the three objects into her pouch.

Rimp's tone was warning. "Because, Shoenia, I too can read mystic mist."

She looked alarmed, so Rimp patted her shoulder to calm her before going on. "My final items have no weight or shape, yet their value extends well beyond all others. Shoenia, I give you my blessing and the gift of unconditional friendship."

The pretty galfolk had never enjoyed unconditional friendship before. Few ever do. Emotion swelled up in her throat, making speech difficult. Her alert, emerald seers moistened. "Isn't it sad, Rimp?"

"Isn't what sad, Shoenia?"

"That we should meet like this. I mean, I was forced into your forest because this beautiful land of ours in currently embroiled in its Second Continental War. Isn't it sad that we mere mortals are so lacking in sense that we actually have to give our Continental Wars numbers? You'd think we'd all learn after the first one?"

Rimp nodded as only those who understand can. "At least we did meet, my young friend. Although, I'm afraid, we shan't meet again. At least not in this realm. Even as we speak, a younger plantimal is taking my place as keeper."

"B – But where are you going?" Shoenia was visibly alarmed.

Rimp squeezed her hand. Sticky sap oozed from its puffy hollows. "Back from whence I came. Or so I hope." He forced a smile.

When Shoenia absorbed her friend's meaning, she suffered the pangs of knotted-up guts. Weepwet seeped from her sockets. Trying to be brave, she gulped hard and swallowed. She was barely able to choke forth her response. "Perhaps we shall meet again in the beyond?"

Rimp smiled to show its lone biter. "Perhaps. I would like that."

Shoenia wiped sap from Rimp's rough cheek and gently kissed it. "I shall miss you, my most special friend."

"Oi." Rimp kissed her brow, noting it felt just as warm being the kisser as being the kissee. "I do wish I'd learned of this strange humanfolk custom sooner."

Shoenia smiled through moist cheeks. "At least you did learn of it."

"Oi. Now it is time for you to set sail. Remember Shoenia; I know you do think as you speak. With feeling and honesty. A most rare quality. Yet always mind what you speak – and especially to whom. A quality magician never wastes words."

Rimp nodded knowingly, and then continued. "Keep honed your wits and your courage. Then when you find yourself in the proper place at the proper time, you shall know to do the proper thing. And always remember, you are loved. Unconditionally."

Rimp kissed her brow for the final time, lest they should ever meet in the unknown beyond. And with that, the plantimal turned and shuffled away.

Weepwet poured from Shoenia's seers, drenching her hangtop. "Rimp!" she choked out in a shaky voice. "Oi!"

The plantimal raised its rush, but neglected to turn about.

Then Zebu barked for them to depart. Thus she set sail with the moody magician. With only his chilly gaze and scowl for company. She silently wished that others had come. Her chestpumper pounded with sorrow and guilt. Only once they were well out to sea did she realize that she had neglected to bid Sneek and Peek farewell. She hoped they knew she adored them, and hoped Rimp knew it too.

Shoenia was unaware that the aged plantimal, too, shared her sorrow, from its final perch upon a stump. Sticky sap flowed freely from both puffy hollows as it viewed the tiny craft carrying its three true friends. It watched in silence as the craft vanished beyond the downaway horizon.

"Fare ye well, my friends. I can only trust in Destiny that I have chosen well, and not risked your being for naught." Rimp whispered. "Yes, fare ye three most well."

Then the most aged plantimal wilted and met Morgue

Tiptin

Wisps of shivermist spindanced across the mountain slope, while biting gusts sneaked about the giant floatwoods that swayed and rolled throughout the deep valleys of The Swallow Mountains. Boughs crackled with cough, or snapped from the weight of glistening wetspikes that hung down from tree limb to freshly fallen chillcream.

"Dung!" the shivering ladfolk cursed, his breath tumbling forth like frosty smoke from between his chattering biters. He drew his fine woolen bratt tightly about his hide vest and torso, trying to trap in body heat. His tough, cloth trousers were tucked into his hide highboots. Blowing breath to thaw his numbing digits, he added, "Shall I ever know warmth again?"

The ladfolk blew breath across his digits once more before dipping them into his vest-pouch. Then he smiled as they felt two hard and familiar shapes wrapped within dry straw. He would soon need them, lest he perish from the cold.

His alert brown seers darted back and forth, seeking the right spot for a much needed rest. A thick tietail of black hair dangled down his back. Although tall and thin, the ladfolk's frame was not lacking in strength. Wiry muscles tauted beneath his smooth brown skin. Thighs and calves burned with each crunching step. Yet on and on he trudged.

For two cycles he had hidden out in the forest, only sneaking into hamlets or Folkton on rare occasions. And always under cover of Black, lest he be captured by the swaddies and shackled for desertion. For he had no intention of ever obeying the sorcerer's decree, or his ban on travel. To him, freedom was well worth any degree of hardship. In fact, he would readily meet Morgue before becoming anyone's servant. Ever.

Yet he had always kept close to home before, always relying on friends or kin for supplies. That is, until his narrow escape from a swaddy patrol took him deeper and deeper into the forest. The humanfolk soldiers had pursued him for almost a quarter palesphere, forcing him to flee upaway and thisaway into the Swallow Mountains. Twice he had barely ducked errant arrows. And once he had even hidden in a floatwood hollow while his unsuspecting pursuers made camp below.

Destiny smiled on him, however, when the swaddy boss finally decided they had wasted enough time chasing after just one lone deserter. Thus they departed promptly at the next break of Bright, leaving the exhausted ladfolk shivering in his hollow. All alone – and hopelessly lost.

Hence he now found himself stomping about in knee-deep chillcream, seeking shelter from the mountains' frigid breath. Believing himself to be all alone with the cold. At least until…

"Beez still, Bam!"

"Snff. Let Biff pull, Bam! Snff."

"Ahhh – schtopz pull. Hurts. Ahhhh…"

"Duh…???"

"Dooz beez stuck!"

"Me knows, Mister Stinks Gross! Snff. Duhh!"

"Me nod stinks gross!"

"Dooz too! Snff."

"Beez nod!"

"Snff. Dooz too!"

"Ahhhhh – schtopz pull…"

"Duh…?????"

The stunned ladfolk could barely believe his seers. Four burly bullybeasts with skinny legs, huge hairy torsos and thick arms, which dangled to the ground, were standing in a nearby clearing. Each was clad in naught but a loincloth. One had a drippy schnozz. While another had his licker stuck to a frosted chopping axe?

"Nod nice sez me stinks gross!" screamed the biggest bullybeast, releasing his grip on the axe handle and brandishing his knuckles high atop his thick skull. "Dooz pologize or ye get hard hurts noogies!"

"Me nod pologize! Snff. Ye get – snff – nasty knocks noogies!" screamed the bullybeast with the drippy schnozz, likewise brandishing a fist high atop his thick skull. "Bam – snff – too sez ye stinky gross like yucky finners! Ha!"

"Ahhh – doozth notth sezth…" started the bullybeast with his licker stuck to the axe.

"See! Me nod stinks gross like yucky finners!" the biggest bullybeast belted out with a smirk. "Bam sez!"

"Bam beez big fibber! Snff."

"Beezth nodth!"

"Beez too!"

"Nodth!"

"Snff – too!"

"Bam nod fibs!"

"Dooz – snff – too!"

"Nod! Nod! Nod!"

"Too! Too! Too! Snff."

The intrigued ladfolk stared with wided seers and bated breathers as the biggest bullybeast and the one with the drippy schnozz started circling about with his hard knuckles raised high. A third bullybeast pouted and wept with an axe frosted to his licker. While the fourth simply looked lost????

"Boog, ye dooz pologize cuzz sez Bam beez fibber!"

"Me nod pologize! Ye stinks gross! Snff."

"Me stinks nice!"

"Gross!"

"Nice!"

"Gross!"

"Nice! Nice! Nice!"

"Gross! Gross! Gro…huh?"

"Dooz ye see…huh?"

Having now spotted the staring ladfolk, three of the bullybeasts scrambled to hide behind each other. Whilst the fourth simply looked lost????

"Don't be scared," the ladfolk stated calmly as the frightened trio kept backing across the clearing in a frantic effort to hide behind one another. Then he stepped out from amongst the floatwoods and began trudging towards them.

"Stop!" shouted the biggest bullybeast, brandishing his knuckles. "Nod hurts Broz! Get nasty knocks noogies!"

"Snff. Ye beez sorcerer? Snff." Inquired the bullybeast with the drippy schnozz. "Beez meeny?"

"No, I'm neither a sorcerer nor a meeny. Nor do I wish to hurt anybody," the ladfolk calmly assured them, exposing his empty palms. "I am just a simple ladfolk. My name is Tiptin of Folkton and I…"

"Dooz ye beez heer?" inquired the biggest bully, still suspicious. He leered askance at the small stranger. "Dooz ye nod beez to Folkton – huh?"

Tiptin granted the bullybeast a warm smile. His tone rang soft and disarming. "Well, actually I am lost and…"

"We beez lost!" the biggest bully interrupted, splashing a great big smile across his face.

"Snff. Got dezzerts?" asked the bullybeast with the drippy schnozz.

The ladfolk was somewhat perplexed by the bullybeasts sudden change in mood. "Sorry, I don't have any food at all. As I was saying, my name is Tiptin and I…"

"Greetz! Me beez Biff!" announced the biggest bullybeast, pointing to his own burly chest. Next he pointed to the others. "Dooz beez me Broz!"

Suddenly the others all felt the need to compete. The bullybeast with the drippy schnozz armswung directly up to the startled ladfolk. "Greetz! Me beez Boog! Snff."

"Uh – greets – er, I mean, pleased to meet you – uh – Boog."

Now Biff also armswung up to Tiptin. "Bam lick cold axe," he informed him.

"Gotsth schtuck," the weeping bullybeast said, pointing to the axe. "Hurtsth."

"Oh, I bet it does," Tiptin acknowledged.

Next, the lost-looking bullybeast armswung over to the stranger and extended a wet and hairy foot in greeting.

Tiptin hesitated, and then played footsies with him as he inquired, "And what is your name?"

"????????"

"Brainless nod sez much," Biff explained.

"Snff. Too much nasty knocks noogies," Boog added, rapping his knuckles loudly upon his own thick skull. "Brainless beez boink."

"Oh, I see," Tiptin began. "Still, I'm pleased…"

"Me see too!" Biff cut in, using his digits to widen his own seers. "See – me got seers?"

"Him see ye seers – snff – Mister Stinks Gross! Snff."

"Me stinks nice!"

"Nod nice – snff – beez gross!"

"Dooz beez nice!"

"Uh-uh. Snfffff. Beez stinky gross like yucky finners!"

"Dooz nod!"

"Dooz!"

"Nod! Nod! Nod!"

"Dooz! Dooz! Snff…"

"Hey!" Tiptin hollered, stepping directly between the circling combatants. He pointed at Bam, causing the latter to flinch. "Instead of fighting, why don't we try and get that axe off of your Broz' licker?"

"Beez schtuck," Bam added with a sulk.

Tiptin drew a deep breath before he resumed speaking. "Listen, if we start a fire and carefully warm up the axe, then it should come off without tearing the skin. It really is quite simple."

"Snff. We bullies like simple."

Tiptin rolled his seers. "I'm certain you do, Boog."

"Dooz ye sez?"

"Uh – I said – um – I said I am most happy to help you."

"Tiptin beez bullybeasts budz?" Biff inquired.

"Uh – yes, sure. I'm your budz. Now let's gather…"

"HOORRAY!!" shouted the bullybeasts, suddenly grabbing the startled ladfolk and rubbing their knuckles briskly across his skull. "Noogie-noogie-noogie-noog…"

"Stop it! Hey! Cut it out! I mean it! Hey! **Dung!**"

Suddenly the Broz stopped.

Biff donned a serious look. "Nod plite sez bad woyds."

The others all nodded with wided seers.

Tiptin rubbed his aching crown and met Biff's serious stare with one of his own. It was readily apparent that the bullybeasts were beginning to rattle his reason.

"Nod plite sez bad woyds," Biff repeated.

"Okay, okay," Tiptin conceded with a sigh. He rolled his seers. I do apologize. It's just that we humanfolk don't much care much for - uh – noogies."

The bullybeasts were visibly stunned. Each dropped jaw and looked to the others in utter disbelief.

"Ye nod even like nice no-hurts noogies?" Biff asked at last.

"Nod ever? Snff." Boog added.

"Bam was equally perplexed. "Beez schik, Thipthen? Ahhh…"

"Duh - ?????" Brainless moved to say something, then lost his sense of thought.

Tiptin felt guilty. "Well – er – no, I'm not sick. You see, my skull is not near so thick as yours and…"

"Stop!" Biff suddenly exclaimed. "Me get it – Tiptin wants to play zings!"

"HOORRAY!!" the others cheered. **"Zings in sky! Zings in sky! Zings in sky! Zings in sky! Zings in…"**

"Hey!" the startled ladfolk screamed to no avail, suddenly finding himself being tossed heels over hearers high into the brisk air. Time after time after time he tumbled back down, only to be caught by huge, hairy arms and promptly 'zinged' back up into the sky. He quickly grew dizzy. Plus very, very angry.

Tiptin's cheeks flushed with rage as he flailed frantically about in mid-flight, grasping at breeze. "Hey! Stop it! I said stop – whooaaa…"

"ZINGS! ZINGS! ZINGS!!"

"Ha! Snff. Tiptin beez high up to trees!"

"I am not …whooaaa…kidding! Stop it! Put me down! Now! I said…whoooaaa…" Tiptin's stomach spinned to spew.

"Tiptin beez green – see?"

"Snff. Too high zings, Tiptin?"

"Schtopth playth zingth!"

"Whoooaaaa….."

"SPLUNCH!!"

All the Broz gawked at the ladfolk's legs kicking furiously above the chillcream.

"Ooopz. Dooz pologize, Tiptin. Boog spozed catches."

"Nod me – snff – spozed beez ye catches!" Boog protested.

"Beez nod!" Biff shouted back.

"Beez too!"

"Beez…"

"Mmmmm !?" "#*!?!"

"Dooz Tiptin sez?"

"Mmmmmm!! '#*!??' "!*#!??!!!"

"Snfff. Sez plays noogies maybe?" Boog suggested with a shrug of his broad shoulders.

"Nodth sez plays noogeeth," Bam said. "Sez beezth schtuck!"

"Oooopz." Biff put in.

Of course, the customary round of 'post-zings' congratulatory knuckle noogies was required before Biff and Boog finally yanked the beyond livid ladfolk free of his frigid fix and placed him gently atop the chillcream. Where he laid panting and shivering and scolding Seed for the very being of bullybeasts. Plus begging forgiveness from Destiny for whatever it was he'd done to deserve meeting this lot.

"Snfff. See, Tiptin. Broz got wood."

"Destiny, grant me strength," Tiptin pleaded, staring up at the distant skysheep while holding onto the spinning ground.

"Dooz him sez?"

The other bullybeasts simply shrugged.

Once the belly spins had stopped and he'd shaken clear the witwebs from his mind, Tiptin winced and pressed astand to encounter four beaming bullybeasts bearing armfuls of busted tree boughs.

"Duh - ?????" Brainless began, but lost his train of thought.

"Got wood," Biff explained enthusiastically.

"Nodth gotsth flintsth?" Bam pointed out.

Tiptin sighed and stuck his numbed digits into his vest-pouch. "It's okay, I have flints and dry straw for starting a fire."

"HOORRAY!!" the four broz shouted, throwing their massive arms in the air.

Tiptin dove for cover as large chunks of busted boughs smacked down all about him.

Pulling his wet face out of the chillcream, the now way beyond livid ladfolk muttered something through gnashed biters.

"Dooz ye sez, Tiptin?" Biff inquired.

"Dig a fire pit!" Tiptin snapped. "Now!"

"Oooopz – kay."

"And find some dry logs for us to sit on!"

"Tiptin beez mad at bullies, huh?"

"Yes!" Tiptin railed, pointing his pointdigit at the bullybeasts. "Now you four Broz listen to…"

Tiptin ceased in mid-shout as all four bullybeasts started to shake.

"Please nod schodes Broz, Tiptin. Pleeeeeze."

"Snff. Broz dooz pologize cuzz beez dense boobs."

All four bullybeasts nodded in agreement.

Lowering his digit, the ladfolk tamed his tone. "Okay then, I nod schodes – er – I mean, I won't scold you."

Instantly, the bullybeasts ceased shaking. **"HOORRAY!!"**

"Hey! No! Ow! Ouch! Aaaa! Stop it!"

"Ooopz. Broz forgot, Tiptin nod like noogies."

"Dooz pologize. Snff."

"That is right. I nod like.....DUNG!! I'm even starting to speak like them!"

"Nod plite sez bad woyds."

"I know. I know." Tiptin bowed his head in prayer. "Dearest Destiny, grant me strength."

"Dooz him sez?" Boog asked of his broz.

"Seth nod liketh noogies?" Bam offered.

"Snff. Plays zings?" Biff suggested.

"No!" Tiptin screamed out in frustration. "I do not want to play zings! I like my belly inside my skin! Or noogies! My skull feels just fine without lumps! In fact, I don't want to play any games! Now, can we simply get a fire burning? Please."

"We like simple."

Despite their apparent lack of wit, the bullybeasts actually proved to be most capable workers. Digging like canines, their large hands quickly cleared away a patch of chillcream. Of course, they inadvertently displaced much of it onto one very annoyed ladfolk.

"Snfff. Dooz beez Tiptin?"

"Hey – dooz him beez! Beez creemfolk – ha!"

"Duh - ?????"

"Zings creemballs, Tiptin?"

"No!" Tiptin snapped, shaking and slapping the white wet from his bratt and trousers. "And be careful where you throw…"

"WHAP!!"

"Hey!" was all Tiptin could manage as a giant slushy creamball landed him on his butt.

"Brainlesth zingth," Bam snitched, pointing at his lost Broz.

"Cuzz ye dooz sez him zings, Bam!" Biff shouted in the lost bullybeast's defense.

"Soth. Brainlesth shtilth…"

"Whooaaa!" Tiptin exclaimed, pressing astand and wiping chillcream from his face. Crimson trickled from one sniffer. "I don't give a – er, I don't care who threw it! One more creamball to the face and I'll leave you all here to start your own fire! Got it! I said, got it!"

Tiptin glared daggers at the muted bullybeasts. "Good. Now dig that pit!"

At once the bullybeasts took to fist pounding the frosted ground and breaking it up into chunks.

"Brainlesth zingth."

"Cuzz ye sez, Bam."

"Deeper!" Tiptin cut in, barely dodging an errant dirt missile.

"Oooopz. Dooz pologize."

"Broz-snff-scoops deep, Tiptin."

"Hey!" Biff suddenly exclaimed, tearing a large chunk of root from the hole. "Beez toober! Me got food!"

""HOORRAY!!"

Tiptin could merely roll his seers as the Broz launched into an excited round of knuckle noogies.

"Dooz nice no-hurts noogies, Tiptin?"

"NO!"

Having finally finished with their noogies, the bullybeasts continued scooping out soil with their digits until they'd dug a deep crater. Then Tiptin grabbed some small sticks and jumped into the hole.

Suddenly Tiptin noticed Brainless wandering off into the woods alone. "Where is he off to," he inquired.

"Brainless got piddle," Biff explained, busily washing his hands with chillcream.

It shocked the ladfolk to discover Boog and Bam were likewise washing their hands. And their faces, too?

Nothing Tiptin's surprised expression, Biff held up the root and explained. "Got toober, so scrubz hands."

Bam and Boog nodded their agreement, while Brainless armswung back with his licker awag. Then he too joined in the ritual.

"Dooz make fire, Tiptin, pleeeze," Biff begged.

"Pleeezth. Axe beeth schtuck," Bam also pressed.

Tiptin took the flints and straw from his pouch. "Yes, it is time we were warm."

Soon the entire group was all warm and cozy, seated on dry logs about a raging fire. Famished flames eagerly devoured the fibrous feast.

"Ahhh – ahhhhhh," Bam moaned as Tiptin gently tugged on the axe.

"It shouldn't be long now," Tiptin assured the sulking bullybeast. "But don't get too close. We don't want the metal to get too hot and burn your licker."

"Uh-uh," Bam agreed, shaking his head so the axe-handle swung.

"Want toober?" Biff asked, offering Tiptin a chunk of charred root.

The famished ladfolk eagerly snatched it from the bullybeast's outstretched palm. "Thank you," he said, before chomping off a chunk and greedily gulping it into his gut.

"Beez yummy?" Biff inquired. "Beez joosee too, huh?"

"Oh yes," Tiptin replied, biting off another chunk.

"Snff. Nod beddar beez dezzerts," Boog remarked.

"No, I don't suppose it is beddar – er – I mean, better than desserts. But given our choices, it is rather tasty. And nutritious, too, no doubt."

"Dooz ye sez?"

"Oh, I mean root – er - toober, is good for us."

"Makes strong, huh?"

"Yes, toober will make us strong."

"Snfff. Me beez strong!"

"Nod strong dooz beez me!"

"Beez too!"

"Dooz nod!"

"Beez…"

"Duh - ?????…..dezzerts!?"

All stopped to stare at Brainless, who calmly went about biting off another chunk of toober.

“Hey, Broz! Axe beez off – see!”

It was true. Bam was standing and proudly displaying the tool high atop his thick skull. Next he commenced wagging one very swollen and very blue licker.

“HOORRAY!!”

Tiptin barely avoided being trampled during the excitement. Yet he got off rather easy this time, only being noogied three times.

After the commotion had finally come to calm, Tiptin asked, “I hope you all thought to save Bam some toober?”

The confused bullybeasts exchanged quizzical glances.

“Broz dooz always share,” Biff finally stated, holding up a large piece of root and passing it to Bam.

“Broz got lots,” Bam added, spreading his arms wide apart. “Beez lots – cuzz be in woods.”

“Oh, yes. I suppose there is plenty more about.”

“Huh?”

“Plenty? Snff.”

“Uh – lots. Plenty means lots.”

“HOORRAY!!”

“Hey! Stop it! No! Don’t! Put me down! Now!”

"Ooopz. Forgot."

"Dooz pologize."

"Duh -?????…lots?"

Having finally filled their bloated bellies near to burst, the group fed many logs to the famished flames. Then they settled down to chat.

The bullybeasts eagerly explained to Tiptin that they had 'swinged' away from Ezu because the sorcerer 'beez big meeny' and 'dooz nod nice things'.

"Mastoor Xebec boss us bout!" Biff exclaimed angrily.

"Snff. Him nod like bullies," Boog elaborated.

All four Broz nodded in solemn agreement.

They also added how much they missed 'swims in sea' and 'dezzerts'. Yet, by far, they mostly missed the 'sheebullies'.

"Cuzz me like hot noogies," Bam explained, grinning slyly and wriggling his brows.

"Ooooooo….," the others teased, smudging their blushing Broz with razznoogies.

The bullybeasts yacked well beyond Black. Incessantly. About everything from 'Ezu' to Xebec to 'snagging finners' to 'skytwinklers'. For the immense above was filled with them.

Eventually Tiptin felt his lids shutting against his will. He struggled to stay with the chat, yet could not. Fighting fatigue to no avail, he let his heavy lids lock and he slowly slumped to one side. Then, just as he entered the relaxing realm of napvisions, he was vaguely aware of strong arms scooping him up and gently snuggling him against something warm, soft and hairy. And his dreams danced to the beat of Biff's breath….

"….nod so squeezes, Boog!"

"….see licker stix out – ha!"

Tiptin awakened to find himself lying atop Biff's pulsing belly. Bright had long forced Black from the sky, triumphant once again in their never-ending battle to rule the above. All the bullybeasts were themselves back in the realm of the real. Angry embers still hissed and cackled within the pit.

"Greetz, Tiptin," Biff said with a welcoming smile. "Boog squishes skulz so licker stix out – see! Ha!"

Tiptin stretched the knots from his frame and palmed his cheeks to awaken. Then he rolled off the bullybeast's warm, heaving belly. Pressing astand, he turned about to find that Boog was now stretching his yap wide apart and wagging his licker at Bam and Brainless, both of whom were holding their bellies and rolling in giggle about the chillcream.

"Dearest Destiny, what'd I do?" he muttered, looking above. The brightsphere was high and warm and the wetspikes were dripping in melt. "Well, whatever I did, I'm sorry."

"Dooz ye sez?" Biff asked, knuckling to his feet.

"Oh – uh, nothing, Biff. Just muttering."

"Huh?"

"I mean, I was just talking to myself."

"Tiptin beez boink?" Biff asked, winding a hairy pointdigit about his hearer.

"I'm fine, Biff," Tiptin assured the concerned bullybeast, while drawing tight his bratt. "Though I really should be getting on now. But it certainly was nice meeting you and your Broz. I do wish all of you well."

Biff's seers wided with shock and misted over with sadness. "Tiptin – ye nod stays too Broz?"

Suddenly the others ceased their antics and all swiftswung over to join Biff. All donned the same look of shocked sadness. Except for Brainless, of course, who simply looked lost?

"Snff. Tiptin nod like bullies?" Boog asked.

Bam added, "Cuzz bullies beez dense, huh?"

"No. No. I really like you Broz a lot. It's just that…"

"HOORRAY!!"

"No. Wait. Hey! Stop! Put me down! Now!"

"Oooopz. Dooz pologize."

"Broz forgot ye nod like zings."

"Nod like noogies too. Snff."

"Tiptin nod like bullies," Biff sulked. "Broz dooz beez lost."

Looking at the brooding Broz, Tiptin realized that there was absolutely no chance of his simply saying good-bye to them and being on his way. With their incredible speed, they'd follow him for certain. And annoy him to no end.

Not that the ladfolk disliked the burly bunch. In fact, he had grown somewhat fond of them. But their ceaseless antics were certain to wind him completely 'round the twist'. And his skull was already plenty sore enough. So he needed to somehow give them the slip.

Still, he felt more than just a tad blameworthy for leaving them all alone and lost in the woods. Except that they weren't really all alone after all, he reasoned. They do have each other, do they not? And they're most certain to find their way home to Ezu eventually, are they not? Or wherever Destiny intends for them to be?

Oh well, he thought, I'm certain they'll forget all about me soon enough. Probably won't even remember my name. Or I theirs for that matter. Besides, what do I owe them, anyway? Or anybody else for that matter? Absolutely nothing.

Is it my fault Xebec found that staff? No. Did I cause him to become evil? No. Am I responsible for the choices made by others? No. One is only responsible for oneself – and I do have myself to think of. Besides, these bullybeasts must learn to solve their own problems. Their current plight is not my prob…"

"Tiptin nod go," Bam pleaded. "Pleeeze."

"Bullies beez lost," Biff again pointed out.

"Snff. Bullies beez Tiptin's best budz. Nod dooz him zings no more – snff – nod ever. Pledges. Snfff."

"Pledges!" promised the others. "We clunks skulz to seals it!"

Tiptin felt his pumper tugging at his chest as the four Broz all clunked 'skulz' to seal their promise.

"Dooz pologize cuzz zings creemball in face."

"Nod go – pleeeze."

"Duhh…..?????…..dezzerts!"

All glanced briefly at Brainless.

"Hey!" Tiptin suddenly exclaimed, stretching a phony smile. "I have an idea. Why don't I stay and we'll play a game?"

"HOORRAY!!"

"Hey! Ouch! Stop it!"

"Oooopz – forgot."

"Dooz pologize."

"Snfff. Play game?"

"Yes, Boog," Tiptin said, stretching his smile. "It is a cubfolk game called hide and seek."

"Hides and see?" Boog asked. "Snff."

"Me dooz see?" Biff noted, pointing to his seers.

"No," Tiptin explained, "not hides – er - hide and see. Hide and seek."

"Hide and seeks? Seeks beez finds, huh?" Bam inquired, beaming with pride.

"Yes, hide and seek. It's really quite simple."

"We like simple."

Tiptin began turning the burly bunch about so that they were all facing the same direction. "Here, I'll show you how to play," he explained. "First you must all look this way…"

"Beez for?"

"Cuzz, Dungskulz. Sheeesh."

"Me nod beez dungskulz, Bam! Ye beez…"

"Whoa!" Tiptin intervened, just as both Broz began raising their knuckles.

"Oooopz. Dooz pologize."

"Me pologize too."

"Okay then," Tiptin continued. "The reason you must all look this way is so you won't see where I hide while you Broz are counting."

"Counts?" the bullybeasts all said with marked concern.

"Yes. First you all count to twenty…"

"Huh?"

Tiptin paused, then rephrased. "Okay, let's make it to ten then. You can count to ten, can't you?"

The bullybeasts hesitated, and then nodded that they could.

Slighting his mounting guilt, Tiptin kept on. "So then, while you Broz are counting, I'll go hide. But you can't turn around and look until you've counted to ten, and you must cover your seers with both hands, like this." Tiptin pressed both palms over his own seers to show them.

"Hides and seeks beez fun?"

"Oh yes, Bam, hide and seek is quite fun. But you must cover your seers while you count."

All four Broz pressed palms to seers, although Brainless needed several attempts to get it right. Each burly beast teetered from side to side as their thin legs buckled beneath their bulk.

"Broz leen to Broz cuzz stop tips."

Following Bam's suggestion, the bullybeasts did in fact start leaning on each other for support. Then they began teetering to-and-fro as a group.

As he started sneaking away, Tiptin said, "Okay, start counting. And no peeking."

"Broz nod cheetz," Biff assured him.

"Bullies – snfff-nod dooz bad things."

"Duh - ?????.....seeks!"

Tiptin felt terrible. He had the knotted-up guts of a false friend. Still, he kept on and trudged in amongst the giant floatwoods. Then he started scaling the steep slope of the rugged mountainside, reasoning that he would have a much better vantage point to view his much swifter pursuers if he was well above them. Thus it would be much easier to avoid the burly bunch.

"One – tree – six – er five – uh..?.."

"Snff. Me thinks dooz beez four?"

"Uh-uh. Beez nine."

"Nod. We spozed sez six again."

"Beez nod!"

"Dooz too!"

"Nod!"

"Too!"

"Duh - ?????"

Tiptin made haste. He had no idea how much time would elapse before any one of the Broz suddenly remembered the number ten. Then the counting sequence would matter for naught. So without even looking back, he continued winding his way in and out of the floatwoods, climbing ever higher and higher.

Soon the slope steeped to a near vertical pitch, and the temp dipped. Dropping to all fours, the ladfolk scrambled like a fleeing animal up a narrow ravine, twice sliding all the way back down over slush and busted wetbricks.

His digits numbed as he clawed his way up towards the growthline. Flesh was painfully stripped from his palms, and bruises throbbed about his battered knees and shins. Weary thighs and calves cramped in revolt. His parched pipe pleaded for drink. Frosty smoke tumbled forth from between his cracked lips. Skindew soaked his garments. He grew giddy with giggles.

Yet on and on and on he climbed. He wondered, would they even pursue him above the growthline?

At last, Tiptin broke free from the floatwoods. The Mountain's frigid breath blasted down from its frozen peak; berating the puny pest for intruding upon its face, and whipping the bratt violently about his shoulders and head.

Peeling the wool from his numbing cheeks, he wrapped the bratt tightly about his shivering torso, and then blew hot breath across his numbed digits. He pondered his dilemma while watching white twisters spindance across the Mountain's cap of packed chillcream.

The determined ladfolk was also aware that Black would eventually charge atop the thisaway horizon, forcing Bright to retreat and, therefore, bringing about a brutal dip in temp. He knew he could not descend back from whence he'd climbed, lest he encounter the bullybeasts. Yet to remain above the growthline would mean a frigid meeting with Morgue.

"Must stay of sense," he muttered. "Mustn't lose control…" Suddenly some familiar voices chopped his thoughts.

"Tiptin! Heer we beez – see!"

"See Tiptin! See!"

Tiptin felt all fight flee his frame. All four Broz were speedily swiftswinging clear of the floatwoods.

"Nod plays hides game, Tiptin! Mountain nod beez nice! Snfff." Boog stopped and began frantically flailing his arms about. "Stop, Tiptin! Snff. Game nod beez fun!"

"Stop! Pleeeeeeze!"

"Pleeeeeze, Tiptin! Stop game!"

"Game beez dense! Snfff. Stop plays!"

“PLEEEEEEEZZE!!!” The bullybeasts all screamed in unison.

“Destiny!” Tiptin shouted out in sheer frustration, charging back down amongst the floatwoods. “Am I to be bound to this bunch for all my being?”

“Stop, Tiptin! Snff.”

“Dooz cum nod like Broz?”

“Broz luvs ye!”

Tiptin could tell by their mounting voices that the bullybeasts were quickly gaining on him. In fact, at any nod he fully expected to feel their hot breath upon his neck. If not their hard knuckles upon his head! Yet the determined ladfolk wasn’t ready to surrender the chase just yet. He thought, there must be some way to lose th…

“Whoooaa!!” Tiptin failed to negotiate the thin crevice in time. He tumbled heels about hearers down the narrow ravine. “Ouch! Oh! Ahh! Ow! Ow! Ouch!…”

A solid slab finally brought Tiptin’s bouncing acrobatics to a jarring halt. But not his agony. He winced and struggled to stand. Fleshscrapes stinged and bruises blued. Warmth trickled down one ankle, which screamed with pain.

Dizzy and disoriented, he desperately high-stepped through the chillcream. He wiped warm crimson from a bit lip. An elbow ached obscenities to him. His stomach spinned to spew.

Melting wet stung his seers as he squinted to sight through fogged vision.

Upon reaching the base of the ravine, he was surprised to find a complete absence of chillcream. In fact, here the Mountain's aura was warm. He wondered, was he still of sense?

Veering clear of some rubble, he hobbled in amongst a family of ferns. With reckless abandon, he flailed vines and branches from his path, and suffered the numbing sting of flesh welts as the Forest, in retaliation, whipped barbed twigs across its tormentor's face and limbs.

Then his screaming ankle failed him, and he pitched face first into an angry thicket of thorns.

For several wince-filled nods the battered ladfolk lay still, holding his ankle while struggling to fill his burning breathers. All too familiar voices shouted to him from somewhere well above. But he no longer cared if they found him.

Then he spied a tight crawlcozy, which was almost entirely obscured by moist moss growing about its stony lips.

Vicious thorns sliced open exposed skin as Tiptin dragged himself towards the beckoning shelter. He hoped the rich aroma from the moss might mask his scent, lest he be found and noogied nutty.

Finally tearing his body free of the determined thorns, Tiptin wriggled into the crawlcozy, wedging himself between both stony lips. Hot gusts blew forth from the blackness, and skindew soaked his torn garments and stung into his cuts. He noted that the floor of the cozy felt soft and – **fleshy!**

"Wha…?"

Too late! The stony lips smacked shut!

"AAIIYYY!!" Tiptin shrieked in horror as something coarse and fleshy curled about him, the pitched him into a dark abyss.

"Whoaaa…!" Down, down, down, down, he plummeted. Down into a deep, deep, deep place. No sounds. No sights. Not even shapes! Only hot black and his own sinking stomach.

Outside, the stony lips parted and belched before spreading into a satisfied smile.

Down, down, down, down………. "**Sploop!**"

Now he plunged deep into a thick soup. A sense of motion indicated he was caught in some sort of swirlpool, which sought to suck him away.

G-Gotta reach surface, he thought. B-Before breathers burst…

Frantically, the frightened ladfolk fought for his very being, thrashing his limbs wildly about and gasp-gulping soup. But to no avail. It was like swimming in swirling sinksand, only worse. He felt himself nodding off into the relaxing realm of napvisions, to be followed by…

Suddenly something nudged his legs. Something lurking in the soup! Then it nudged him again! And again! And yet again!

“No, Tiptin realized, I’m still of breath. This thing is real!

Panic seized his mind as the something slammed into him from beneath and surged for the surface. Then, immediately upon breaking through, it flung him into the black. Discarding him like distasteful chow!

Tiptin slapped against a spongy barrier, and then slid slowly into a sit atop some soggy stuff. He gasped for breath and tried to shake mush from his mind, while straining his seers to sight shapes, or anything.

His nostrils burned as he inhaled the stinging stench of ammonia. Evidence of blackwings?

However, nothing stirred inside the Mountain’s belly. Not a sight, nor a sound, save for the occasional dull ‘sploop’, and his own pounding pumper.

“Destiny, guide me,” he whispered. Upon pressing astand, his battered knees buckled beneath the weight of his saturated garments. Thus, he discarded the heavy bratt and spilled ‘soup’ from his highboots.

Squishing back into his footwear, he groped about in the blackness until his palms found a barrier. Then, tracing his dirty digits along its spongy plane, he trudged slowly across the soggy 'stuff', completely unaware that high above, two stony lips parted to giggle.

"Schmuck-schmack-schmuck-schmack…"

After a few labored steps, Tiptin paused to rest his injured ankle.

"Schmuck-schmack-schmuck-schmack…"

The sound seemed to come from behind him. An echo? No. He hadn't been walking that slowly. Was the something from the soup stalking him?

Tiptin took several exaggerated steps, and then stopped abruptly.

"Schmuck-schmack…" Silence...

Once again, the leery ladfolk took a few cautious steps. Then he stopped and spun about, honing his hearers.

"Schmuck-schmack…" Silence…

Next he tried stepping in place. *"Schmuck-schmack-schmuck-schmack…"* Silence…

"Wh – who's there," he asked meekly.

Silence…

"I – I mean nobody any harm. I'm just lost." Tiptin thought of the vile tree beast, Snarky Snotnicer. Legend stated he dwelled in The Swallow Mountains. Could it be him? Tiptin had always thought that Snarky was only a myth. But was he?

Again, Tiptin tried stepping in place. Then honed his hearers for naught.

A few paces forward…stop.

Silence…

It seemed that he was alone with his breath and the blackness after all. Perhaps fear and fatigue were teasing his mind. "Yes, that must be it," he whispered. Shrugging his shoulders and blowing out breath, he restarted on his way.

"Schmuck-schmack-schmuck-schmack schmuckschmackSCHMUCK!!!"

That was definitely not his imagination! He fled across the soggy stuff, tracing the spongy barrier. His mind was now a tangled mesh of thoughts. None of them clear.

What was the something? Where was he going? Where was he coming from? Would he, at any moment, collide with an object? How would he ever escape the Mountain's belly? Was there even a way out? Was the something still chas…"

Run! Forget the pain in your ankle! Just run and don't think! What's that? Light? Thank Destiny; there is light up ahead!

It was true! There was a faint glow of light up ahead!

Tiptin raced for the light, kicking his heels high atop the soggy stuff. He ignored his screaming ankle.

The light shone through a cleft in the spongy barrier. Could he squeeze through? Probably, but what lay beyond?

"SCHMUCKSCHMACKSCHMUCKSCHMACKSCH…"

Who cared! Tiptin near dove into the narrow slit and barely squeezed through, tearing his vest and scraping flesh from his back. One foot caught a snag, sending him sprawling across rock on the far side. Real rock! Hard and cool and – **beautiful!"**

Tiptin propped his aching frame upright against a solid wall and scanned his new surroundings. He was now inside an immense cavern, which sprawled out as far as his seers could sight!

It's ceiling was of clear, sparkling stone, which glittered like stained pearls. Peculiar scarlet fibers spiraled from floor to ceiling, throbbing forth both heat and red light. Petrified tentacle trees with long faces wiggled their stony feelers and watched him with wided seers.

Silkspinners nets were festooned between the spiraled fibers and pillars of fungi-clad stone. Yet there were no silkspinners about?

"Dearest Destiny!" Tiptin exclaimed, forgetting all about the something beyond the cleft.

Pressing astand, he took to hobbling about the cavern. He weaved in and out of the spiraled fibers, while keeping clear of the tentacle trees, lest he be snared.

Eventually, he grew weary and felt need of nap, but the vacant silkspinner's nets kept him nervous. Somehow, he sensed he was not alone. So he picked up a heavy chunk of stone, just in case.

Creepy shadows teased his mind. Some stretched and shrank as the scarlet fibers throbbed forth their heat and light. Others simply loomed stoic.

Then he heard it. It was faint and distant, but unmistakably the sound of claws clicking upon rock. And they were coming closer!

Now Tiptin began to panic! Without success, his seers scoured the vicinity for a better weapon or a suitable hiding place. Suddenly he wished he'd stayed with the Broz.

He wondered, should I flee? But to where? No, sound will only give away my location. But I can't stay here…

"Ouch!" he exclaimed, as his arm brushed up against a searing fiber, singing his skin.

Suddenly, the clicking ceased.

"Dung," Tiptin cussed beneath his breath, before clamping his errant yap mute.

He began slowly backing away from the area. Ever so cautiously. Upon tippydigits. With clenched biters and darting seers. He feared there would be no tricking his way out of this latest fine mess.

Both trembling hands gripped firm the heavy chunk of stone. His chestpumper pounded, and beads of skindew blazed trails down his filthy cheeks. The very thought of becoming a silkspinner's snack made him shudder and gulpswallow, hard.

"Come to me," he muttered, trying in vain to summon up false courage. "I'll bash at least one of you senseless."

Back and back, he crept, still upon tippydigits. Slowly. Cautiously. Stealthily. Tiptin was fully unaware of the huge form already looming over him, mocking each of his backwards steps.

"AHHH!" Tiptin screamed as he bumped up against the unmistakable feel of flesh! He spun about with the crude weapon held high.

"AARG!!" roared the giant, brandishing a log-like club high atop its head. **"AAAAARRRGGG!!!"**

"Aiyeee!" Tiptin wailed as he dropped the heavy stone upon his digits. In ragewild agony, he commenced to hop, scream and cuss. "Ah! Eee! Oh! Oooooo. Ouch! Dung! Ow! Ow! Ow! Oh my dearest Destiny! Dung! Ahhhh…."

"HARR! HARR! HARR!" roared the giant in a booming belly laugh. "HARR! HARR! HARR! HARR!"

Tiptin fumed as he studied this jovial joker in a jungle-jumper, who really seemed to revel in another's pain.

Although stooped over in hysterics, the annoying giant still stood some thirty hands in height. Tall, even for his kind. Plus his brawny body would probably tip the stone scale at about seventy. Even bigger than a bullybeast.

His blotchy skin bore a greenish tinge. Frizzes of coarse orange hair covered much of his broad back and shoulders and chest. Ditto the top of his meaty forearms.

Pointy hearers perked atop his shiny dome. One bushy, orange brow bridged a gleaming green seer. A large schnozz hooked down past two fat lips. His mouth was filled with sharp, pointy biters. He almost lacked a neck.

His fists were big as boulders, and his knuckles near as hard. Muscles ripped within thighs thick as sinkwoods. Enormous feet were each complimented by a trio of clawed digits. His enormous belly bounced in laugh beneath the hide jungle-jumper.

"HARR! HARR! HARR! HARR!" Glee drops now flooded his face. "Wow! Were you scared, or what! HARR! HARR! Y-You shoulda seen your face! Ooooweee! Too much, I tell ya, toooooo much! HARR! HARR! HARR! HARR!"

Tiptin finally ceased hopping about and addressed the jovial joker. "Y – You're a Cyclops?"

"Wow, you're quick! HARR! HARR! HARR! Too much! Simply toooooo much! HARR! HARR! HARR!" The giant lowered his club and grabbed his bouncing belly. Then he slapped Tiptin's back, nearly dislodging the startled ladfolk's pumper. "Oh, Destiny. "HARR! HARR! HARR! HARR! Tooooo much, I tell ya! This puny guy is simply tooooo.... **EEEEYYYOOOWWWWWWWW!!!"**

While the now not-so-jovial joker hopped about clenching one clawed foot, Tiptin gloated and patted the solid chunk of stone.

"OUCH! OUCH! OW! OW! Oh mighty Morgue, it smarts! Ah! Ow! Eee! Ooooo, my aching toots..."

"Serves you right," Tiptin scolded, "sneaking up behind folk and terrifying them. Not to mention stalking them through black tunnels."

"Ooooo – huh? Black tunnels? What black tunnels? Oh, dearest Destiny it smarts. Ooooo..."

Tiptin gulped, and then warily scanned the vicinity. He could almost feel somebody watching them. Or something?

Thump! The moaning Cyclops plopped about and stuck a swollen digit between his fat lips. "Mmmmm..."

"So," Tiptin continued, "what in Ranidae would a Cyclops be doing sneaking about a mountain's innards, Hmmmm?"

"Ooooo..." The giant took to rubbing his toots. "Ahhhh..."

"Well?" Tiptin pressed.

The giant's face was flushed. "I – ahhh - I was fleeing a bunch of batty bullybeasts I had encountered at the base of this mountain."

Tiptin smiled knowingly.

Using his club as a makeshift crutch, the Cyclops struggled astand and hobbled closer to the puny ladfolk. Then he returned the smile and extended a huge hand in greeting.

Tiptin was skeptical, and hesitant to shake.

Sensing such, the Cyclops withdrew the gesture. Yet he continued to smile. "Anyway, I spied the mouth of a large cave and figured I'd give them the slip. I managed to sneak into the cave without them seeing me. All seemed to be going well and soon I could no longer hear them calling my name. Then I accidentally rubbed up against the side of the cave and it – uh, well it…"

"Smacked shut and swallowed you?" Tiptin asked.

"Yeah!"

"Then you landed in some soupy sinksand, right?"

"Uh, wrong. Then I landed in a silkspinner's net. A right sticky one, too. Took forever to gnash free." The Cyclops chomped his sharp biters for effect.

Tiptin soured face in disgust before speaking. "I am Tiptin, Stonemason from Folkton. "What is your name and title?"

"What is my title?" The giant smirked silly, then snapped straight his spine and palmed his chest. "I am Thwack, Fleshfeed For A Mountain's Innards! HARR! HARR! HARR! HARR! Oh, Destiny! Too much, I tell ya! This puny ladfolk is simply too much! What is my title? HARR! Like it almost matters down here! HARR! HARR! Ha.... **EEEEEEYYYYOOOOWWWWWWW!!!!"**

"Har – har – har," Tiptin mocked with noted sarcasm. "How about Thwack, Smarty With Twin Throbbing Toots?"

Eventually Thwack ceased howling. Again he stuck a swollen digit between his fat lips, moaning as he sucked. He viewed Tiptin with hurt pride, the silly smirk seemingly silenced for good.

"Well, nobody likes to be poked fun at," Tiptin rebuked, massaging his own sore ankle.

"Certainly not!" a dignified voice concurred from above. "Nor does one usually favor having one's digits bashed with stones."

Thwack and Tiptin exchanged panicky gapes before scrambling astand.

Dangling from the ceiling was the strangest silkspinner either had ever imagined! Its plump body was mostly covered in coarse hair, white as skysheep except for a pink bald patch in the center of its back. Eight skinny arms led to eight pinkish pods with long, hooked digits. Two stubby legs joined with a pair of pinkish feet.

Its scalp was wrapped to the temples by a broken wreath of white hair. Its lush face was wrinkled with knowledge. Wise, pink peepers popped from deep, puffy sockets. A long, warted sniffer twisted to one side of its pinkish face. Sheeny fangs parted its braided beard from a curly stache. Black holes served as hearers.

The muted pair continued gawking agape as the strange silkspinner reeled out more cord and dropped towards them. Thwack tightened his grip on his club, while Tiptin clenched the stone with both hands. Both were intrigued, yet uncertain. Silkspinner's knew naught of speech? At least, so they had always believed.

"What – er – who are you?" Tiptin asked as the silkspinner touched solid. Nerves tangled his licker. "I – I…"

"Nap your nerves, Tiptin, I've no desire to do you damage. Nor you, Thwack."

"H-How do you know our names?" inquired the suspicious Cyclops.

The white stranger chortled. "How? Hee, hee. You pair were only raising enough racket to raise a comatose arachnid."

"Ara –Ar…"

"Arachnid, my dear clops. Or, if you so prefer, silkspinner."

"But who are you?" Tiptin re-asked.

"Oh, dear. It does seem that I have neglected to formally introduce myself. Tsk. Tsk. How unbelievably improper of me. I do offer only the humblest of apologies. Really. Just haven't quite been myself of late. But no excuses! This boorish behavior simply will not do. It is most unbecoming of an arachnid of noble stature." The silkspinner placed a hooked digit alongside its fanged eathole and lowered its voice to a whisper. "Not to mention, it's downright rude."

Thwack and Tiptin shared amused looks.

"Ahem! I am Spidey Smeals - Master Magician and Metal Forger. Besides being your humble host." Placing its four right arms behind its back and simultaneously sweeping the four left across its plump body, the strange silkspinner executed a most gracious bow.

"Smeals?" Thwack bit his lip hard, lest he launch into laughter. Despite a savory smirk stewing about his face, he somehow managed to pot a brewing belly burst. Only one drop bubbled beyond the lid.

"Correct. Spidey Smeals. But my friends just call me Spidey."

"Master Magician and Metal Forger?" Tiptin was uncomfortably conscience of the Cyclops cooking up a quip next to him.

"Indubitably. I am considered to be amongst the foremost in both ancient arts."

Thwack spouted a saucy squeak. Which surely would have boiled over into a bouncing belly burst, were it not for a heel scrunching the tip of his already throbbing digit.

"Ahhh! Ahh-ahhh…"

"Pardon me, Thwack?" Spidey asked.

"Ahhhh…."

"He's awed speechless by the presence of a real master magician," Tiptin explained, glaring daggers at the wincing Cyclops, and grinding down his heel even harder in warning. "Isn't that right, Thwack?"

"Ahh – yaahhh!"

Tiptin grinned and palmed up. "See?"

"Hmmmmm?" Spidey stroked his beard as he examined Thwack's face. "Interesting. I've never seen green skin turn to purple before."

"Ahhhh…"

"Anyway, I'm not behaving like a proper host. Tsk. Tsk. Come, my lair is quite comfy. There, Tiptin can clean up from his dip in the whirlpit. Then we shall all break bugs. I do hope you've both brought along ample appetites. Hmmmm?"

Tiptin's stomach wrenched and his face soured in disgust. "Break bugs?"

Spidey forced a sort of smile. "Or bread and fruit if you so prefer. I can never keep it straight which species consumes which grub."

"Can we still put bugs on our bread?" Thwack drooled with obvious concern.

"Certainly, my dear clops. Also, I have been told that I prepare the best pestzels anywhere. Hee, hee. Hardly surprising when one considers that I probably bake the only pestzels anywhere."

"Mmmmmm." Thwack rubbed his enormous belly and smacked his fat lips.

"Gee, Tiptin thought, I can hardly wait. "Yechhh."

"Pardon me, Tiptin?"

"Uh – er – ahhhh…"

"He says he'd feel most privileged to try some pestzels," Thwack said with a smirk, squeezing the back of Tiptin's neck until the puny ladfolk gagged out his licker. "See?"

"Marvelous. Then I shall bake up an extra big batch. And prepare a light insectasalad, too. Along with creeper cake for dessert. Come, we shall feast!"

Thwack released Tiptin's neck and patted the choking ladfolk's back. "You also have digits," he warned in a whisper, supplemented with a show stomp.

Tiptin was too busy sucking for wind to reply.

"Come. Come." Spidey beckoned with sweeping arms. He stretched his eathole into a sort of smile. "Don't fret, Tiptin, for I do have ample bread and berries as well. In case you change your mind about the bugs."

Thwack's tone was once again tinged with concern. "But you shall still bake pestzels?"

"Of course, my dear clops. We do aim to please. Come. Come to my lair. But do avoid being snagged by the tentacle trees. They don't get on very well with strangers, I'm afraid."

Together, they weaved in and out of the spiraled fibers and pillars of fungi-clad stone, often brushing silkspinner's nets from their path. Until they at last came upon a hole in the rock floor.

"I'll spin you a sturdy climb cord," Spidey explained as he commenced circling a pillar. "Fear not falling. My silk does stretch, but it shan't snap."

"Naaaww," Thwack replied. "Idav never guessed."

Spidey carefully attached his silk cord to the stone, then scurried across the floor and jumped into the hole. "Wheeeeeeee…"

Tiptin motioned for Thwack to descend first. Should their host be in error, he had no intention of landing beneath seventy stone worth of cynical Cyclops.

The climb down proved to be much easier than they'd imagined. Numerous rocky crags provided for secure footing until the pit sides veered into a soft slope. Sparkling silknets lighted the tunnel, assisted by an effervescent spring of frigid wet.

Eventually Thwack and Tiptin caught up with their host, who was standing before silkspun curtains with bugbeads woven in for décor. With puffed pride, the plump arachnid parted the curtains, then bowed and armswept for his guests to enter. "Welcome, fine friends, Welcome to my lovely lair."

Both jaws dropped as the stunned pair absorbed the awesome splendor of Spidey's large lair.

A tiered chandelier swung from the glittery ceiling. Woven of magic sparkle silk, it lighted the entire lair as if it were midbright above.

The floor was of solid gold tile, inlaid with polished gemstones and covered in many areas by oval mats of mistbow moss. Several silkspun cots swung between petrified pillars. The furniture was of petrified framing, with padded sitcushies spinned of fine silk.

An intricately carved table was set with wooden goblets and plates, along with a large bowl of citrus-balls and curved, yellow pulpy. A second bowl was packed to the brim with an assortment of stemmed coremushies. Fine, silver cutlery was arranged in a neat row.

Iron pots and skillets dangled from metal hooks. An aged iron stove squatted before a brick 'suckstack'. Solid sinkwood shelving supported many clay jugs. Four barrels were lined up along the wall, labeled: **BUGS, BIG BUGS, BIGGER BUGS,** and **BIGGEST BUGS.** Two spouted urns bore the inscriptions, **'WASH'** and **'THIRST'**. Drying cloths hung from wallpegs, marked with the insignia: **S.S.** and **GUESTS**.

In a far corner, suspended above a brick hearth, a huge caldron chain swung from a heavy iron tripod. Beside it stood a thick, sinkwood cabinet.

Adjacent a 'ventsucker' crouched a stone workbench, littered with the tools of metal forgery.

A round, silkspun tapestry covered almost an entire wall. It depicted an alert seer.

In one corner hung a huge painted portrait of a plantlike creature with shinesilver skin, grassy hair, a mossy beard, and purple peepers set deep within puffy hollows.

"Who is this?" Thwack inquired.

"A very old and very dear friend," Spidey replied.

"Where does your friend dwell?" Tiptin asked.

Spidey sighed with obvious sorrow. "Nowhere, anymore. Least not anyplace that we still of breath would as of yet comprehend?"

"Oh." Both guests responded in one voice. "Sorry."

Spidey sort of smiled. "Sorry? Whatever for? All that begins must end. Whatever arrives must eventually depart. Lest there could be no order in the universe, nor space for those yet to follow. Besides, perhaps the beyond is better? Sort of like we're all climbing a stepwell through different levels of being? I often ponder such matters."

"So what's at the end?" Tiptin asked.

"End of what?"

"Of the stepwell?"

The arachnid stroked his beard. "I honestly don't know, Tiptin. A chute back to the very beginning, perhaps? Only Destiny, Seed and Morgue know the solution to this time worn riddle.

"But it is okay for mere mortals to still ponder such matters?" Tiptin inquired. "I mean, they wouldn't mind?"

Spidey produced a lopsided grin. "They'd probably be much more amused than mind. Maybe to wonder is in fact the primary purpose of our being? I've little doubt that Destiny itself has often wondered about the antics of us mere mortals. I know I do."

"Perhaps eating is the primary purpose of being?" Thwack cut in. "Like, I wonder when we're gonna? Can we bake some pestzels now, Spidey? Please."

"Hee, hee. Perhaps for some it is." Spidey rubbed his own plump belly and winked at Tiptin. "We can converse about such perplexing problems another time. For the moment, somebody's primary purpose growlbegs for bugs."

"Uh – perplexing?"

"Puzzling, my dear ladfolk. Perplexing means puzzling." Spidey explained, retrieving a very big bowl and a wooden chowpounder from one of the many shelves and handing them to Thwack. "Whilst I flame the stove, do be a dear clops and start crunching bugs into fine pellets for our pestzels. I've found that the biggest bugs bake best."

"Sure, Spidey!" Thwack beamed a big smile, exposing all his pointy biters. Then he merrily thumped over to the appropriate barrel.

"Help yourself to fruit and drink, Tiptin. But be certain to peel the skin from the crescent pulpy. And remember, the unripened green ones taste horrible."

"Okay," Tiptin acknowledged, snagging one of the drying cloths enroute to the wash urn.

Together, Spidey and Thwack prepared a fabulous feast of insectasalad, pestzels, and chocolate-coated creeper cake. Almost all of which the famished Cyclops eagerly devoured, while Tiptin routinely soured face in disgust.

With bellies brimmed and nerves relaxed, all three then settled on sitcushies before the tapestry; which watched their every movement.

"Ahhhhh. That was deeeeee – lisheeoous!" Thwack exclaimed, smacking his big lips for effect.

"Glad my pestzels passed your approval, Thwack." Spidey sort of smiled at Tiptin. "I trust the bread and berries were likewise satisfactory?"

"Mmmmmm." Tiptin replied, rubbing his bloated belly.

Spidey chortled. "Splendid. Now perhaps we can converse free of belly distractions."

"Converse?"

"Chat, my dear clops. Chat?"

"About what?" Tiptin inquired.

"Hmmmm..." Spidey stroked his braided beard and focused his pink peepers upon the floor. "Well, for starters you both might share with me news of events up above. I nearly never venture atop the surface – and absolutely never during Bright. However," he paused and pointed at the vigilant tapestry, "my silkspun Seeing Net has recently revealed to me that all is not well in the Land Of Ranidae. I do wish to know more."

Now both guests proved most eager to chat. Often they interrupted one another in their vivid and emotional accounts of the 'New Order'.

Details of how a sorcerer, bearing a staff of white gold, had encroached upon their peaceful communities and invoked his decrees intrigued the arachnid, who listened patiently until each guest had exhausted his own version of events.

"...and now many of us are in hiding," Tiptin sighed out upon completion.

"Hmmmm." Spidey stood, and, interlocking all eight arms behind his back, commenced pacing back and forth across the gold tiles.

Thwack and Tiptin exchanged shrugs, yet kept mute. Neither wished to divert their kind host's flow of thoughts.

Finally, Spidey ceased pacing and stopped the silence. "This sorcerer you speak of – what exactly does he look like?"

"I don't know," Tiptin replied. "I've never seen him."

"Few actually have," Thwack put in. "Although all have heard tell of him." "Oh? And just what have you heard?" Spidey asked.

Thwack was most eager to reply. "That he has the wickedest grin and most sinister stare that ever will be. Tell is he owns a laugh of madness and dons naught but garments of black."

Now Tiptin offered his remarks. "Talk also tells that he rides a magnificent flying beast with solid gold wings and the head of a bird of prey. And it is said that his staff can hurl forth blue beams of searing light so hot that they burst timber into flame!"

"And even melt stone!" Thwack added. "I've viewed the evidence with my own seer."

"I, as well," Tiptin said. "That is why the sorcerer is able to rule over Ranidae. Because of the staff."

"My kind are most frightened of him," Thwack put in. "Clear out of their wits."

Spidey nodded his head in sympathy. "I can hardly blame them, Thwack. I am also frightened."

"You?"

"Yes, Tiptin. I know this sorcerer well."

"You do?" inquired two voices.

Spidey's tone sank solemn. "Oh, yes. Also, I know of this staff of which you speak. Together, they are a most dangerous and frightening pair. Xebec has found The Staff of the Demon Chaser. Oh my dearest Destiny. My previous lack of judgment has played its own role in creating this fine mess that we all now find ourselves in. And it is a right fine mess, indeed."

"Staff of whom?" Thwack asked.

"You know Xebec?" Tiptin asked, appearing somewhat alarmed.

"No. Not really." Spidey sighed and bowed his head. "Although I once thought I did."

Both guests blinked uncertain.

"Please permit me to make a thorough explanation." Spidey directed their attention to the Seeing Net, then commenced clapping and chanting in cadence.

"OH MAGIC SEER WHO EVER PEEKS…

SPIN FORTH TO VIEW WHAT MY MIND SEEKS…

REVEAL XEBEC'S FORM FOR US TO SEE…

SHOW US WHERE THAT SCROLLTHIEF BE!"

Slowly, the net began to spin. Next, the seer snapped shut and, ever so gradually, a shape began to take form.

"Yikes!" Tiptin shrieked as a fanged jawcrusher snapped at his head. Only Thwack's reflex yank spared the lucky ladfolk a messy meeting with Morgue.

"OH SPINNING NET, I CLAPPED IN ERROR,

NOW WISK THIS BEAST AWAY FROM THERE!"

With a slicing shrillscream, the fanged jawcrusher vanished. Then the net slowly ceased spinning and the seer blinked alert.

Spidey flushed in awkward abashment. "Oops. Sorry about that. Hee, hee. Sort of clapped out the wrong cadence there. A minor mistake. Hee, hee. Much time has passed since I checked up on that scoundrel. You see, the very sight of him causes my biters to clench. But no matter. I'll just opt for a second swat at the skitter."

Both guests stepped backward and poised to bolt.

"OH MAGIC SEER WHO EVER PEEKS,

SPIN FORTH TO VIEW WHAT MY MIND SEEKS,

REVEAL XEBEC FOR US TO SEE,

SHOW US WHERE THAT SCROLLTHIEF BE!"

Once again, the net began to spin. The alert seer snapped shut and, ever so gradually, a sinister shape took form. It was a glumdreary figure, in a black cloak and matching skullcap, standing alone upon the balcony of a pink tower and clenching a staff of white gold.

"There!" Spidey exclaimed. "Feast your seers upon the slimiest schmuck to ever skulk about civilized Ranidae! A bona fide scoundrel, that one!"

As the pair stared at the dim sorcerer, their obviously resentful host told them of Xebec's treachery and how his former lead apprentice had sneaked unannounced into 'this very' lair while Spidey swinged in trance, and stole from him the sealed tubes, which contained the Webscrolls of Dim Sorcery. He also related to them how Xebec escaped by dissolving virtually all of the lesser apprentices into putrid moo-pies! Before fleeing to an island.

Next, Spidey related to them the Legend of the Demon Chaser. Both had heard it as youngsters, but had long forgotten.

"…so you see, my dear guests," Spidey warned in conclusion, pointing at the sinister shape, which smirked and pointed back, "…unless that slimy schmuck is somehow defeated and the staff flung into The Saline Sea – well, I'm sure you both understand fully the dire consequences should you fail."

Thwack and Tiptin exchanged leery looks. "Uh – fail?"

"Certainly." Spidey parted all his arms. "Well you can't just watch from here while that clout crazy cuckoo becomes madder and madder, until he starts raising all of Ranidae just for chuckles!"

Thwack raised a pointdigit. "Ah, excuse me, but I thought you just implied that we two are somehow supposed to tackle this task?"

Spidey beamed with enthusiasm. "Absolutely, my dear clops! Rather challenging concept, don't you agree?"

"So just what is wrong with your own legs?" Tiptin asked with overt suspicion.

"Well, nothing really. You see, it's my skin."

"Your skin?"

"Yes, my skin. You see, should I ever be exposed to Bright's penetrating rays, my skin will melt. No, really. Honest arachnid."

"Yeah, sure."

"Uh-huh."

"No, it's a fact. I wouldn't dung ya. Absolutely not. That is why I dug the tunnel. Honest. Swear on my mama's eggs and hope to be squashed."

"Tunnel?" Tiptin raised a skeptical brow.

"Now, obviously I didn't dig any tunnel all by myself. Let's be realistic, here. No, to undertake this engineering endeavor, I've enlisted an entire army of gravel gulpers!"

"Gravel gulpers?" Tiptin asked, growing more skeptical.

"HARR! Sure Spidey. And Tiptin can lift more than me!"

"No, fellas. I speak the truth. Gravel gulpers are obese, limbless wigglers with mushy heads and many, many rows of crunching chompers. Each shift, they gorge down thrice their enormous body weight in dirt. Put Thwack to shame. They even devour rocks and slate. Terrific workers. Always eating, never complain. How could they? Their mouths are forever full. And any biters that they break or lose are quickly replaced with new ones."

"Uh – and just where does this supposed tunnel lead?"

"Why, straight over to Xebec's Island, of course. Where else would it lead? Originally, I'd intended to tunnel clear through to his coral castle and retrieve the Webscrolls myself. According to my calculations, it would have taken another forty cycles to complete the dig. By which time, Xebec may well have met Morgue, but the scrolls might still be there. As they were my responsibility to safeguard, it is likewise my responsibility to get them back. Although all has changed now that the staff is found. There is no longer ample time to dig the breadth of the entire island. That is why you two must go. If not for myself, then for all those you love. You do love, don't you? Besides, if somebody doesn't unpower the staff, then all shall soon be lost anyway. As it is, you have already lost your freedom."

Spidey's pink peepers pleaded with them to consider carefully his words.

Both did so in earnest, drawing away from their host and whispering amongst themselves. Yet no matter what excuses to refuse his request seemed almost perfect, the arachnid's last statement rendered them invalid. "*As it is, you have already lost your freedom.*"

Finally, the pair agreed to go. Not out of bravery, but rather out of fond feelings for their loved ones and their own kind, who were still suffering under Xebec's harsh rule. Proof, once again, that love does indeed wield more power than fear - and forever shall.

"Splendid! Splendid!" Spidey clapped his eight pods like a small audience. "Then we shall be off, forthwith! Ah – but first I've gifts for each one of you. Come."

They followed the arachnid over to a wall shelf, where he procured a tightly rolled item of hide. After fang-snipping a silkspun tie cord, he held the hide up high. It flopped over and over, unrolling to reveal a big bag, complete with silk drawstrings to seal the mouth, and a hide sling-strap for easy carrying.

Handing it to Thwack, Spidey sort of smiled and pointed to the bug barrels. "Help yourself, my dear clops."

Thwack beamed with delight. "WOW! A BIG BAG OF BUGS!! Thanks, Spidey!"

Next, Spidey led Tiptin over near the hearth. "You shall require some mode of defense," he explained, swinging the cabinet doors open to reveal a dazzling arsenal of assorted weaponry.

There were twin-bladed axes with golden handles, and gemmed hurling daggers. Spiked balls on chains and jeweled javelins. There were many maces molded of various metals, all shiny and smooth.

Tiptin squinted as Spidey reached in and removed the most impressive weapon of all – a spectacular sword with a shimmering blade and a honeycombed hilt. It radiated forth both light and heat.

"Ahhh," Spidey remarked with prided pleasure. "My fiber masterpiece. Weightless and with pulse, it can wield itself. Here, take it."

"But I know nothing of weapons," Tiptin said.

Spidey grabbed the hesitant ladfolk's wrist. "So what is there to know? You swing your weapon at your foe, they swing theirs at you. Whoever dispatches the other first, wins. Too easy."

Tiptin gulped as the somewhat cynical arachnid sort of smiled and pressed the honeycombed hilt into his palm. Instantly, he felt the weapon's charge vibrate up his arm and spill into his body.

"Now about that swollen ankle," Spidey remarked, stooping to get a better look. He gently lifted his young guest's knee and moistened the dangling ankle with hot breath.

His patient could actually feel the torn tendons tingling in repair.

Spidey lowered the foot back down. "There, now. So how does it feel?"

Tiptin hopped up and down on the ankle. It no longer screamed in pain. In fact, it was as though it had never been injured at all. "Wow, it's entirely healed!"

Spidey beamed. "Another triumph for the science of magic medicine. Now come, let us be off. Ready, my dear clops?"

Thwack raised the big bag of bugs, which he'd crammed near to burst. Along with his bulging cheeks. "Schorr, Schpidey."

They stood before the seeing net, and the arachnid commenced to clap and chant. Both guests prepared to duck and bolt.

"OH MAGIC SEER, OF SILK AND BLUE,

MY NEWFOUND FRIENDS HAVE A DEED TO DO,

BY MY COMMAND, I ORDER YOU,

TO OPEN WIDE AND SEE US THROUGH!"

Immediately, the seer snapped shut and the Seeing Net took to spinning. Slowly at first, then faster and faster and faster. Until a strong wind threatened to blow Tiptin backwards. But a meaty forearm held him in check.

A vacuum suctioned behind the spinning net as a tiny black hole opened in its center. It expanded wider and wider until the silk had completely dissolved to expose a downsloping shaft.

"Come," Spidey beckoned, stepping into the passageway.

No sooner had the others followed suit, when the shaft entrance snapped shut behind them. Beyond it, the alert seer resumed its blinkless vigil.

The shimmering blade breathed forth ample light as the trio wound their way down the steep slope. Spidey scurried on ahead. Tiptin strided with newfound energy. Thwack thumped along in the rear, stuffing his yap with bugs.

Eventually the shaft led them to a main artery. Its walls were of slate and dark dirt. However, ample light was produced by luminous jellglow trees. Lacking in bark and foliage, they swelled and shrank in breath, supported by see-through stems and fully exposed roots.

"What unusual trees," Tiptin commented.

"Ah, they are that," Spidey concurred. "To exist where bright does not, plants must produce their own. The seeds to grow these jellglow trees were given to me by an old friend."

"The thing in the portrait?"

"Yes."

"Issth thith the tunnel to Schebecth Island?" Thwack wanted to know, while munching down yet another fistful of bugs.

"Absolutely. And I'd conserve those crunchy delicacies, my dear Clops. It's really quite an arduous journey to the other end of this tunnel."

"Oh, I wouldn't fret too much over him, Spidey. None of flesh can match the stamina of a cyclops. It is myself who lacks nourishment."

Spidey sort of smiled at Tiptin. "Don't fret yourself, my young friend. While you hold the pulsing sword, you shall seldom require neither nap nor feed. The blade's own energy shall enter into you. That is why I chose it."

"I have noticed I seem to feel somewhat more vibrant than ever before?"

"You are, Tiptin. You are."

True to Spidey's warning, the journey through the tunnel proved to be long and arduous. But even more so, it was boring. Boring! Boring! Boring! Naught about the immense tunnel ever changed. The rough walls of slate and dark dirt went on and on and on and on and on and......

Until, just when Thwack thought they'd be thumping through the pale passageway forever, his pointy hearers pricked to snag sound. "Wait. I hear something?"

"Such as?" the arachnid inquired.

"It sounds like – ummmm…"

"Like deep music, perhaps?"

"Yeah!"

"What is it?" Tiptin asked. "I don't hear anything?"

"You shall," Spidey assured him. "It's the gulper bosses trumpeting orders to the diggers. They blow blasts of bass through their horny hearers. Of course, they all take turns being boss and digger. Thus each gets a chance to feel weighty. Hee, hee. Which, as you shall soon see, they certainly are."

And they most certainly were! **HUMONGOUS!!**

Both guests gaped agawk at the obese, limbless beasts with horny hearers sticking from their mushy heads. They greedily devoured soil, stones and slate; their many, many rows of crunching chompers grinding each into powder. Burping and slurping and gassing, they paid the newcomers no heed.

"Gross!" Tiptin hollered, pinching tight his nostrils.

"Revolting!" Thwack concurred in obvious disgust.

"Absolutely!" Spidey readily agreed. "Terrific workers, though! Always chewing! Never complain! But keep your distance, my friends! They are blinder than blackwings – and they'll gobble up anything!"

Thwack embraced his big bag of bugs.

"Follow me! There's a vent shaft to the surface!"

Tiptin scrambled after the arachnid, with Thwack hot on his heels.

"Hey! Quit shoving, Bugbreath!"

"Well, hurry up! It stinks worse than whitestripes down here!"

"Come!" Spidey beckoned, scurrying into a diverging artery. "This vent shaft leads to the surface!"

They ascended up and up and up some more, panting and grunting and digging in with their dirty digits.

Then, just when Thwack thought they'd be trudging up the steep slope forever, his hooked schnozz sniffed the sweet scent of soil and bush.

They stepped out onto the surface, into a dark and mysterious place. The treefolk grew so large that creatures could get lost in their trunks, and peepers blinked from the shadows. The only colour was shapes and strange sounds shivered their skin. It was apparent by scanning the vague canopy of foliage above that sphereshine seldom touched soil in this eerie place.

"Er – wh-where are we?" Tiptin inquired, firming his hold on the honeycombed hilt. His cheeks glowed beside the shimmering blade.

"This place is called The Baobabs," Spidey explained. "Be calm, both of you. The critters hereabouts are probably much more frightened of you."

"Gulp – probably?"

"Of course, I can't speak for certain," Spidey continued. "But you do have your weapons and your wits and each other. Now, don't forget, to get to Xebec's coral castle you travel due thisaway until you reach the distant seashore. Then you trek straight upaway as far as you can go. You'll find it easily enough."

"But however shall we know which way we are trekking beneath this thick canopy? There is no palesphere to…"

"The sword shall guide you, Tiptin. It knows. Now remember, you must toss the staff into The Saline Sea. And, if at all possible, try to retrieve my Webscrolls for me. But the staff matters utmost. It must. Or else all shall soon be lost, anyway. Do you understand?"

Tiptin and Thwack both nodded that they did.

"Very well, then. Venture forth in high spirits. Your quest is a most noble one. Walk with Destiny, my brave friends, and you shan't fail. Now go. Go! Too much time has passed by already. Go!"

Neither uttered a reply as they set forth to find their fate. Although shielded from the crackling flashbolts that ripped open the unseen above, both were quite aware of the angry skybangers battling for space well atop the canopy, announcing the arrival of violent skyshowers.

Never had the pair experienced such a torrent. Soon raging rivers of muck flooded the forest floor. To trek further was futile. To stay put was to perish.

Using the blade as a lantern, they began climbing one of the broader trees. With Thwack boosting his puny pal from bough to bough, eventually they came upon a platform of sorts. There, they both slumped asit.

"I can't believe it," Thwack said.

"C – Can't believe - ahhh – can't b-believe what?" Tiptin panted.

"Those massive boughs. Even the droopy ones didn't bend one bit beneath my weight."

"Well, they – ahhhhh – they are thick as t – trunks, Thwack. I wonder how aged a tree such as this…"

"Whooooo?"

Chills shivered their spines as both jerked towards the voice.

"Whooooo? Whooooo?"

Thwack dropped his precious bag of bugs and two-fisted his log-like club. He blinked in disbelief.

Tiptin heeled his body backwards until his back bashed against a bough, belting all wind from his weary breathers.

"Whooooo?"

Finally, the defensive cyclops untangled his licker. "Wh-Who are you?"

Taleteller

"Hi! Hi! Hi! Hi, You! It's me, Me! So, so, so what can one possibly say about those bullybeasts? Except maybe, dense dee dense dense. Dense dee dense dense – DENCE!! Personally I'd give sticks a slight edge in an aptitude test.

"Now, where were we? Oh, yes. Yes. Yes. Xebec now has both the staff and the Webscrolls. Dearest Destiny, what a scary combo. Like granting one of your Earth Officials an unlimited expense account and an open mandate. Geeeee – do ya think they'd abuse it?

"And what of this cold character, Zebu? Poor Shoenia. Imagine undertaking a long sea voyage with only old scowlface and his odd seers for company. EEEYIKES!! If I had lips, I'd bobble them. I mean, it's certainly not my idea of a choice cruise. Uh-uh. Noper! No way! Not at all!

"Lastly, we have Thwack and Tiptin trapped high up in a baobab tree. Cornered by a – "Whooooo?". Which I suppose is better than a "GRRRRR!" or an "AAARRRGH!!" Or even a "whaaaaat?". Is too! Is so! For certain! For sure!

"But you shall never find out more of what happened if I keep yackity-yack-yackin! Uh-uh! Noper! No way! Not a chance! So I shall, as you Earth types would say, put a smog in it! Will so! Will too! Will! Will! Will!

"SO BYE FOR NOW!! Hack! Gag! Cough! Choke!"

Baobabs And Beakers

With tidypalm sails bulging and dandytower masts bended by gusts, the boulderpea pod pitched and dipped and listed its way across the blue, rolling wetscape. Capable digits gripped the chute tiller, steering the sturdy vessel safely through the swells.

A lanky figure in a blue and red robe peered far downaway from the pod's bow. Streamers fluttered from the peak of his pointy cap. His wrinkled hands clenched firmly a wand of pink crystal.

"Uhggg," Shoenia grunted, heaving hard on the tiller. Bright had battled Black an entire wars worth of times since she and the moody magician had bid the kind plantimal farewell and cast off from the Divided Continent.

She had long passed the point of weary, although not of energy. Titanroot sap was quick to replenish any dip in stamina. Rather, she had grown weary of her muted companion's constant scowl and arrogant attitude.

Seemingly indifferent to her presence, he had barely even acknowledged her since they'd weighed sinkstone. Not once had he even offered to spell her on steerage or assist with trimming the sails. Nor would he even respond to her questions. In fact, he behaved as if she wasn't even there.

All the moody magician did was peer downaway from the bow and occasionally chant to his wand. Or point out a slight change of direction, without so much as looking back at the laboring galfolk; which actually suited her just fine, since his odd seers only served to chillgaze clean through her anyway.

Tossing her white hair back behind her shoulders, Shoenia savored the fresh sensation of fine splashmist caressing her skin. Shutting her emerald seers, she licked saline droplets from her lips while enjoying a beautiful piece of natural music titled 'The Waltz of the Whispering Winds'.

Even the boulderpea pod took part, dancing in bob to the tempo. It leaped to peak at high pitch, and then swooped quickly downward during the hushed chorus of spray, hitting deep-swell right on cue at each rest. Then it climbed back up to the roll of the sea's skin, only to once again leap to peak at high pitch.

Re-opening her seers, she spied a blue spouter far in the distance. Then it was gone, and she again felt the dumps of alone.

Tying the tiller in check, she reached for her stalkhollow and granted herself a satisfying sip of titanroot sap. Next, procuring the scrapstick, she stroked the attached shinebulb to glow; then giggled as she returned the pretty object to its spot at her feet.

Suddenly movement snagged her sights: neither of spouters nor her moody companion. No, this movement was mid-pod, amongst the supplies. Wasn't it? She couldn't be sure.

Then it happened again. One of the fluorescent acurns shifted slightly and its stemmed lid jiggled. It wasn't her mind playing tricks on her out of boredom after all. Something lurked inside the acurn!

"Wh-Who's in there?" she demanded, snatching up her scrapstick. Ever so cautiously, she started soft-stepping towards the now-stoic container.

Upon gripping the acurn's stem in one hand, she readied her weapon with the other. Then she quickly lifted the lid. "Don't mo…?"

Shoenia gasped. A pair of red, furry faces blinked up at her. One bore blue, mask-like facial markings, and the other bore a blue patch about one seer. Each chattered uncontrollably, while pointing an accusing paw at the other. Then, together, they scampered free of their hiding place and clutched hold of the startled galfolk's loose hangtop.

"Sneek! Peek!" she shouted. "What a joyous surprise!"

Shoenia scooped the furry pair up into her chest and began to laugh as both smuzzles licked moist her cheeks. "I don't believe you two, hiding inside an acurn all this way. Why…?"

"Ooooo. Cootchy-coo, I love you. Now I'm traveling in a zoo," Zebu taunted. "But rest assured those stowaways are getting off at Orange Island!"

"Stowaways? But they're not stowaways." Shoenia protested.

"Oh?" Zebu said. "Then tell me, dear apprentice, what else are they to be? Hmmmm?"

Although the magician's green and blue seers both sought to chillgaze clean through her, Shoenia bluffed a stern reply. "They're – they're stowfriends."

Zebu actually smirked amused. "Stowfriends?"

"Yes," Shoenia said. "Stowfriends. And I'm not your apprentice anymore, either. In fact, I don't even like you."

Now Zebu toned cynical. "Well wiggle my wand. Shoenia doesn't like me. Boo-hoo."

That's right, and neither do my stowfriends."

Both smuzzles tugged hard upon her hangtop.

"Not many do like me, Galfolk. In fact, I can't think of any. So what? And you can call these two whatever you wish. They're still getting off at Orange Island. Also, I'd mind my flippant licker if I were you..." Zebu wielded his wand in a most menacing manner. "...lest it should become tied in a bow!"

Bellybees buzzed about Shoenia's knotted-up guts and her knees felt weak. She knew the moody magician had the magic means to carry out his threat. Yet two innocent friends were clinging to her for protection, so somehow she summoned up more courage.

"Do so, Zebu, and you can just find somebody else to sail this pod!" Shoenia spat, bluffing a brave front. "And help you to unpower that stupid staff, too!"

Zebu rolled his odd seers. He knew of spells that could entrance and make mute the saucy galfolk, plus make her do his bidding. Except such spells would numb her mind and body to a point where she may very well function well below what was required to trim sails properly and steer the craft safely. Besides, he rather enjoyed having another tend to all the toil. Thus, he decided to tolerate her as far as the coast of Xebec's Island. But no further!

"Very well, then," he grumbled. "Your stowaways can stay..."

"Stowfriends."

"Those!" Zebu snapped, pointing his wand at the trembling smuzzles. "But they'd best chop the chatter and keep clear of mischief, or else into the drink they shall go! Understand?"

Shoenia merely nodded. This battle she'd already won, but she knew to push the enraged magician any further could mean losing the entire war. Therefore, she pressed a pointdigit to her cherry lips to signal silence to the smuzzles.

Both acknowledged the gesture by paw pinching their short snouts.

"Good! Glad we're all agreed! Now get back on that tiller! Move!"

All three obeyed at once.

It quickly became apparent to Shoenia that her furry friends were indeed very quick to learn. With very little instruction from her, they took to trimming sails like skilled seafarers. Plus each learned with but one demonstration how to tie the knots necessary to secure the vine sheets. They even climbed aloft to untangle crossed rigging.

Shoenia, herself no slouch at sailing, had experienced several catch seasons before her family ever permitted her to attempt such a risky undertaking. Even then, she was learned her skills upon the much tamer wetrollers of The Bay, and only after ample dockside practice: all the while enjoying the added security of a safety line.

Yet the nimble rodents scurried up the swaying stems with neither a slip nor a fear. In fact, they seemed to rather enjoy doing it.

Their voyage took them due downaway, through soft seas and toss torrents. Climbing up steep wetrollers and sledding down into deep swells, they saw naught but sky, wet and some blue spouters; plus one titanic tentacone with suckers on its wiggly bouquet of arms. Until, immediately following one of Black's thataway retreats, they found themselves bobbing in calm off the coast of a lonely isle.

The isle's plants were a bright orange and a dull orange, as well as an in between orange. The shore silt was striped many hues of orange. High, stony bluffs were of a glittery orange. Even the stilted longbeakers wading through the surf were orange. Ditto the flying finfloppers splashing about the breaking wetrollers, and the various gilled skaylees which now swam alongside the pod.

Yes, virtually everything about the isle was orange. Orange! Orange! Orange! Orange! Orange!

Throughout Bright, they bobbed off the coast, while Zebu conjured up barely enough breeze to keep the craft from drifting abeach. Then, just as Black launched its scheduled counterattack upon Bright, the winking winds awakened and, by the time Bright regrouped and charged back atop the thisaway horizon, the lonely isle had long departed.

During especially tough tosstorrents, when crackling flashbolts spread their crooked digits and angry skybangers deafened the very sea, Zebu would calmly chant and wave his wand. His actions always conjured up an overhead shield of solid light, which kept them all dry and warm and safe from zappers. Although wetrollers still spit whitecaps into the craft, thus forcing the three to bail.

Yet they persevered regardless of the ever-changing elements. After all, what choice did they have? They were just four specks on a spot surrounded by sea.

At one point during the long and arduous voyage, they encountered an unfriendly spouter. Unlike the blues they had so often observed from afar, this rather nasty nemesis was entirely black except for its ivory biters and mean, red seers. It soon took to rambashing the pod, once even lifting the tiny craft clear of the drink and pitching its crew about like loose lumps.

As Shoenia and her terrified friends prayed fast and loud unto Destiny, while scrambling to find gripholds, one extremely irate magician sought revenge upon their tailed tormentor. Securing himself by grabbing hold of a broken sheet line, he pointed his wand at the wet and slowly began gyrating the tip.

Almost instantly, the choppy drink began to swirl. Next, as he chanted and increased the tip's speed, the wet aptly accelerated in swirl until an awesome, spinning hole sucked wind into a void.

Then Zebu directed the sucking swirlpool directly into the path of the charging spouter, which squealed with fear as it struggled to swim free of the vacuum. But the black beast's slapping tail was little match for the power wielded by the wand, and it was soon siphoned from surface to …?

As the foursome journeyed further downward, the temp gradually climbed and they started crossing paths with many intriguing forms of sea beasts.

There were groupings of gilled flatflappers with thin tails like whips, plus a cast of dancing crownbreathers that performed talented back flips and tricks.

They viewed shell dwellers with fins, and squish sacks with eight arms, plus surging skaylees with sworded beaks, who meant none any harm. And they spied drifting croonspongees, who sought only to charm, as well as colorful corals of sea polyp farms.

There were floating pinchers with stemmed peepers, and sea serpents, which skimmed past lit up in shock. Even a school of scalewingers flew by in a flock. They sailed alongside gillers with spots, and finners with stripes, plus subsurface shadows of all shapes, sizes and types.

Bright battled Black battled Bright battled Black battled….. Entire palespheres passed by with neither fanfare nor note. *Yet, still no sand of land?*

Until, late one shine-filled bright, they spotted a smoky haze well in the distance. Shortly thereafter, a fuming peak rolled atop the thisaway horizon, accompanied by a lesser, docile peak.

Downthisaway from the Summit Sisters stretched the white ribbon of a sandy beach. It served as a welcome mat to a much larger landmass, which sustained a dark forest of towering, titantrunk trees.

"Dung!" Zebu snapped, realizing his error. "The Baobabs. I've hit the thataway coast. Stupid skytwinklers!"

Deciding that the boulderpea pod was now much too battered to risk sailing around the entire treacherous coast of Xebec's Island, the moody magician ordered the weary crew to put ashore. Which they managed to accomplish with little difficulty, thanks to favorable gusts and the advance tides that creepscouted along the silty shore in preparation for their post bright assault upon dry sand.

The pod rode the rolling surf into a shallow cove, drawing alongside a partially submerged trunk of rotwood. The experienced smuzzles quickly vinelashed the battered craft to some decaying bough stubs, while Shoenia gawked at the mysterious forest about them.

Treefolk grew so large that creatures could become lost in their titantrunks, which far surpassed even those of the Fluorescent Forest. Peepers blinked from the shadows and the only colors were shapes. Strange sounds shivered her skin. It was readily apparent that sphereshine seldom struck soil in this eerie place.

"You three stay put!" Zebu growled, stepping atop the rotwood.

"Wh-Where are you going?" Shoenia inquired, suddenly feeling quite unsafe and wondering if perhaps she hadn't been a tad hasty in dismissing her former mentor.

Zebu neither broke stride nor looked back. "To investigate. Remain in the craft until I return. These Baobabs hide hordes of hideous horrors! All who enter shall perish!"

Shoenia gulped and her furry friends embraced her shaky legs. Each of them sensed something strange in the magician's manner. Especially when he paused to tap tree vines with his wand. Yet none could see the wicked gloatgrin on his face or read his wicked mind.

After Black had yet again conquered Bright in their perpetual war for control of the above, the three trembling friends cuddled together for comfort. Each tried to stave off fatigue as best they could, trying in earnest to keep their senses primed. However, Shoenia wanted to conserve the titanroot sap. Plus she was afraid to use the shinebulb, lest its glow attract the hordes of hideous horrors.

Thus, as each in turn succumbed to Fatigue's fog and nodded off into the relaxing realm of napvisions, they were entirely unaware of the tree vines slithering from their boughs and crossing the soil towards the rotwood. The slumbering trio never noted the muffled plop of the stringy stalkers dropping into the pod, nor felt them winding about torsos and limbs.

Bright had long returned by the time Shoenia awakened. Immediately, she saw their desperate dilemma. Sneek and Peek were tied together into one furball with seers. Even their short snouts were lashed shut. She, herself, was bound from shoulder to feet.

The furball blinked at her, its moist seers begging for help.

However, the galfolk fared no better than they. The harder she struggled, the tighter the vines squeezed, choking her wind and gagging her speech. All she could do was stare at the pathetic bundle of fur, and pray of Destiny for help before the searing rays past midbright baked flesh from her face.

Silently, she wished they'd ignored Zebu's order and taken refuge beneath the canopy. There, at least, they would be spared the wrath of the brightsphere. But what other horrors would they know?

Then she recalled the magician's strange manner as he'd departed and how he had wand-tapped the vines. Realizing that it was he who was responsible for their plight caused her to grow angry. She struggled to scream and burst her binds, but to no avail. They simply squeezed even tighter.

Oh, how she wished that Rimp had come. Wait! That may be the answer. Perhaps, she thought, my dear and departed friend may still be of help?

She remembered the glass vial in her skirt pouch. Why had Rimp given it to her, if not for a fix such as this? But how was she to retrieve and uncork it? And whatever was contained in its emptiness?

Stretching with all her strength, she attempted to scoop even a pointdigit into her skirt pouch. It was no use. The vibrant vines constricted even tighter about her wrists, cutting into the flesh and numbing her digits. Squinching in pain, she ceased trying to overpower her captors. Conscience of wet trickling trails down her cheeks, she began to ponder her plight.

Suddenly, a hopeful thought leapt to mind. Her limbs may be bound, yet the vines only lashed about her body. She might still manage a roll!

Shoenia began rocking her body back and forth until she was finally able to roll onto her belly. Then she started squirming about like a wounded wriggler until three objects slipped free of her skirt pouch.

In an effort to halt her movement, the vines latched onto one of the masts and commenced reeling their catch across the pod, while squeezing ever tighter about her torso and limbs.

Shoenia choked and gasped for breath. She saw that she was sure to swoon. She must dislodge the cork, or else…

Snagging the vial with her licker, she tried to scoop it into her mouth. But it rolled away from her lips. She was becoming dizzy.

Dung, she thought. To Morgue with the cork!

Squirming enough to backbend her torso, Shoenia opted for one final try. Out of sheer desperation, and despite the certain pain, she whipped her brow down hard upon the glass vial. Red shot throughout her blanking mind. Defeat all but engulfed her aching limbs as the vial rolled away almost intact, save for a slight crack.

However, a slight crack proved to be all that was needed. Never one to quit at anything, Shoenia fought to keep from sinking in swoon. She was much encouraged by the spectacle now unfolding before her.

A slight wisp of smoke appeared within the vial, fed by the inseeping air. Gradually, it expanded into a glowing green haze. Then the container itself puffed near to burst.

"POW!" The cork shot clear of the vial, and instantly a glowing green fog spewed free of its tiny prison. Within its mass hunched a creature with a mossy beard, shinesilver skin and purple peepers.

The creature wasted no time in pointing its walking rush at the vines. "Be gone!"

Without a blink of delay, the vines unwound to release their captives. Then they speedily slithered from pod to rotwood to soil to boughs. Not once did they pause or divert. Each knew that to do so would mean being made into mulch.

Sticky sap flowed freely from its puffy hollows as the creature's apparition floated over the gasping galfolk. It tapped her with its rush to refill her breathers. "We've not much time, Shoenia. Already, my own breath is waning."

"Rimp?"

A red licker flickered from the plantimal's mouth, but his tone had withered flat and distant. "No, my friend, I have long wilted. You now view my specter."

"But I do not understand?"

The plantimal pressed a twiggy digit to its black hole. "Oi. That stinkstalk Zebu knew I was fast wilting from age, and thought his magic would soon surpass my own. He only wanted to use me for my far superior ability to read Black's twinkler map, so I would lead him directly to Xebec's castle. He never could grip astrology. Paid too much attention to conjuring spells, I suppose? Anyway, he has never intended to unpower the staff in the sea. I had hoped he might alter his plot, but now I weep over a student's betrayal."

"But why did you send me with him?"

Rimp's specter was fading quickly now. "I knew my time for wilting was near and needed an honest entity to stop him."

"How, Rimp? I wield no magic?"

"Oi. Not yet," the specter replied. "But you will. Now listen carefully, Shoenia. You must remember these words I speak above all others. Do you understand?"

Shoenia nodded that she understood.

Then the specter offered her a riddle:

"WHEN NEXT YOU MEET UPON A SHORE,

HOW SHALL FLAMES LICK CLOTH NO MORE?"

"I – I do not understand? Rimp, what does that riddle mean?"

"My influence over future events has its limits, Shoenia. I can aid you no further. Remember…." The specter paused and smiled, exposing one ivory tooth. "….in the proper place, at the proper time, you shall know to do the proper thing. And perhaps you may learn something of Love's magic along the way? I miss you, Galfolk. My smuzzles are most fortunate."

"Did you send them along, too?"

Now the specter was almost gone. "Oi. To help ease your dumps of alone."

Shoenia scrambled for the right words just as the vision vanished. "Rimp….I love you!"

A fading voice responded from the nothingness above.

"OI! WHEN NEXT YOU MEET UPON A SHORE,

HOW SHALL FLAMES… LICK …CLOTH… no… more…."

Both smuzzles whined and whimpered and sniffed the remaining wisps of haze. Providing proof beyond doubt that pain over loss indeed transcends species.

Shoenia gently stroked her little companions' fur. Then she gathered up the flint and striker, before palming the shinebulb aglow. She was now determined to settle several scores. "Come on, you two. We have to find and unpower that staff. Somehow?"

Together, the three friends trod warily beneath the canopy and entered the dark forest. Sneek and Peek clung to Shoenia's neck and shoulders while she dangled the shinebulb from the tip of her scrapstick.

Peepers blinked from the shadows and strange sounds shivered their skin, but the brave trio trekked onward. Doing their best to ignore their eerie surroundings, they strolled beneath root archways draped with mangy moss, and they clambered over broken branches by the batch. Shoenia wondered just what type of hideous horrors belonged to the peepers?

Soon it became readily apparent that they were hopelessly lost. Nor could they even claim to know who presently ruled the sky atop the canopy. So, in utter frustration, Shoenia wiped her skindewed face with her hangtop and sought out a soft mattress of moss at the base of an exposed root. There, she and the smuzzles snuggled up to take rest.

But just as she reached to palm out the shinebulb....

"Whooooo?" a firm voice inquired from somewhere overhead. "Whooooo are you?"

Fisting tight the scrapstick, Shoenia scanned the shadows for shapes. While Sneek and Peek scrambled beneath a fallen tarpleaf.

"Whooooo?" the voice repeated.

Shoenia braced her back against the root and prepared to swing at the slightest hint of movement.

"Whooooo?" This time the voice was chorused by rustling and flapping.

"Go away! Or I'll swat you!" Shoenia warned.

"That wouldn't be very nice," replied the voice. "Would it, Dearest?"

"No, Dear," concurred a mellow voice. "Not very nice at all."

"G-Go away!" Shoenia deepened her tone in an attempt to sound menacing. "I'm big and I'm bad!"

Several lengthy nods elapsed before the firm voice shattered the silence. "You don't look very big to me. Does it to you, Dearest?"

"No, not at all, Dear. Nor does it appear to be very bad. Does it appear bad to you?"

"No, Dearest. I'd suggest it appears somewhat more frightened than bad. Wouldn't you say so?"

"Most definitely, Dear. Not that I blame the poor…."

"Well, I am very, very bad!" Shoenia retorted over her pounding pumper. "And – And I grow much bigger when I get angry! So you had best both leave me alone!"

Another prolonged silence ensued before the firm voice spoke again. "It doesn't appear to be growing bigger to me. Does it to you, Dearest?"

"No, Dear," replied the mellow voice. "Perhaps it is not really angry at all and simply fibs out of fear? Wouldn't you agree?"

"Absolutely, Dearest. But it certainly has nothing to fear from us."

"Of course it doesn't. The poor thing is simply afraid of that which it cannot see. Perhaps it is best if we swoop down there and show ourselves?"

"Yes. Let's," concurred the firm voice.

"No!" Shoenia screamed as unseen flapping approached. Then she was awed mute by the two figures that descended into the glow of the shinebulb.

Circling above her was an unusually big, bespectacled beaker bearing bold, brown blinkers. Tipped hearers and tiny horns topped its wide head. A pair of powerful flappers kept it aloft. Sharp talons dangled at the ends of its bony legs. Short arms led to pudgy palms with stout digits.

Fluttering in place was a beautiful beaker batting brilliant, blue blinkers. It had soft down and feathers like fresh fallen chillcream. White and clean. Its widewise stare was somehow disarming.

"No, it certainly isn't very big," observed the bespectacled beaker in its firm voice.

"Nor bad," noted the beautiful beaker.

"I do believe I've read of this species in the Scholarship Chronicles."

"Is it an ape?"

"No. No. Given the lack of limb and facial fur, I suspect it to be a humanfolk. And given its shape, I'd guess it is female."

"Are you sure, Dear?"

"Not fully, Dearest. But it does fit the description as best I recall."

"Perhaps you should ask it?"

The bespectacled beaker nodded, and then looked down at Shoenia. "I say – you down there. Are you in fact a galfolk?"

Shoenia barely managed an affirmative nod.

"Well, go on," prodded the pretty beaker. "Ask her name."

"Yes, Dearest. Galfolk, do you have a name?"

Shoenia managed another weak nod, simultaneously lowering the scrapstick.

Both beakers exchanged bewildered blinks.

"Well?" pressed the bespectacled beaker, touching talons to moss. "Might we hear it?"

The beautiful beaker landed beside its apparent mate. "Can't you see she's still frightened, Dear? Perhaps we should introduce ourselves first?"

"Absolutely, Dearest." Extending a pudgy palm, the bespectacled beaker introduced itself. "Hello, Galfolk, my name is Hoot Beaker."

Shoenia stared in silence, but shared the shake.

Hoot then gestured to the beautiful beaker. "And this is my missus, Hweet."

Hweet stepped forward and executed a flapsweeping bow. "I do hope we didn't scare you too badly. We were really quite startled ourselves. Strangers are most rare here in the Baobabs."

"Perhaps she's gone mute?" Hoot suggested.

"Yet her hearers seem to function just fine," Hweet pointed out.

Finally Shoenia unknotted her licker. "I – er – we were already scared."

"It speaks again!" Hoot declared.

"I can hear, Dear."

"Sorry, Dearest. Young galfolk, do you have a name?"

"Shoenia."

Hweet clapped her palms together. "Oooooo, what a nice name."

"And do your rodents have names?" Hoot asked, pointing at two shivering lumps beneath the tarpleaf.

"Uh, yes they do. Their names are Sneek and Peek."

"They certainly look tasty," Hoot remarked.

Hweet smacked him hard on the chest, then firmly pinched shut his beak. "Pay ole growlguts no mind, Shoenia. We are not in the habit of devouring our guests."

"Guests?"

"Well, certainly," Hweet confirmed, releasing her tacky mate's beak. "You really can't expect us to simply abandon three lost visitors, now can you?"

"Especially with some serious skyshowers approaching," Hoot added.

"Uh-no, I guess not."

"So, it's settled then. You and your puny pals may sit out the coming flashfloods in the dry safety of our hollow."

"Flashfloods?"

"Yes, there's no skyshowers like Baobab skyshowers," Hoot explained. "Where we now perch shall shortly be a raging river of muck. Isn't that right, Dearest?"

"Oh, absolutely. Now spread your arms so I can transport you, while ole growlguts fetches the rodents."

"Smuzzles," Shoenia corrected her. She spied Hoot with distrust. "They're called smuzzles and I adore them."

"Smuzzles then," Hweet acknowledged, winking at the nervous galfolk. "Perhaps it would be best if I brought them along, instead?"

Shoenia smiled and pressed astand. "Thank you. Sneek! Peek!"

Two furry faces poked out from underneath the tarpleaf, viewing the beakers with obvious skepticism.

"Come on, it's okay. The Beakers want to help us. Come on out. That's it."

Hoot gently clamped his strong talons about Shoenia's outstretched arms, while Hweet snagged the shivering smuzzles. Then they all flapped aloft, dodging and dipping about barely visible shapes.

Only when the group neared an obstacle, did the shinebulb's glow reveal it to Shoenia. Yet the feathered pair's big blinkers enabled them to sight well beyond the luminous object's short range. To those who dwelled in the Baobabs, blackness posed no barrier. Indeed, it was a blessing that had long protected them from rare intruders. Time and time and time again.

Shoenia rather enjoyed the caressing gusts from Hoot's powerful flappers, which whooped quietly enough to permit conversation. "Hoot, what belongs to all these blinking peepers?"

"Oh, a great many different creature's dwell here, Shoenia. More than we together could half count during all of our being."

"Are you not afraid? I mean, this forest is so dark and spooky."

Hoot chuckled. "Maybe it is spooky to you, Shoenia. I once ventured above the canopy, just for a few nods. Now that was spooky. My blinkers went blind and the missus had to guide me home to our hollow. That's how I came to need specs. Much worse, though, I was forced to listen to 'I TOLD YA SO' so many times that I nearly leapt with wings wrapped!"

"I heard that, Dear."

"Sorry, Dearest." Hoot winked at Shoenia.

"But don't any of the other creatures here pose a threat?"

"No, not really. Beakers pretty much rule here. There are a few howlers, but only the Ohmees are really dangerous. Thankfully, they're reputed to be very poor climbers and they are even rarer than strangers. Personally, I've never even seen one.

Nor do I know of anybody who has actually seen one. Although I've heard they do come in all colors, shapes and sizes."

"Ohmees?"

"Yes. Miserable, phony critters that pretend to be one's friend, only to destroy one at the first possible opportunity. All they require is a justifying excuse."

"Such as?"

"Such as a slight difference of opinion, maybe. Or a minor altercation, which they are always quick to provoke. Of course, Ohmees perceive themselves as forever right."

"But why would anyone destroy a friendship over somebody's right to their own opinion?"

"Because hurting others is the only thing that makes miserable critters feel less unhappy. Ohmees especially like to gloat over others' pain and suffering."

"Sounds pretty silly to me."

"Ah, yes, but the Ohmees are a very sad lot. Always blaming others for it, too. Shoenia, have you ever noticed that whenever you focus heavily on another's faults, you become blind to your own?"

"Uh, yeah? Kinda, I think."

"Well, the unhappy Ohmees would never pause to ponder about such. They believe themselves forever right, and even encourage by example for their younglings to likewise cheat and lie. Shoenia, take care to avoid Ohmees at all cost, and, if you should ever encounter some by misfortune, remember - never, ever trust an Ohmee, or lodge in their dwelling. If you should so much as see one – Flee!"

"What do they sort of look like?"

"I've heard they are ugly beyond words. But they can fool you because Ohmees always carry spare faces. Especially the males, who can quite easily hide their many faces behind bushy beards!"

"Were they always like that?"

"Ugly?"

"Yeah, and mean?"

"I'm not sure, really? I'd have to study the Chronicles. But I suppose one would well feed the other. I mean, expending all that energy always out to *'get'* somebody must surely take its toll upon one's features. Don't you think?"

Shoenia sighed. "Now I understand. There exists some humanfolk like them, too."

"Really?"

"Unfortunately, amongst my kind Ohmees are not so rare."

Hoot suddenly switched topics. "Keep your – er – talons poised, Shoenia. We're very soon to touch solid."

"Feet. We humanfolk have feet."

"Hmmm? Interesting. According to the Scholarship Chronicles, so do Ohmees."

Hoot gently touched solid on a large boughcany, just as the first opposing skybangers blasted into each other high atop the canopy. Hweet landed mere nods later, bearing two gladchirping smuzzles.

A natural archway had been split open in the Baobab's titantrunk. It was sealed by black drapes fashioned of fine feathers.

"Welcome to our den hollow," Hweet stated, drawing aside the droopy barrier and gesturing all inside.

Their bespectacled host led them down a narrow shaft, through a tight corridor and on into a large vault with shelved walls and an arched ceiling. Tattered old scrolls were rowed neatly upon every single shelf, each bound by ribbons and tagged for quick reference.

The floor was shingled with strips of bark, diligently arranged to make it level. Any cracks had been painstakingly patched with red clay. Two nest-like cots were neatly positioned against one of the walls. A petrified stump squatted in the center of the vault, supported by a stand made of roots and encircled by six smaller stumps. Two wooden bowls, brimming over with assorted nuts, were positioned near its center. Fluorescent, pink ferns in hanging vases supplied lighting.

"Relax, you three." Hweet's widewise stare and mellow voice set the trio at ease.

"Yes, please treat our home like your very own," Hoot encouraged. "First, we shall munch nuts dipped in bumblesweet, and then you can share with us where you hail from and why you've come to the Baobabs?"

"If she so chooses," Hweet scolded him. "Don't be so beaky."

"Uh, oh yes. If you so choose, of course."

Shoenia smiled and unstrapped the stalkhollow. "I don't mind. Perhaps I'd benefit most from sharing it. Does anyone care for a taste of titanroot sap?" she offered, smearing dabs on her bruised brow and wrists.

Madness

A glumdreary figure in a black cloak and skullcap fixed his sinister stare upon the blooming bush before him. It was all that remained of the numerous floral fixtures that had once beautified his castle courtyard.

Directing his staff of white gold upon this bright's final target, the figure grinned most wicked. It had certainly been a most splendid bright, at that, filled to a feast with much useless destruction. Many useful objects were now no more.

Xebec stretched a smirk as he mumbled the command. Instantly, a blue beam of hot light was hurled forth from the awesome weapon, and, in less than the bat of a blink, the pretty bush was burned into dust. Then the sinister sorcerer launched into the distinct loco laugh of a loony gone completely 'round the twist'.

"AH-HA-HA! HO-HO-HEE!" he howled, with glee drops squirting from his sacky seers. "OH-HO-HO-HO-HO! HEE-HEE-HEE-HEE-HA!"

Abruptly, the loco laughter cut. Two vacant seers darted back and forth while a muddled mind sought to seek.

Procuring a vial from his cloak, the sorcerer scowled silly and flung it forcefully against the remnants of a stone chirp-dipper, where it smashed into slivers.

A brownish smog poofed into place, and Xebec commenced to chant.

"OH SMOG OF SIGHT, I SET YOU FREE,

TO SHOW MINE SEERS WHAT THEY MUST SEE,

EXPOSE MINE EN-E-MIES TO ME,

REVEAL WHERE THEY HAPPEN TO BE!"

The brownish smog curled and shifted until it revealed the distinct outline of Scald and Slumber Summit. At their base bobbed a craft carved of a pod. Four forms occupied its hull.

Xebec squinted and leaned closer to the fog. "Ohhh, and what have we here? Hmmmmm? One moody magician, plus one galfolk, plus two furballs – equals four dopes for the dungeon! AH-HA-HA! OH-HO-HO! Hee, hee, hee…huh?"

"What have we now?" Xebec bit a knuckle and drew crimson. "My old nemesis Spidey Smeals scurries through his tunnel. The old fool! Does he really think I'm unaware? Hee, hee. But wait! Who else shares his trek? Ohhh – well I'll be a goblin's goo if ole Spidey hasn't enlisted the help of a tall ladfolk and a one-seered giant in a jungle jumper! Hmmmmm? Yes, we'll have to expand our facilities to accommodate Mr. Hookschnozz. And we'll require a special spinestretcher for sure. Ha! So all Destiny can manage to gather against me is this pathetic gaggle of geeks? Oh, goody, goody, gleeglobs."

Entirely overwhelmed with joyous anticipation, the loco-laughing loony did an enthusiastic rendition of the 'Lipsbobble Boogie' clear across the courtyard and on up the long, winding corridor that ascends in stages to a coral antechamber.

He paused briefly to staff dust one of the few remaining wall paintings, the meanings of which are known only to magicians and sorcerers. Then he savored fully the portrait's splendid squeals before sillyskipping with satisfaction on through the antechamber, fully indifferent to its charred furnishings.

After taptwirling merrily beneath the narrow archway, he next wackowaltzed up a spiraled stairwell, past two heavy sinkwood doors, and on into his tower chambers. Flopping onto his floatress, he now performed a horizontal version of the 'Lipsbobble Boogie' until he finally giggled himself deep into the delirious domain of napnuttery!*?!!#@*??!!!

TALETELLER

"Wow! Wow! Wow! Wow! Wow! What a spincase! Nuts! Nuts! Nuts! Nuts! Koooookoooooo! Gone completely round the twist, he has. Whew!

"That's what becomes of any who bear the staff. Is so. Is too. Oh well, Xebec can't claim he wasn't warned by the very legend itself. Uh-uh. Noper. No way. Not a chance. And the longer he possesses the staff, the madder he'll grow. For certain. For sure. Cross my beams and hope to get snuffed by a comet.

"And what of poor Shoenia and the smuzzles? Dumped on a foreign coast by a greedy splop. That's alien speak for dungskull. No, more like double-disgusting dungskull. Can you just imagine if Mr. Personality ever gets his greedy digits on the staff? Eeeeeyikes! He'll make Xebec look like a psycho wannabe.

"Thank Destiny for Hoot and Hweet Beaker. Two fine beings if ever there be. Not to mention Rimp's cagey foreplanning. Shrewd! Sly! Quick! BRILLIANT!

"Anyway, you still won't ever discover the outcome of this adventure unless this humble taleteller gets on with his primary function. Taletelling, that is. So on with our tale. On! On! On! On! On!"

Thisaway Then Upaway

Finally, the defensive cyclops untangled his licker. "Wh-Who are you?" he inquired of the bespectacled beaker, who parted some feather drapes with one hand while extending a vase of fluorescent, pink ferns in the other.

The beaker blinked and stepped out from the archway. Colliding skybangers atop the canopy, and the incessant roar of tarpleaves wetslapping the wind, forced it to shout. "Well I'll be a howlpack's chow! A young ladfolk, I do believe? In fact, I'm near positive! But I'm not at all familiar with you features, my green friend! Might I inquire as to your species?"

Thwack slackened his grip on the club, and exchanged a glance of bewilderment with Tiptin before responding. "I-uh-I'm a Cyclops! My name is Thwack, and this is my partner, Tiptin! We – uh – er…"

"Who are you?" Tiptin inquired, pressing astand.

"Pardon me!"

"I asked, who are you?!"

"Hoot Beaker's the name! Although my misses has several creative substitutes! Hee, hee. She's inside with our guests! You have taken refuge upon our boughcany!"

"What!" Tiptin hollered to top the wailing wind.

"He says we're on his boughcany!" Thwack shouted, pointing to the drapes. "And he has guests inside!"

Tiptin nodded. "We are so sorry if we have intruded! It's just that we had no place else to…"

"Follow me!" the beaker interrupted, parting the drapes. "This drizzle dampens my specs!"

Even on all fours, the brawny giant barely managed to squeeze through the natural arch split in the baobab's trunk. He was forced to remain crouched in the narrow shaft beyond; however, at least the cramped cubicle was warm and dry. Plus, the thick feather drapes greatly muffled the roar.

Hoot set the vase of fluorescent ferns in a small nook, then employed dry fronds to wipe dry his specs. After pinching them back atop his beak, he folded his arms behind his back and gave the two strangers a detailed study.

"Hmmmm," he remarked. "You humanfolk sure look a mite better than what I'd pictured. Some entries in the Scholarship Chronicles are very vague at best. Uh – Tiptin, is it?"

"Yes, I hail from Folkton."

Feeling somewhat left out, the one-seered giant cut in. "And I hail from Cycity."

"Folkton and Cycity, you say?"

Both nodded.

"My, you two have journeyed from afar. Albeit, not near so far as our galfolk guest. She…"

"Galfolk?" Tiptin said, his seers betraying an overabundance of enthusiasm. "One of your guests is a galfolk?"

"Hee, hee. I suspected that might interest a young ladfolk such as yourself." Hoot exaggerated a sly wink. "Only, I must caution you that her beauty is far surpassed by her wit. I would strongly suggest an honorable modus operandi with this…"

"Dear, who are you spea…..king too?" A beautiful beaker batting beautiful, blue blinkers rounded a bend in the narrow shaft. She had soft down and feathers like freshly fallen chillcream. White and clean. Her nervous stare was locked upon Thwack.

Hoot took his mate by the hand. "Dearest, I'd like you to meet Tiptin, a ladfolk from Folkton. It's a place on the downaway shore of The Sweet Sea, I do believe?"

"Exactly," Tiptin confirmed, extending a hand in greeting.

The beautiful beaker acknowledged the polite gesture without straying her sights from the giant.

"And this rather large fellow is Thwack, a Cyclops from Cycity. Now I do seem to vaguely recall the Chronicles have such a place plotted on the bank of The Sweet River, is it not?"

Thwack rudely ignored their host and offered Hoot's missus a huge hand in greeting.

Although somewhat hesitant, the nervous beaker reluctantly extended her own.

"BOO!" Thwack suddenly blurted, forming a scary face.

"Freeeeep!" shrieked the startled beaker. She fluttered in fright and feathers filled the shaft.

"HARR! HARR! HARR! HARR! Gotcha! Wooeee! You shoulda seen your face! Your very blinkers near bolted! HARR! HARR! HA-huh? Hey, where are you all going? HEY!"

Hoot turned and glared daggers over his specs. His tone went way beyond cynical as he retrieved the vase of ferns. "You'll have to excuse us, Mr. Clops, if we don't share your sense of fun. We're all going to retire to our cozy little den hollow. Much too little for you, I'm afraid. We would offer you some nuts dipped in bumble sweet, and knit a special quilt just for you, however, my missus can't seem to recall where she misplaced her downyarn and serving bowls. You see, she has had a most terrible fright of late. But I'm sure you'll fare just fine here in the dark with all your friends. Adieu."

As the three rounded the bend, an irate ladfolk turned and pointed at the puzzled cyclops. "Later," he promised, acting out an exaggerated stomp. Then he hurried to rejoin his host and hostess.

"Hey!" Thwack hollered from the blackness. Upon trying to follow, he conked his skull. Then he got himself wedged tight in a squeeze. "Hey! Hey! At least give me the ferns! Hey! Aw, come on, it was just a little prank… Tiptin. Tiptin! **Tiptin!**"

His calls were greeted with stony silence.

"Oh, yeah! So be that way! See if I care! **I'VE GOT BUGS!!**"

The highly embarrassed ladfolk tried to apologize, but Hweet wouldn't hear of it. "We are not at all responsible for the behavior of others," she explained in her mellow voice. "If that were the case, none of us would ever nap at ease. Isn't that right, Dear?"

"Absolutely, Dearest."

The Beakers led Tiptin down a narrow shaft, through a tight corridor and on into the large vault where many scrolls were kept rowed neatly upon shelves, each bound by ribbons and tagged for quick reference.

However, Tiptin noticed naught of his strange surroundings. His sights were stuck solid upon the most gorgeous galfolk he'd ever seen, or even imagined. Although her striking appearance was most unusual in that her smooth skin was fair like cream and her hair even whiter. But her full, cherry lips, ivory biters and sparkling, emerald seers tied knots in his licker. And strange feelings fluttered about his empty belly. He completely overlooked her many scars. His pumper pounded and flesh tingled with want.

The galfolk lowered her head to disguise a grin.

"Ahem," Hweet injected. "My mate and I certainly seem to be meeting many strangers of late. Tiptin, perhaps you might set aside your shimmering thing to munch nuts at our table and share with us news of your travels before we retire?"

Hoot couldn't resist. "If he so chooses, Dearest. We mustn't be beaky."

She shot her smug mate a look. "Of course, only if you so choose."

"Oh, I don't mind," Tiptin replied, at last prying his seers from the galfolk.

"Um, I'm Shoenia," the galfolk blurted, not yet ready to forego the brown lad's attentions. "I hail from Ga."

"Ga? I've never even heard tell of Ga."

"It's very far upaway, beyond The Saline Sea," Hoot informed him, obviously proud of his knowledge of such things.

"Oh? And are all of Ga's galfolk so – uh – inspiring to behold?"

Shoenia flushed, while two jealous furballs rolled seers and pawtended to spit up. They scurried to embrace Shoenia's legs, thereby diverting her attentions to themselves.

Hoot motioned them all over to the table and, while Hweet fetched a jar of bumble sweet, Tiptin began his tale.

He started with Xebec's invasion of Ranidae, and how he'd fled Folkton to avoid obeying the sorcerer's decrees. All but the suspicious smuzzles were thrilled by his account of how he had outwitted the bullybeasts in the Swallow Mountains before plunging into the swirling sinksand. Of course, none were at all surprised by the details of his first encounter with Thwack, but his description of Spidey Smeals and the gravel gulpers kept them captivated.

"… and that is how we came to be on your boughcany," he finished.

"So now you and this cyclops seek to unpower the staff?" Shoenia inquired, adding, "All by yourselves?"

"Better two try than none," Tiptin replied.

The Beakers exchanged agreeing nods.

Shoenia decided to risk telling her own tale for Tiptin. She explained that her homeland was embroiled in a brutal war between her kind and their Ape allies, against the foul Lizarme.

Then she noted how she, too, had fled into a strange place. In fact, her tale near paralleled his own – from them both meeting master magicians, to being granted items to aid in the same quest. They even shared the same worries over kinfolk, and the dumps of alone.

Tiptin caught himself clenching both fists and biters as she told of Zebu's treachery and how he's abandoned her for an early meeting with Morgue. The ladfolk wondered how any being could be so crass and cruel? And he secretly wished he could have been the one to find and save her.

"… so you see, Rimp diverted our meeting with Morgue, but my departed friend can aid us no more." Shoenia paused, remembering Rimp's warning about the objects in her skirt pouch. She was to mention them to no one. "So now we must make do with just my scrapstick, hurling dagger and a shinebulb," She said in finishing.

"And now each other," Hoot added.

"And now…" Shoenia almost concurred before catching herself. As yet, she did not trust the brown ladfolk, or his as yet unseen companion.

Noting her concern, the bespectacled beaker sought to sell her on his viewpoint. "But since you both seek to do the same thing, surely it would make more sense to seek out this staff together? After all, three is better than two?"

"Five," Shoenia corrected him.

"Ah, yes. Five. We mustn't forget the rode – er –smuzzles. Anyway, it seems to make much more sense to me. Doesn't it to you, Dearest?"

"Absolutely, Dear."

"We could even help by guiding you to the edge of The Baobabs," Hoot offered. "After the skyshowers have ceased and the muckrivers have dried, of course. Couldn't we, Dearest?"

"Of course, Dear."

"But now it is time to nap. Why don't you share my napnest this black, Dearest? And allow our guests to share yours?"

"For sure!" Tiptin accidentally blurted out. Palming mute his mouth, he blushed like a breaking brightsphere.

"Perhaps you should check on your friend?" Shoenia suggested. "He's been awfully quiet for quite some time now?"

"Ha! Probably stuffing his yap with bugs," Tiptin quipped. Then her seers moved him to sigh, "Okay, perhaps you are right."

"Take a filament fern," Hoot suggested.

Tiptin grabbed hold of the honeycombed hilt and, instantly, his fiber blade breathed ashimmer. "Thank you, but my sword shall guide me."

"Sword, Dear?"

"A battling tool of sorts, Dearest."

"Oh."

With Spidey's sword lighting his way, the ladfolk exited the vault, strolled through the tight corridor, and longstrided up the narrow shaft. He encountered the cyclops still wedged tight in the squeeze.

"Well, it's about time!" Thwack scolded, twisting his large head about to get a better look at Tiptin. Both his arms were firmly jammed tight to his sides. "Now get me out of this!"

"Ha!" Tiptin scoffed. "You're hardly in any position to be giving orders, Mr. Smarty. Besides, it serves you right, scaring Hoot's kind missus like that."

"HARR! But did you catch that look on her face? Simply too mu… Hey! Where are you going? Hey! This isn't funny! I'm stuck!"

"At least this way you won't get into any more mischief."

"Hey, come back here you puny…huh? What are you doing? Hey? HEY!!"

Tiptin turned and marched right up to the stuck giant. "Now, let's see how Mr. Smarty like being on the receiving end of a prank?"

"Ow!" Thwack yelled as Tiptin employed a pointdigit to flicking a pointy hearer. "Ow! Hey! Ow! Ouch! Stop it! Ow! Hey! Ouch! No fair, I'm stu…**OW!!**"

"Harr-Harr-Harr," Tiptin teased. "You should catch the look on your face."

"OW!!"

"Simply 'toooooo' much, I tell ya. 'Tooooooooo' much."

"OUCH! HEY! OW! OW! OW! OW! OW! OW! **EEYEOW!!!!**"

Propping the sword against the wall, the ladfolk finished up tormenting his wedged victim by performing a serious slapping palm roll upon his shiny dome, followed by a severe cheekie. Then he grinned and walked away. "Harr. Harr. Harr."

Thwack was furious. He twisted and kicked and grunted and groaned; yet he was still unable to break free. "I'll get you for this! **You hear me, TIPTIN OF FOLKTON! ?!!"#*$$!"?!*#?!*?**"

Light and the undaunted ladfolk both vanished around the bend, neither being the least bit concerned over Thwack's threats; the former being indifferent to such things, and the latter having much more important matters on his mind.

Upon re-entering the den hollow, Tiptin noted that the filament ferns had dimmed. Hoot and Hweet were already asnore in one nest-like cot, while three bumps hid beneath the quilt on the other. Slipperboots, a hangtop and a rust skirt were folded and placed neatly against the wall.

Donning a smirk of anticipation, the eager ladfolk sat on the quilt and removed his highboots and vest before releasing his long tietail. Trembling digits seemed to make everything a chore. His pumper pounded to pain his chest, and his breathers raced as he drew one leg free of his trousers. Now the other…

"Ah!"

"Thud!"

In painful confusion, Tiptin looked up into emerald seers. Shoenia's lips were stretched into a challenging grin.

"I – I thought we were going to share?"

"We are," she explained. "This black, I shall take the napnest. Next black, you can have the napnest. Rest well, Tiptin of Folkton." With that, Shoenia turned away and drew the warm quilt about her firm and shapely form.

A pair of furry faces poked out at Tiptin. Each stuck out its licker. "Ppptttthhh."

While wiping the smuzzle spray from his face, the humiliated ladfolk pondered over which hurt worse – the bruise from her heels, the bruise from the bark floor, or the bruise to his ego?

Either way, he dared not try that again soon. Stretching out on the rough bark, he mumbled, "Hmpff. Who wants to nap with two furballs anyway?" Then he drifted off into the restless realm of nearnap, waking often to stretch kinks from his sore neck and massage the numb from his limbs. Now he wished he'd been more forgiving of Thwack, so he could curl up on the big guy's soft, warm belly.

Finally, his discomfort was disrupted by the arousal of all. After washing up and downing a big wakechow of nuts dipped in bumble sweet, Tiptin summoned up the courage to approach Shoenia. "I must apologize for my lack of manners, Shoenia. Even though it is my turn to next use the cot, you and your smuzzles may enjoy it instead."

Shoenia smiled knowingly. "Do not fret over us, Tiptin of Folkton. We have managed thus far with neither yourself nor a cot. However, I might be swayed to engage in meaningful dialogue during our trek. Of course, I'm not promising such."

Tiptin gulped. He had a shot after all. Then he recalled Hoot's advice regarding an honorable modus operandi. "You are very beautiful, Shoenia. And keen of wit. If you please, I request the privilege of properly wooing you?"

Shoenia broadened her smile, inadvertently betraying her own enthusiasm. "We'll see."

Two jealous furballs pawtended to spit up.

"Yesiree!" Hoot shouted down from a ledge near the ceiling, where he had been peeking out through a sight slit. After sliding the floatwood shutter back into place, he descended to explain his excitement. "The skyshowers have ceased, so now we can depart."

"Excellent!" Tiptin exclaimed. "We are without the luxury of time."

"Uh, but what of the forest floor? Will it not still be a river of muck?"

Hweet addressed the valid concern. "The floor dries most quickly here, Shoenia. Baobab roots are forever thirsty, and they can store many times their own weight in drink."

"Greedy, too," Hoot added. "They race to out-slurp one another. The ground may remain soft for a short while, but Thwack shall fare well. We can carry the rest of you."

Within a few nods, they were all ready to depart. They hastened through the tight corridor and on up the narrow shaft, where they encountered a huge, motionless form, which appeared to be wedged tight into a squeeze.

"Thwack?" Tiptin inquired with concern. He gently nudged the giant's shiny dome. "Thwack, are you okay? Speak to me, big buddy. Thwack?"

Perhaps the squeeze squashed his breathers?" Hoot suggested.

"Thwack? Buddy? I'm sorry, Thwack." Tiptin knelt and lifted the cyclops' sealed lid.

"Aaaaa!" Tiptin screamed as a fist as big as a boulder yanked him through the squeeze.

Both smuzzles puffed fur and leapt onto Shoenia's back. Feathers filled the shaft.

"Schmmaaaaack!" Thwack planted a big slobbering smooch across the startled ladfolk's face. "Gotcha back! HARR! HARR! Aw, I never knew ya cared. Schmmaaaaack! HARR! HARR! HARR! HARR! WOW! Shoulda seen your faces! Tooooo much, I tell ya. Simply tooooo much. HARR! HARR! HA…"

The others faces were simply 'naaaaawwt' amused.

Each shot the jovial giant a dirty glare as they paraded past, shoving him back against the wall. The smuzzles even granted him a rigid 'long-digits up' as they went by. Then the group all filed out onto the boughcany, and made preparations for flight.

Both beakers stretched their flappers, touching tips to talons to loosen things up, while the competing rodents entered into a tumbletussle to decide who would fly with the galfolk.

Eventually, two firm pairs of humanfolk hands tore the chattering furballs apart. Sneek then gloated as a sulking smuzzle with a blue patch about one seer dangled from the tall ladfolk's arm. Such was the contest decided.

"Hey, what about me?" Thwack voiced in protest, suddenly catching on. "I'm too heavy to carry?"

Hoot toned well beyond cynical. "My dear Mr. Clops. Before wakechow I took the liberty to study up on your kind. According to the Scholarship Chronicles, no being of breath can match the stamina of your species. Apparently, none can match your atrocious manners, either. I must remember to write that in. Do remind me, Dearest."

"Oh, I certainly shan't forget about that, Dear." Hweet glared daggers at Thwack.

"Therefore, my dear Mr. Clops, you should have very little trouble keeping up with us battered, old beakers. The sword and the shinebulb shall guide you, and you do have your precious bugs to nourish you. Although, the monster bugs of The Baobabs don't take too kindly to bugsquishers."

"M-M-Monster bugs?"

"Oh my, yes. Megamonster bugs, even. The forest floor is crawling with megamonster bugs. They're simply 'tooooo' much." Hoot flapped aloft and clamped his talons about Tiptin's outstretched arms. "That's why we're all flying. However, you shouldn't have too much trouble. If they surround you, just entertain them with your sense of humor. I'm certain they'll be most impressed."

"S-Surround me? M-Megamonster bugs might surround me?"

"Quite possibly, Mr. Clops. Quite possibly. But given your hefty bulk, you really need only beware the poisonous bite bugs."

"Gulp.... p-poisonous bite bugs?"

"Oh, yes. And do mind their sharp fangs, will you."

"F-Fangs?"

"Yes, fangs. They are exceptionally long and..."

Thwack gulped, hard. "And what? Hey! And what? I said, **AND WHAT! HEY!**"

"Do hurry down, Mr. Clops. You surely don't want to lose sight of our lights!"

"AND WHAT? HEY! WAIT UP! AND WHAT!"

"That should add to his stamina," Tiptin noted with a slight trace of amusement. "Please don't lose him, though."

"What, and have him remain here in The Baobabs with us?"

A brief silence ensued before all six burst into laughter.

"AND WHAT!!!!"

"Careful, Mr. Thwack!" Hoot hollered into the blackness below. "I've spotted some movement behind you!"

"AAAIYEE!!!!"

Again, all six burst into laughter.

"HEY! DON'T GO! C'MON, WAIT UP! THIS ISN'T FUNNY! AND WHAT! HEY.........AND WHAT!!!!!!"

Peepers still blinked from the shadows, but the strange sounds no longer shivered Tiptin's skin. He felt quite secure in the big beaker's talons, plus there was the added security of Shoenia's shinebulb floating slightly ahead of them.

On several occasions, Hoot even exchanged pleasantries with some of the peepers. "That was my eldest chick's ex-mate," he would explain, adding, "Young beakers sure don't tough through their troubles like we old beakers did. Such a shame, sometimes, although sometimes I imagine it's for the best." **OR,** "That was old Busy Buckbiter, chief chatteryarn amongst the Gliding Bushytails. Knows almost every rumor about everyone. Small wonder, she started most of them."

"Gliding Bushytails?"

"Yes, Tiptin. They are much like regular bushytails, but with pliable skin stretched between their legs so they can glide from treetop to ground. Must climb back up, though."

"So they can't fully fly?"

"Precisely. Maybe Destiny hasn't quite figured out what they're eventually supposed to be yet? Hey, how's it going between you and the galfolk?"

"Uh – I'm working on it."

"That bad, eh?"

"Well, I'm certainly open to suggestions."

"Hmmm. I'm no expert on the riddle gender, however, I can't stress too much the importance of your being real."

"Being real? I am real."

"Are you, really Tiptin?"

"Hoot, I don't quite understand?"

"You must always be yourself, Tiptin. Above all else, you must allow yourself to be who you really are. Because if you are phony at the outset and Shoenia does fall in love with you, then it's not really you she will actually love."

"It isn't?" Tiptin said.

"No. Then she will love the phony you've pretended to be. Which means you'll have to try and keep up the act. But one can only pretend to be somebody else for so long before one's true self returns. Thus you won't get to keep her love, anyway. If you and her are meant to be, then she will love you despite yourself. If not, then neither of you will have lost anything."

"Sort of like how a being can only fool others for so long before they fool themselves?"

"Actually, the instant you even plot to fool others, you have already fooled yourself."

"Oh? Hoot, you are well learned. Tell me, why is her skin so fair?"

"I truly don't know, Tiptin. Why is yours brown? Why do Hweet and I have feathers?"

"Uh…?"

"Does it even matter?"

"Well…no, of course not."

"Bzzzzztt! Correct answer!"

"It is?"

"Of course. We should never pass judgment on another based upon skin colour or texture. It is of much greater importance to view the being by character. If you don't like someone, at least try to get to know them a bit better before entirely dismissing their friendship, or their views. And always give somebody who's wronged you a second chance."

"Like Thwack. He's forever frightening others."

"I said a second chance, Tiptin. That's only one past a first."

"Hoot?"

"Yes?"

"You're really wise."

"No, I just study hard."

"Hoot?"

"Yes?"

"What about the Ohmees? I mean, should they be given a second chance?"

"From what I have read, trust an Ohmee once and you won't get a second chance. As far as I know, they are the only exception. Yet, I've never actually met one. And it is not wise to believe everything just because you read it in books."

"It isn't?"

"No. Beings who speak untruths can also write untruths. Always try to think for yourself."

"Hoot?"

"Yes."

"I'm glad we met."

"Ditto, my young friend. Ditto."

In The Baobabs, none can ever say for certain who rules atop the canopy. Therefore, the group could not know how long or far they'd traveled.

Shoenia drew energy from the titanroot sap, while Tiptin was constantly charged by the blade's breath. Thwack, hollering up from somewhere in the blackness, proved the Chronicles were correct. Indeed, no mortal being can match the stamina of a cyclops. Although big beakers do come close.

Finally, beams from the brightsphere began to penetrate the thinning canopy and waltzed within a cool mist between the shrinking trunks. Here, the beakers touched down.

"We can go no further," Hweet informed them.

"It's our blinkers," Hoot elaborated. "Brightsphere rays damage our sight. I tried to look directly at the brightsphere once before, and now I need specs."

"Well, I told you so," Hweet reminded him.

"Yes, Dearest. You certainly did." Hoot rolled his blinkers.

"It's really unwise for anyone to stare at the brightsphere," Shoenia informed them. "Not just those accustomed to darkness."

"See? I told you so."

"Yes, Dearest. You did at that."

Suddenly something bulky came crashing through the bushes. The entire group turned to sight upon the spectacle.

Huffing and puffing and dripping with skindew, a beefy cyclops bounded towards them. His spanning smile exposed two rows of sharp, pointy biters. In one hairy fist, he gripped a log like club, while the other held high an enormous, limp crawler.

"Well I'll be a howlpack's chow...?"

"WOW!" Thwack exclaimed. "You weren't just chirping delicacies. Check out the size of these bugs!" Next, the ecstatic giant motioned to the big bag, which was packed near to burst and slung over his broad back. "I bagged a batch!"

All spun in disgust as Thwack chomped out a chunk. "Mmmmmm – thendar too."

"We'll be on our way now," Hweet said. "I have kinbeakers just upaway from here. Please take care of yourselves."

"I do hope you'll come see us again," Hoot put out. "After you've completed your quest, of course."

"If, you mean?"

"No, Tiptin, I mean after. Be realistic, but be positively realistic. You shall always succeed in a noble quest if you trust in Destiny and truly try. Always."

Both beakers fluttered aloft. Before soaring back up into the dark, Hoot turned and winked at the ladfolk. Remember, be real."

Tiptin smiled and waved to his wise friend - while Shoenia wondered what the beaker meant?

"Hey, anyone want a taste? Your choice, juicy or crunchy? HARR! HARR! HARR! HARR…"

All turned away in disgust.

"Rogue," Shoenia mumbled.

"A really revolting rogue," Tiptin elaborated.

The smuzzles nodded their agreement.

They quickly emerged from The Baobabs and waded directly into marshyland. Thatches of purple slurpweeds reached up from still pools, which were bounded by moist mounds matted with squooshmoss. Black foulferns with white stripes squirted out stink. Tiny, winged borebugs drilled deep into skin, while annoying botherbugs buzzed about heads, expertly dodging swats and occasionally chomping out chunks of free flesh.

Always, the questers were stalked by armored snoutsnappers, whose evil peepers popped atop pools. On several occasions, the devious creatures attempted to sneak up and snack on a smuzzle. Only to swim swiftly away with large lumps between their crossed, spinning peepers. Courtesy of Shoenia's scrapstick. Or to meet Morgue with bellies-up. Courtesy of Thwack's club.

The petite galfolk packed a wallop worthy of one well beyond her weight, and she wouldn't hesitate to protect her furry friends. Plus nobody, but 'nooooobody', was going to get anywhere near Thwack's big bag of bugs. Noooo way.

On and on and on they trekked, wading through frigid pools, and slogging through muck that sucked at their feet. Bright after Black after Bright after Black, by both brightsphere and palesphere, under both blue above and bleak. On and on and on…

Eventually the soil dried firm and they entered the Fern Forest. The thick musk of rotting vegetation stung their nostrils and irritated their seers. Fuzzy fronds licked skindew from their flesh.

Here they began to see big-footed fuzzballs with long floppy hearers, who hopped about munching orange spears; plus trunked pest suckers, with abnormally big rears. There were wood-munching puffers bearing needles with barbs, and nattering fern dwellers with bent, bushy tails. Along with giant rat hoppers, complete with pouches for tots, as well as tusked snort-squealers with tails coiled into knots.

There were whip-tailed squeakers that scurried by in a dash, and furry chatcheekers who buried nuts in a stash. They heard a choir of hop chirpers, that just knew how to groove, and caught sight of antlered bellowers, clopping by on split hooves. Plus they were once entertained by a slapstick ensemble of bug-seer buffoons.

Buckbiter slaptails constructed sturdy log dams, while bumble buzzers turned nectar into sap sweeter than jam. Chirpers built nests, and cheek pockets dug dens. A croak hopper squatted on a shell snapper, so they might have been friends?

"Wait!" Thwack suddenly blurted. "I hear something coming?"

Shoenia cast a skeptical stare at Tiptin.

"He does have far superior hearing," Tiptin confirmed.

"What kind of…?" Shoenia began.

"Shhhh." Thwack pressed a pointdigit to his fat lips. "It sounds like many feet marching. Many heavy feet."

"From which direction?" Tiptin whispered.

"Behind us," Thwack informed him, palm muffling his voice. "Probably Xebec's bullybeasts patrolling his island?"

Shoenia firmed her grip on her scrapstick. "But way out here?"

"This is still Xebec's Island," Thwack reminded her.

"Yeah, but…?"

"What shall we do?" Tiptin cut in, hoping to avoid at all cost the delay and aggravation of dealing with a bunch of dense bullybeasts.

"Hmmmm? Ah, I know. I can stride faster than even they can swing, and my stamina greatly surpasses theirs. I'll go back and act as a decoy. By the time I'm finished leading them astray, they'll be too pooped to piddle. HARR!"

"Shhhh."

"Oh, yeah. Sorry. Now you hurry along and I'll try to catch up later. Go on. Go. They're coming closer."

"But what if they should catch you?" Shoenia asked, her tone expressing alarm.

"Then Thwack can always fool them by playing hide and seek," Tiptin pointed out, making amused.

"Yeah, well suppose they're not these bullybeasts after all?" Shoenia smugly noted. "Suppose they're mean beings instead?"

Thwack was undaunted. "Then you'll simply have to carry on without me. Now get on before they can hear us. Go. Go," he urged, shooing them off with his large hand.

"But-But…"

"Go."

Tiptin grabbed Shoenia's arm and, together with the smuzzles, they stole in amongst the ferns.

"Thwack?" Tiptin called after him. But his voice was answered only by the whispering wind. "Walk with Destiny, Thwack. And do be wary."

Tiptin and the others began sneaking silently between the skinny ferns talks, soft-stepping with care. Each felt their pumper pounding in beat to their fear. They'd journeyed too far now to be delayed by a bunch of bullybeasts. Assuming it even was bullybeasts?

Finally, they stopped to grant their sore digits a much needed rest.

"Do you hear anything?" Shoenia asked.

"No, nothing. Look, Bright is retreating thataway across the sky. Soon Black will rule."

"Can these bullybeasts see in the dark?"

"I don't really know, Shoenia, but they do have a keen sense of smell. Yet they could not think any slower, and they really aren't a bad lot. Providing one has ample patience, of course. I worry more about hurting their feelings than I do about them harming us. Of course, they could be under some sort of spell. Or simply terrified of Xebec. Fear can make anybody do things that they normally wouldn't even consider doing. Still, Thwack should fare well."

"You worry about him, don't you?"

"Only because the big guy never matured beyond cydolescence. This quest might prove to be a dangerous time for him to resist growing up."

"Well, I think he's a complete dungskull."

Both smuzzles nodded in agreement.

"Then perhaps you three should get to know him better before entirely dismissing his friendship and views."

"But why is his skin so green? Is he ill or something?"

Tiptin shrugged. "I don't know why? Why is mine brown? Why is yours white? Does it really matter?"

"No, of course not. Why should it matter?"

"Bzzztt! Correct answer!"

"Shhhhh," Shoenia cautioned.

"Sorry, I just feel it is much more important to view beings beyond their colour or species. It's character that coun...."

"AAAAARRRGGGHH!!!!"

"Eeeeyikes!" the terrified pair screamed in unison, each grabbing onto the other in fear.

Sneek and Peek froze in fright. Each thought its wee ticker might tok!

"HARR! HARR! HARR! HARR! Oh, dearest Destiny! I can't believe you actually fell for that ole 'we're being followed' routine! HARR! HARR! HARR! What a bunch of saps, I tell ya! Ooooweeee! Simply tooooo much, I tell ya! Simply…. huh?"

This time Shoenia had had quite enough of the jovial joker in a jungle jumper and his cubbish pranks. With sparks spitting from her seers, the well beyond livid galfolk poked his belly hard with her scrapstick. "And having thus gained his immediate attention, she launched into a long overdue licker-lashing of truth.

"You may be big, Buster, and carry a log, but I bet you just tremble at the thought of others looking down on you! That's the real reason you're forever making slycut remarks to put others down, and always plotting to humiliate or frighten them! Just so you'll feel a mite less lonely and miserable in your own skin! Because deep down inside, lonely ole Mr. Smartyclops doesn't even like himself! Which I hardly find surprising, Mr. Nofriends! Do you?"

The giant was stunned silent. His armor of attitude had just been stripped clean away. His fat lips quivered, yet he could neither speak nor lock sights with the fuming galfolk. Weepwet began to seep from his misty seer. Never had he even suspected that shame could make one physically ill, or that the simple truth could cut so deep. Never had he felt so vulnerable.

"Any more trouble and we go on without him!" Shoenia railed at nobody in particular. "From what I've seen of his character, we'd all probably be far better off without him along anyway. Who needs his nonsense? Now come on. He's wasted quite enough of our precious little time already."

Before scampering up onto Shoenia's back, both smuzzles paused briefly to kick the weeping green prankster in one of his digits.

"Weren't you a tad tough on the big guy?" Tiptin asked meekly.

"No!" Shoenia spat. Then, realizing that Tiptin was not the source of her ire, she tamed her tone. "Listen, Tiptin, I like you. Really, I do. But this quest is not a stupid game; at least not to me. If we are to have any success and unpower that staff, the key ingredients for our success shall be courage, unity and trust. So far, your cubbish pal has displayed none of those qualities. As things are now, we'd really fare better without him."

Thwack started sobbing uncontrollably.

Tiptin knew he couldn't dispute her point. Nor was he willing to risk upsetting her further than she already was. However, he fully understood her feelings. He too had grown weary of Thwack's cubbish humor. After all, a second chance is only one past a first.

The sullen cyclops sulked along in the rear, without uttering so much as a peep. His mind was still haunted by the shaming echo of truth, and the realization that he had succeeded in fooling only himself.

Black won again. Then lost again. Ruled. Then retreated. Yet on and on they all trekked. Up hills and down. Through families of fuzzy fronds and around rippled ponds.

Until eventually they stopped to soak their tender tootsies in one of the many shinesilver aquaveins which nourished the emerald and blue body of The Fern Forest.

"Ahhhhh...." Shoenia sighed in relief as the crystal clear liquid cooled her sore soles. She shut her seers and wiggled her blistered digits.

"Ahhhhh...." Tiptin also sighed, likewise savoring the soothing sensation of cool wet flowing across burning digits and heels. "I needed....huh? Ouch!"

"Ouch!" Shoenia mimicked.

Thwack also yelped, and the smuzzles chattered and swatted.

"Charge!" sang out a high-pitched voice from above.

"**Charge!**" replied a chorus of thousands more. "*Stickem! Stickem! Stickem!*"

The questers stared in utter disbelief as a dark mass descended upon them. It was composed of tiny flyfolk with transparent wings and tipnut helmets. Each brandished a tipnut-cap shield and a thorn sword. All shouted, "*Stickem! Stickem! Stickem! Stickem!*"

"Ouch!" Shoenia shouted, swatting to snatch one of the pests. "Ouch! Stop that! Ow! Ow! Careful, you could poke somebody's seer out with those – ouch – things! Ow!"

"*Stickem! Stickem! Stickem! Stickem!* Poke em in the rear! Jab em in the neck! Prick em in the hearer! *Stickem! Stickem! Stickem! Stickem! Stick.....?*"

"WHOOOOOAAAAAHH!!!" Thwack suddenly screamed, blasting all breath from his powerful breathers.

Calm ruled as the tiny tenors truced. They exchanged bewildered glances, completely uncertain of their next maneuver.

"Now then," Shoenia demanded in a terse tone. "Who exactly is in charge of this ornery outfit?"

The tiny flyfolk mumbled briefly amongst themselves before an especially puny member winged forward. "The Sheebazz is in charge."

"Sheebazz is in charge!" echoed the chorus.

"But Sheebazz not here," added another.

"Oh? And just where is this Mr. Sheebazz?" Tiptin inquired, angrily rubbing his wounds.

"Not Mr. – The Sheebazz," corrected a reply.

Tiptin was growing annoyed. “Well, where exactly is ‘The’ Sheebazz, then?”

“Sheebazz not here.”

“I know that…..”

Shoenia motioned Tiptin mute. She adopted a gentler tone, infused with patience. “But who are you? And why did you attack us?”

“We are The Weetykes,” answered the especially puny flyfolk.

“Weetykes!” echoed the chorus.

“But why did you weetykes attack us?”

“Because we don’t like strangers anymore.”

“We don’t like strangers anymore!”

“That’s not very fair,” Tiptin put in. “You don’t even know us.”

“But we’d certainly never harm you,” Shoenia assured them.

Thwack and the smuzzles all shook their heads.

“The funny folk did,” said the especially puny flyfolk.

“The funny folk did!” echoed the chorus.

“Please, just one speak at a time.” Shoenia looked to the especially puny weetyke. “Do you have a name, young lady?”

The puny weetyke looked nervously about.

"Go on and tell her," encouraged another.

"Tell her!" echoed the chorus.

"I'm Pint Little," replied the puny weetyke.

"Pint Little!" echoed the chorus.

"Hush. I can hear her just fine."

"Hear her just fine!" echoed the chorus.

"Now, Miss Little…."

"What are your names?" Pint Little interrupted, fluttering a bit closer to Shoenia.

Shoenia paused to allow for an echo that never came. "My name is Shoenia. This here is Tiptin and my furry friends are named Sneek and Peek."

Each bowed in turn.

"So who's the big greeny with the attitude?"

"Mega attitude!" echoed the chorus.

"Oh, I'm sorry. That is Thwack. He's a cyclops."

"He's even bigger than bullybeasts," Pint Little observed.

"Even bigger than bullybeasts!"

"Shush!" Pint Little shouted. "She did say she could hear just fine!"

"Oh, yes. She did say she could hear just fine…" mumbled the chorus.

"You know of bullybeasts?" Tiptin asked.

"Of course," Pint Little replied. "They come swinging about our forest, sometimes. Swatting and smashing our twigshelters. On purpose."

"On purpose!"

"Well that's certainly not very nice."

"No, Shoenia, but it's not really their fault."

"Not their fault?" Shoenia was visibly puzzled. "But you just said they smash your twigshelters on purpose."

Pint explained. "The bullybeasts aren't really mean, Shoenia. They're just afraid of the sworcerer and fear makes them sometimes do not nice things."

Shoenia's tone was terse. "No excuse. One cannot blame another for one's own actions. If this sw – er, sorcerer told them to go leap off a bluff, would they do it?"

"Yes."

"Oh. Anyway, do tell me more of this funny folk," Shoenia pressed.

"He skulked through our forest just this past palesphere. We didn't much care for his moody manner, so we swarmbombed to *stickem*. But he knew magic. He waved his funny pink stick and made The Sheebazz slumber with locked lids. And she is very slight of breath." Pint Little bowed her head in sorrow. "We think The Sheebazz might meet Morgue."

"Uh, this funny folk, does he have odd seers?"

"Uh-huh. One seer is green and the other is blue. Is he known to you?"

"Oh yes," Shoenia replied with obvious disdain. "He is Zebu, a most mean and moody magician; and certainly no friend of ours."

Tiptin thought, it seems like this Zebu should be crowned ruler of all dungskulls.

"Where is The Sheebazz now?" Shoenia asked.

Pint Little eyed the galfolk with more than a tint of distrust.

"Perhaps we can help her?" Tiptin explained.

"Swarmhuddle!" Pint Little shouted, suddenly winging asky.

"Swarmhuddle!" echoed the chorus.

The dark mass lifted well clear of hearshot before closing ranks into a tight, multileveled scrum. Quite some time elapsed before the scrum finally dispersed and wound its way back down like a long, black whip.

Pint Little led the column, winging directly down to Shoenia. "I've been elected Proxy during Sheebazz' slumber. Although most are staunchly opposed, I exercised my 'Option of Override'.

"What is an Option of Override?" Tiptin inquired.

"It means even if the majority are opposed, the proxy in charge can do whatever he or she wills." Pint Little explained.

"Sounds like a silly rule," Tiptin said.

"Then you'll bring us to The Sheebazz?" Shoenia cut in, quite honored by Pint Little's trust.

"Not exactly," Pint Little glanced at Thwack. "We voted to fetch The Sheebazz for you. My peers fear for their twigshelters. You see, even a proxy must compromise – or face recall."

"Sounds like a sensible rule," Tiptin noted.

"Here comes Sheebazz!" announced the chorus.

About a dozen weetykes emerged from amongst some ferns, bearing a fuzzy frond. A silent form lay upon the makeshift stretcher. Her stiff arms were folded across two nut breast cups, and her flesh was ghoulishly pale. Both of her lids were locked tight and her pumper seemed stilled.

She was clad in a short skirt, fashioned from silkwiggler thread and dyed berry blue. Limp, colorless locks dangled from her wee head, upon which was placed the shell of a brownish burrnut. Its smooth surface had been painstakingly polished to a fine sheen.

Yet, despite her current plight, it was readily apparent that The Sheebazz was normally quite vibrant and lovely.

Donning expressions of hope, the weetykes gathered about the determined galfolk and started singing sweet songs in a group effort to help out.

First, Shoenia tried to revive The Sheebazz by moistening her dry skin with blasts of hot breath. All to no avail. Next, she dabbed a drop of titanroot sap between the still form's tiny, cracked lips. Still, she got no response. Chants also failed to work, as did pleas unto both Destiny and Morgue. So Shoenia tried the breath and sap routines again and again and again, fully determined to break Zebu's cruel spell.

Each attempt only netted more disappointment than the last. Sad and discouraged, Shoenia finally turned to Pint Little. "I'm so sorry, my tiny friend."

Pint Little smiled and patted the galfolk's shoulder. "Sorry for what, Shoenia? Never apologize for trying your best to help somebody."

"Never apologize for a precious pumper!" replied the chorus.

"Wait!" Tiptin suddenly blurted.

"What?" Shoenia responded with a start.

"What!" echoed the chorus?

"Spidey's sword!" Tiptin's tone was tinged with newfound hope.

"The sword?"

"The sword?"

"Yes!" Tiptin exclaimed. "The sword! Its fiber blade pulses with breath. And it was fashioned by Spidey Smeals, himself a most learned master magician!"

"Well, try it!" Shoenia exclaimed, her voice infused with fresh hope. "What have we to lose?"

"What have we to lose!"

Tiptin began wavering the shimmering blade just slightly atop the silent form.

"The Sheebazz stays still," Pint Little noted.

"Shhhh!" Shoenia shushed. "Try again, Tiptin, while I offer up a chant."

Again, the ladfolk began wavering the shimmering blade just slightly atop the still form.

Shoenia commenced with her chant:

"OH BLADE ASHIMMER,

DO SERVE US WELL,

LEND OF YOUR BREATH,

PLEASE CAST OFF ZEBU'S SPELL?"

All watched with wided seers and locked lips, but the still form did not stir.

"Try a different chant or cadence or something," Tiptin suggested, and Shoenia opted to try again.

And again.....

And yet again.....

"OH BEING ASHIMMER.....

DO SERVE ME WELL.....

LEND OF YOUR MAGIC.....

AND UNCAST ZEBU'S SPELL!"

No sooner had Shoenia completed her latest chant, than the blade cast a white glow over the frond. Wisps of hot mist floated free of the pulsing fiber and swept into The Sheebazz' tiny nostrils.

Immediately, her still chest inflated in breath and her pale skin bronzed. Golden shades began fluttering through her fluttering locks as she slowly unfolded her wee arms. Her moist lips parted a moan. Both seers blinked in bewilderment.

"Sheebazz! Sheebazz! Sheebazz!" echoed the chorus. **"Sheebazz! Sheebazz! Sheebazz!"**

"Welcome back into being," greeted a tall ladfolk.

"How do you feel?" Shoenia inquired, wondering if she shouldn't perhaps bow or something?

The Sheebazz drew her tiny torso upright and smiled at the strangers. Soft words flowed smoothly from her throat. "Like I've been remade by a breathbeam. Who, pray tell, are you?"

Shoenia and Tiptin took turns telling The Sheebazz exactly where each of their group hailed from and what they were about. She proved to be a most polite listener, as did the rest of the weetykes. None dared speak past The Sheebazz. Besides, they were all kept quite intrigued by the humanfolks' tales.

"…and now we are here with you," Tiptin finished.

"And you are certain the sworcerer's staff can be unpowered in The Saline Sea?" inquired The Sheebazz.

"Absolutely," Shoenia assured her. "Only we may not have enough time."

"Zebu is well ahead of us," Tiptin pointed out. "And his intentions quite differ from ours."

"I have observed this coral castle," The Sheebazz informed them.

"You have?"

"Oh yes. A very long time past. It is an ugly place, and the sworcerer is most glumdreary."

"You have actually met him?"

"No, but I have observed him from afar. His brand of scowl does carry."

"But whyever would you even risk going near there?"

"I went to voice a protest about his bullybeasts always swinging through our twigshelters during their travels to and from the thataway coast. However, one glance at his wicked stare and I knew not to waste words. You five certainly have courage. It will require nothing short of an army to penetrate the walls of that castle, I can assure you of that."

"But we don't have an army," Shoenia pointed out. "Besides, then Xebec would know well ahead that we are coming. After all, an army is quite visible."

"Hmmmm." The Sheebazz briefly pondered a thought before turning to Pint Little. "Swarmhuddle."

"Swarmhuddle!" announced the Proxy.

"Swarmhuddle!" echoed the chorus.

A dark mass lifted well clear of hearshot before closing ranks into a tight, multileveled scrum. Yet hardly any time passed before the scrum dispersed and winded its way back down like a long, black whip.

The Sheebazz flew directly up to Shoenia and Tiptin. "The vote was unanimous with no abstentions. We are very hard to spot, therefore, we shall be your army!"

Shoenia and Tiptin exchanged fond looks.

"You really don't owe us anything," Shoenia assured them.

The Sheebazz smiled. "Agreed. I have long contended that the silliest saying ever spoken is, you 'OWE' me a favor. But we really do want to help out. Besides, we've long grown weary of constantly rebuilding our twigshelters. And you can certainly use our help, can you not?"

"Yes, I suppose we could well use some tiny seers inside the castle to let us know what Xebec's about. But it will be very dangerous. Are you sure…"

"And to let the staff remain in the hands of either the glumdreary sworcerer or the funny folk with the odd seers is any less dangerous?"

Tiptin and Shoenia looked at one another and simply shrugged. For both knew their tiny friend had made a most valid point.

"When can you be ready to march – er – fly?" Shoenia asked.

"Now," replied The Sheebazz. "As you yourselves have noted, there is no time to doddle."

Thus the five questers were joined by an army of tiny flyfolk with transparent wings and tipnut helmets. Each of which brandished a thorn sword and a tipnut-cup shield. Together, they flymarched throughout the foliage like a dark mass. All were very eager to engage the bullybeasts. And *stickem!*

Eventually, their travels brought them out from the rolling emerald and blue carpet that was The Fern Forest, and they ventured into a new marshylands.

This new marshylands was very much the same as the previous marshylands. Once again, thatches of purple slurpweeds reached up from still pools, which were bounded by moist mounds matted with squooshmoss. And there were more stinky foulferns.

A brief battle erupted between the weetykes and the buzzing bother bugs, but the well-armed flyfolk won victory with ease. However, the tinier but much nastier bore bugs proved to be a much worthier foe. Several furious clashes were waged; pitting thorn swords against snout needles, before the vile suckers finally retreated.

Then there appeared a new species of snoutsnapper. Considerably smaller than the former, they enjoyed superior swamp sneaking skills and swim speed. As with their larger kinkind, they too tried to snack upon smuzzles. And, as with their larger kinkind, they too were sent swiftswimming away with large lumps between their crossed, spinning peepers.

Finally, the questers and their army cleared the marshylands and arrived at the coastal bluffs. Damp chillwind cooled their cheeks as the weary lot sighted thisaway across the wetrollers.

A black spouter with mean, red seers was lurching and lunging its way upward along the shore. Shoenia thought it looked familiar?

A family of crownbreathers performed talented back flips and tricks, broad-smiling with joy as they splashed back down into the wet. Stem-seered, red snippers clashed claws over sand, while white-of-wing shoresquawkers swooped low over both sea and land.

"Shoenia!" Pint Little shouted to top the breeze. "We weetykes must remain well hidden within the foliage!"

Shoenia nodded.

"These gusts are quite blowy!" Tiptin conceded.

"It's not the wind!" Pint Little hollered in his hearer, pointing at a distant squawker. "We must beware of those!"

Tiptin nodded that he understood, and then motioned the other questers to follow him back in amongst the short, seaside shrubbery.

Thwack crawled along on all fours, lest he be sighted from afar. And he continued to pout by his lonesome.

While hovering near to soil, the tiny flyfolk maintained a constant upward vigil. All held their thorn swords at the ready as they scouted above for any sign of movement. They had battled squawkers before. Always, some of their number would meet Morgue.

They traveled due upaway for well more than a palesphere. Gradually the terrain became hilly and forested with tall needlers.

Yet they neither sighted nor heard any creatures? It was as if none dared to dwell there.

Then, from a good vantage in a small clearing, they caught sight of a pink structure squatting stoic and foreboding atop a faraway plateau. **Xebec's castle!**

"Only one valley left to cross," The Sheebazz noted in encouragement.

"I hear someone approaching," Thwack suddenly warned.

"Yeah, sure."

"Right."

"Pppttthhh."

"No, really. I mean it this time."

"Uh-huh."

"Sure you do, Thwack."

"What does it sound like?" The Sheebazz inquired with noted concern.

"It sounds….."

"Ignore that fibchucker," Shoenia cut in. "He's filled to his seer with plant fodder."

"No, really," Thwack pleaded. "I'm telling the truth this time."

"Yeah. Uh-huh. Sure you are."

"Nice try, Thwack."

"Pppttthhh."

"No, really. They're almost upon us. I'm not fib…."

"Maybe it's a herd of wild tuskwoolies?" Shoenia suggested, stretching a sarcastic smirk.

"Or a gaggle of gravel gulpers come to help out?" Tiptin quipped.

"No, really…."

"Perhaps it's a herd of snouthorns doing a dance?" Shoenia started to side split.

The smuzzles gleechattered and expanded their reach. Then they flapped their limbs and wided their seers. Lastly, they touched their snouts and paw pointed at Tiptin's blade.

"Ooooooo, good one, Sneek and Peek. Maybe it is in fact a confused flock of winged phantoms with shiny beaks."

"Ha!" Tiptin kept on. "Sounds more like glowgoblins in squishy galoshes. Hee, hee."

Now the weetykes likewise decided to play.

"Or big beakers bearing bark blowhorns, perhaps?" Pint Little offered up with a grin.

Soon even The Sheebazz could no longer resist joining in the fun. "How about singing slimeslugs sliding across soil?"

All began to laugh and ridicule the blushing fibchucker.

"No," Thwack pleaded in earnest. "It's true, I tell you. Somebody is sneaking up on us. Really. Why won't you believe me? Honest, I'm not spinning tales this…."

"SEE!" an unwelcome voice suddenly shouted. "Them they beez!"

"Beez prizners!" exclaimed another as a hairy horde of bat-wielding bullybeasts knuckled free of the surrounding bush. "Mastoor Xebec sez!"

"Charge!" commanded The Sheebazz.

"Charge!" echoed her army. "*Stickem! Stickem! Stickem!*"

"Flee!" Pint Little shouted at Shoenia.

"To where?" came a panicky reply. "We're completely surrounded!"

"Then fight!"

Conflict erupted all across the clearing, as bullybeasts swatted to miss at the helmeted flyfolk, who jabbed them with thorn swords. Taking care, of course, to avoid poking any bullybeasts in the seers.

Thwack and three bullybeasts began exchanging taps with their clubs, each apologizing profusely after each blow.

"I am terribly sorry. Does it hurt very bad?"

"Nod hurts much. Dooz dings in tik skulz."

"Ouch!"

"Dooz pologize. Hurts?"

"Naw, just a slight bruise. Hey, look at the flying pink mooer!"

"Me nod see?"

"Me nod see?"

"Me nod see?"

Conk! Conk! Conk!

"Owz!"

"Owz!"

"Owz!"

"HARR! HARR! HARR!" Thwack howled as all three bullybeasts sprouted lumps and slumped for a nap. But the big guy was entirely unaware of a fourth approaching from behind. "HARR! HARR! HA…."

"WHAP!!"

"….rr, ha…..tweet, tweet, tweet…." Thwack chirped as he slumped to the soil. Where he continued to keep count of imaginary whirling wingers.

Tiptin easily vaulted and ducked many a bat as he somersaulted between his awkward aggressors' thighs, poking their big butts with his blade. Of course, he was careful not to cut anyone.

Being fully experienced at real combat, Shoenia casually employed the shrewd tactic of pitting one's enemies against each other. Sneaking up behind one preoccupied bullybeast, she would smack his broad back with her scrapstick. Then, when the annoyed bullybeast swung about to retaliate, she would point accusingly at one of his brethren. Instantly, the irate bullybeast would retaliate by slugging the unsuspecting other, who, without fail, would always respond in kind. Thus, the two bullybeasts would become engaged in a heated slugfest amongst themselves, while the unscathed galfolk moved on to instigate elsewhere.

As the bleedless battle wimped on, the sly weetykes started untying the bullybeasts loincloths. Soon the clearing became littered with discarded buttwear. Meanwhile, some super serious shrieking filled the forest as blushing bullybeast after blushing bullybeast palmcupped their groin and hopknuckled in haste for the foliage, lest the galfolk should see their wee thingseez!

The fight soon fizzled, as the bullybeasts were all either cowed behind bushes or busy clubbing each other. So, with the enemy thus distracted, and Thwack again able to focus, the questers prepared to escape.

"KAAAPPOW!!!" A searing beam of blue light blasted a crater in center clearing.

Instantly, the weetykes scattered and Tiptin dove into the brush.

"No!" Shoenia screamed as the situation unfolded.

Two hairy bullybeasts stood beside the sorcerer. With saddened seers, they each dangled a smuzzle.

"No! Please, Mr. Xebec? Please don't? Please?"

Xebec pointed his weapon directly at Sneek. "Anyone for some roast rodent a la staff? Ha! Ha! Ha! Perhaps dipped in clops sauce?" Pointing the weapon at Thwack, the spun sorcerer launched into the distinct loco laughter of a complete loon.

"HA! HA! HO! HO! HEE! HEE! HA! HO! HEE!"

Desperate, Shoenia resorted to outright begging. "Please, Mr. Xebec, oh greatest of sorcerers? Please spare my friends? I beg you, please?"

Suddenly Xebec cut serious, donning one of the wickedest stares that there ever was. Or ever will be. "You grovel good, galfolk."

Xebec shifted his evil seers to Thwack. "Welcome, Mr. Hookschnozz! Welcome to your worst napmare! I've been expecting you for quite some time. In fact...." Xebec dropped his voice into a whacko's whisper, "....I've even enlarged my dungeon to accommodate you. HA! And in case you decide to give me any trouble, I've constructed a special spinestretcher just for you! HA! Ha! HA! Ha! HA! Ha! Oh, goody, goody, gleedrops! Ha! Ha! Ha! Ha! HO!"

While the beyond spun sorcerer dropped to perform a horizontal version of the Lipsbobble Boogie, Shoenia looked about at their hairy captors. None were without wetted seers, and all hung their heads. At great risk to themselves, the pair holding the smuzzles released them to join Shoenia.

"Disarm them!" Xebec ordered, hop-skipping into the bush. "Then march them straight to the dungeon! And they had better not get away! Or it is a scolding for each of you! Or worse!"

Stuffing their compassion, the bullybeasts encircled the trembling foursome and began marching them across the clearing.

"Then catch me that ladfolk! Or else! Ha! Ha! Ha! Ha! Hee!"

Once Xebec was gone, Thwack placed the others upon his massive shoulders, where they all clung to each other for comfort.

As they marched up the valley towards the coral castle, the bullybeasts all began to sing the bullybeast song:

"We beez big bullies,
We like dooz noogies,
Pon are tik skulz!

"Noogie, noogie, noogie, noogie,
Bully, bully, bully, bully,
Noogie, bully, noogie, bully – BEASTS!!

"Nod beez so smard,
Dooz thinks beez hard,
Cuzz we dooz beez dense!

"Noogie, noogie, noogie, noogie,
Bully, bully, bully, bully,
Noogie bully, noogie, bully – BEASTS!!"

Shoenia was completely shocked that such big beasts could sing so sweetly. She began to sing along, while Thwack and the smuzzles clapped out the cadence.

They all continued singing until they came to the base of the plateau. There the bullybeasts abruptly ceased singing.

"What's wrong?" Shoenia inquired. "Why have you stopped singing?"

"Mastoor Xebec nod like sings too castle," one explained.

"Him schodes us," added another.

"Or worze," included yet another.

"Worse? How worse?" Shoenia wanted to know.

The bullybeasts merely hung their heads and commenced to climb up the rugged footpath towards the stoic structure at the top.

Finally they all filed across a lowered spanplank, which warped beneath their bulk. Then one of the bullybeasts rapped his hard knuckles against the thick sinkwood door that blocked entry to the castle.

A seeshudder slid open and an annoying voice squeaked out. "Pazzwoyds?"

"Uh – um…?"

"Cum on, Taddler, ye know dooz we beez!"

"Pazzwoyds?" restated the squeaky voice.

"Uh – um - me sez! Dooz beez us!"

Upon hearing the proper passwords, the shudder slid shut. Then the thick doors slowly creaked open, exposing an unusually skinny bullybeast, who was holding a black ring with numerous keys.

Before entering the castle, Shoenia gave a quick look into the trench that completely encircled its foundation. Snoutsnappers of both types grinned up at her.

Inside the castle, it was dark, damp and dingy. Smoke from wall torches stung into seers as the bullybeasts escorted their prisoners down a narrow, winding stairwell. A grimy wall, moist with green slime, bounded the group on one side. The other offered a deep abyss.

"I'm scared," Shoenia whispered into Thwack's hearer, trying not to alarm the smuzzles.

The big guy responded by patting her back, while Sneek and Peek each offered her hugs.

Keys jangled as Taddler fumbled to unlock an iron door. Upon swinging it fully open, he pointed and rudely commanded, "Gets in!"

"Hey!" exclaimed one of the biggest bullybeasts, grabbing Taddler's loincloth and lifting him clear off the floor. "Galfolk beez nice! Show erspect!"

"Dooz!" yelled the others. "Show erspect!"

Taddler wiggled to adjust the loincloth, kicking his legs in the air. His face blued and his annoying voice climbed from squeak to squeal. "Ah-ah-ah – me pologize, Shmash! Dooz pologize! Stop twists gacheez – Pleeeeeze!"

"Ye dooz beez plite, Taddler," Shmash warned. "Beddar!"

"Dooz beez!" yelled the others. "Beez plite!"

After slamming the skinny bullybeast against the slimy wall, Shmash turned to Shoenia. "We hid fruits too stretch thingy. Quilts too. Mastoor Xebec nod see."

"Clopz nod beez frade. Stretch thingy nod works," added another.

"Me snaps spinzle by oopz," another bullybeast informed them with obvious pride. "Nod like nasty hurts things."

All the other bullybeasts nodded their agreement.

"Dooz pologize," Shmash stated in a most sullen tone. "Mastoor Xebec sez put ye six in so nod scapes."

"Five," another bullybeast corrected him. "Dooz beez five."

"Beez three," argued another.

"Four," Shoenia corrected them both. "Thwack, set me down."

"Bullies dooz pologize, galfolk."

"My name is Shoenia," she replied. "I know it's not your fault."

All the bullybeasts bowed their heads as Shmash clanged shut the iron door, sealing the four prisoners in the dungeon.

"Beddar nod snitches beez fruits and quilts, Taddler," warned a serious voice from beyond the door.

"M-Me nod snitches, Munch," squeaked an annoying voice.

"Beddar nod, cuzz nod let ye plays noogies!" Shmash warned. *And he wasn't bluffing.*

"M-Me nod snitches."

"Pledges?" demanded the voice belonging to Munch.

"Pledges."

"Dooz clunks skulz too sealz it….."

Shoenia listened until the voices had completely faded away before turning to view the damp and dingy dungeon. Then she slumped to her knees and wept along with her furry friends.

Thwack gently scooped the sobbing trio up into his massive arms. "I'm so very sorry, Shoenia. If I hadn't lied so much, maybe you would have been able to believe me and we could have escaped. It's all my fault."

Shoenia snuggled tight into the big guy's warm belly. "Xebec already knew we were coming, Thwack. Besides, you're not to blame for his madness. We are not at all responsible for the conduct of others. If such were the case, none of us could ever nap at ease. Isn't that right, you two?"

Both smuzzles nodded their short snouts.

"Thwack?"

"Yeah?"

"Didn't your cyfolk ever learn you the tale of the ladfolk who hollered howlpack?"

"Shoenia, my cyfolk met Morgue when I was still a cycub."

Shoenia stared up into Thwack's seer. "Then who reared you?"

"My unclops, I guess? Well, sort of?"

Shoenia sensed Thwack's discomfort, yet elected to pry anyway. "What do you mean by sort of?"

"Unclops Tippler didn't much like me. Or anyone else for that matter. He just wanted to guzzle his jabber juice and yell a lot. You know of jabber juice?"

"Shoenia sighed. "Oh, yes. I don't care for it."

"Me either," Thwack said. "Although I suppose for many it is okay to drink it. Not for Unclops Tipler, though. Not a bad clops when he was in his right mind, but once he'd popped the plug from his jug, none could tell what he was going to do. Especially not him."

"You must have some friends, though?"

"Naw. I was big and clumsy. All the other cycubs called me 'Cyclod'. And cygals just giggled and pointed at me."

Shoenia hesitated before delving deeper. "So what did you do whenever your unclops started into his jug?"

Thwack turned his head away. "What any young being would do. I hid and made believe I was someplace else. Or even somebody else. At least 'til I ran away and became a vagaclops."

"Oh?" Shoenia decided not to press any further, opting instead to kiss his bruised brow.

The giant blushed.

"Do you want to know what I think?" she asked.

"What?"

"I think the real Thwack is a kind, gentle, caring fellow who's terrified somebody might find out and hurt him real bad. I do hope to spend more time with the real Thwack in the future."

Thwack blushed again. "I've never had any real friends before."

Shoenia and the smuzzles snuggled in even tighter. "Well, now you have three. Actually, four counting Tiptin. Stop behaving like such a smarty and you'll even meet that special cygal as well. Just be real. Trust me, gals know when you're not."

Thwack patted her head. "Don't fret, Shoenia. He will save us."

"Who?"

"Tiptin, of course."

"I so hope he's safe?"

"He will come for sure. I know because he is in love with you."

The galfolk lifted her head. "Oh? And just how would you know that?"

Thwack grinned. "Simple. Whenever he watches you, he gets that look. And he watches you aaah-lot."

"Oh?" Shoenia was intrigued. "What type of look?"

"The exact same type of look you get when you watch him." Thwack stretched his grin. "Which you also do aaah-lot."

Now it was Shoenia's turn to blush.

Braindolt's Boob

A glumdreary figure tossed and turned on his floatlimbo mattress, slowly returning from a twisted chucklenap. His trembling hands began groping through blankets and quilt, seeking the firm shaft of his most prized possession; but without success.

Two sinister seers snapped alert. Instantly, he jerked asit and yanked all the cloth from the mattress, flinging it over the side. Nothing!

Scrambling to the edge, he checked the floor beneath. Nothing! Panic-stricken, he leapt to his feet and scanned the entire chambers. The door was slightly ajar.

His mad mind struggled to recall. Yes, of course he had placed the staff down beside himself: as always when he napped.

Always! Somebody had scoffed it while he chucklenapped in trance! But who would dare do such a despicable deed?

He commenced pacing. "Hmmmmmm? Dung! **BRAINDOLT!!!**"

But the bullybeast was nowhere near the castle.

Braindolt mumbled with pride as he knuckled about a heavily forested glen at the seaside base of the plateau. His voice rose above the crashing hush of breakers assaulting the nearby shore. "Dooz got stav! Dooz got stav! Me beez strong, cuzz dooz got stav! Dooz got stav! Dooz got stav! Dooz got…huh?"

The elated bullybeast suddenly froze in surprise. He vigorously shook his thick skull to refocus his seers. No, his simple mind was not playing tricks on him. Mere strides away, perched atop a boulder, stood a lanky humanfolk in a blue robe and peaked cap. A phony grin parted his bushy beard. "Well, hello there. Grand bright for a stroll through the forest, don't you think?"

"Me thinks sum. Dooz ye beez?" Braindolt inquired, cocking his head to leer low on trust. "Dooz cum seers nod same?"

"Oh, but I am a friend," replied the stranger, stepping down to touch soil.

"Stop!" panicked the suspicious bully, aiming the staff. "Me blasts!"

Zebu smiled and palmed up. "But I have no weapon."

"Dooz beez pink thingy, huh?"

Zebu glanced briefly at the wand in his robe pouch. "What, this silly old thing? It's – it's a – but what does it really matter anyway, my dear friend? I mean you no harm."

"Ha! Ye sez."

"Well, I wasn't hiding on you, was I?"

"Duh – nod hides."

"I'm not clad in black like the sorcerer, am I?"

"Duh – nod beez."

"There then. I did not try to hide on you and I am not clad in black. That proves I'm honest. You can trust me. Uh, might I get a closer look at that interesting item in your hand?"

"Beez magic stav."

"Oooooo, a magic staff. Might I possibly hold it, if only for a moment?"

"Duh – ye nod holds."

"But why not?"

"Duh – cuzz."

"Because why?"

"Cuzz sense sez ye beez big fibber. Stav!"

"Whoaa! Hee, hee. Careful where you point that thing, my dear friend…"

"We nod beez budz!"

Zebu nearly lost his composure. "Just give….uh, I mean, just grant me a chance to eat some citrus pulpy. Then I'll be on my way."

"Zitrus pupee?"

"Oh, yes. Citrus pulpy tastes better than anything. Mmmmmmmm."

"Beddar dooz dezzerts?"

"Oh, much better than desserts. Would you care to try some?"

Braindolt remained skeptical. "Duh – dooz see zitrus pupee?"

Zebu reached for his wand.

"Stops!"

"Whoaa! Hee, hee. I'll need my tap tool to cut the pulpy."

"Duh – nod dooz trixez. Cuzz me dooz blasts."

"No tricks," Zebu assured the suspicious bullybeast while slowly removing his wand. Then he dipped a wrinkled hand deep into his pouch and procured a strange oval fruit with green skin. "Ahhhhh, it even smells better than desserts."

"Stinks beddar dooz desserts?"

"Oh, much, much, much better," Zebu assured him, tapping his wand to the green skin. Immediately, the oval fruit split into perfectly equal halves.

"How ye dooz?"

The master magician wanted to roll his odd seers. "Cycles of practice, my dear friend. Many cycles of practice." He re-pouched the wand to free up both his hands, and then held up the halves for the curious bullybeast to view.

Braindolt inspected the stringy fruit. "Beez joosee?"

"Ah, but the juice is where the flavor is. Mmmmmmmm."

"Got seeds too, huh?"

"The seeds taste like candy. Mmmmmmmm."

"Beez yummy like candy?"

"Mmmmmmmm," Zebu enticed with puckered lips. "Most yummy."

"Beez beddar dooz dezzerts?"

"I'm not clad in black, am I?"

"Duh – nod beez."

"So then, smell for yourself," Zebu urged, extending his arms. "After all, what can one little sniff hurt?"

"Duh – me dooz cuzz ye nod beez clad too black. Nod hides too."

Zebu smirked with laughing seers and bated breath as the simple bullybeast bent low to sniff the pulpy. Then, the very instant his victim's seers came into range, the mean magician shoved one half into each socket and squeezed tight his crooked digits.

"**OW! OW! OW!**" Brainless screamed as the sour juice squirted into his seers. He dropped the staff and buried his face in his palms. "Dooz stings! Me nod see! Me nod see! Me nod see! Dooz stings! Me nod see!"

Zebu chuckled as he snatched up the staff. "You bullybeasts certainly aren't the sharpest sticks in the woods. Ha! Smart like dirt wigglers. Ha! Ha! Ha!"

"Ye fibs," Braindolt whined, trying to rub the burning from his seers. "Nod fair!"

"Fair is for losers!" Zebu snapped back as he strode away with his new prize.

"Dooz stings! Pleeeze helps! Me nod see! Pleeeze helps! Pleeeeeze…"

Zebu responded to Braindolt's frantic and frightened pleas for help by gloatgrinning and taking careful aim with the staff. "Amuse me!" he commanded.

A stifling scream silenced even the winds as a terrified bullybeast bounded through brush with his bare butt burned black, still unable to sight through pain and blur.

Hugs And Taglez

Unseen hands parted a slight peep space in a small bush, while alert brown seers carefully studied the stoic and foreboding structure directly before them. Slowly, the seers shifted to scan along the structure's pink walls, noting in detail the location of each seeslit, ledge, corner and angle. At last, they locked upon the curved shell of the structure's lone tower, and traced up its stem to a balcony near its peak. A dark archway suggested a possible way in.

Satisfied that they'd viewed everything necessary, the alert seers pulled away and the peep space rustled shut.

"Well?" The Sheebazz inquired, hovering before the ladfolk's face. "What do you think of my scouts' reports?"

Tiptin rubbed his chin. "Hmmmmm. And your scouts are absolutely certain it was Xebec himself who flew from the castle?"

The Sheebazz frowned sarcastic. "Riding a flying monster? Black cloak and skullcap? Frail? Glumdreary? Scowl? Sinister stare? Screaming cusses like a lunatic gone completely round the…"

"Okay. Okay. I'm sorry I doubted them. But why didn't Xebec have the staff?"

"Stumps me?" The Sheebazz answered with a shrug.

"Maybe he forgot it?" Pint Little suggested.

"Or broke it?" another proposed.

"Shush," The Sheebazz cautioned. "Do you want the bullybeasts to find us?"

An army of helmets shook that they did not.

"No," Tiptin continued. "Xebec may be mad, but he'd never part with the staff. It just doesn't make any sense."

"So why doesn't he have it then?" The Sheebazz asked.

"That, my tiny friends, is exactly what we must find out. Hmmmmm. And the only access is through that tower?"

"Unless you want to knock on the door, it is. The seeslits are too small for you to fit through."

Tiptin looked to Pint Little. "And you're absolutely certain you checked everywhere?"

The especially puny flyfolk nodded. "We scouted real good, Tiptin. Honest. We spent all black."

Tiptin's tone tinged apologetic. "I know you scouts did a splendid job. It's just that I'm worried about the others, something awful. Who knows...."

"Sheebazz! Sheebazz!"

All sighted upon an incoming flyfolk with wided seers.

"Sheebazz! Shee...."

"Shush!" commanded The Sheebazz.

"Shush!" echoed the chorus.

Tiptin extended a landing palm for the excited weetyke.

"What is it, Mite Diver?" The Sheebazz inquired in a cross tone. "And where have you been?"

Thoroughly exhausted from his frantic flight, Mite Diver sank to the ladfolk's flesh and gasped to fill his breathers. He raised a wee hand for patience. "I – I –gasp – I was catched prisoner by a-a – gasp – a bullybeast."

The Sheebazz granted the puffing scout a chance to completely regain his breath before pressing for an explanation. "What do you mean you were 'catched' by a bullybeast?"

Mite Diver stood and sighed heavily. "I was eavesing on some guards discussing 'prizners', when a sneaky bullybeast catched me like this." He cupped his palms and slapped them together with a pop.

"Ohhhhh…" awed the chorus.

"But however did you escape?" inquired Tiptin.

"Yes, how?" The Sheebazz wanted to know.

"I tricked him," Miter Diver explained, using hand gestures to demonstrate. "He really wasn't too bright. I told him I knew a secret. Then, after he promised not to tell anyone else, I told him to lower his face because I had to whisper it. When he did, I *stickem!*"

"I do hope you minded the poor beast's seers?" Tiptin stated with noted concern.

"Oh, I'd never *stickem* in seers. I *stickem* in fat nose!"

"Shush!"

"Sorry, Sheebazz."

"Don't be sorry; just keep your voice low. Now, what were the guards saying about prisoners?"

"Sheebazz, the guards say that prisoners are being kept in a place called dungeon?"

Tiptin paled. "In a dungeon?"

Mite Diver nodded.

"You know the meaning of such?" The Sheebazz inquired.

Tiptin nodded. "Dungeons are dark and dingy places beneath castles. We must get them out."

"But how?" Pint Little asked. "The trench is filled with hungry snoutsnappers and the only way in for you is up on that tower?"

"Hmmmmm?" Tiptin commenced pacing back and forth. "There must be a way."

"Why don't we simply fly him up?" advanced a voice from the chorus.

"Thank you," Tiptin replied with fond amusement. "Your pumper is indeed most precious. However, I do believe I'm just a tad too heavy for you to lift,"

"Not me," corrected the voice. "We. Sometimes us little weetykes combine our might to lift logs."

"That's right!" Mite Diver enthused.

"Shush!"

"Sorry, Sheebazz."

Tiptin was puzzled. "But whyever would you need to lift logs?"

The Sheebazz smiled. "To defend our shelters from the bullybeasts. We drop the logs onto their thick skulls before we swarmbomb to *stickem*."

"That's what really riles them nasty," Pint Little mused. "When they get conked by a log. Not one near so big as Thwack's, though. All of us weetykes together could never lift his."

"Not a problem," Tiptin said. "I'm much lighter than the big guy's club, anyway."

"Then what are we all doddling for?" The Sheebazz noted. "Let's go."

"Let's go!" tenured the chorus.

"Shush!"

"Sorry, Sheebazz."

After depositing their tipnut-cap shields into frond sacks, the weetykes swarmed all over the nervous ladfolk. Each brandished a thorn sword in one hand, while gripping firm a piece of Tiptin's garments in the other. Except for The Sheebazz, and those that were tasked with transporting the sacks of shields, every single flyfolk was assigned to help transport their large ally to the tower balcony.

"Flymarch-ho!" Pint Little ordered.

"Flymarch-ho!" echoed the chorus.

"Shush!" How often must I warn you?"

"Sorry, Sheebazz."

"Don't be sorry, just remember to keep quiet. All of you. Do you want the bullybeasts to know what we're about?"

An army of helmets shook that they did not.

"Then just fly – don't speak. Understand?"

All nodded that they understood.

With a group grunt, a dark mass rose up from amongst the bushes and advanced upon the castle. Some seers kept watch below for bullybeasts, while most scanned above for squawkers.

Tiptin bated his breath and sealed both lids. Unlike his flight through The Baobabs, here he could clearly see the ground. He knew exactly how far he had to fall.

Yet the tiny digits gripping his garments did not fail him. Nor did the many droning wings, which blew blasts of brisk breeze as they flashfluttered to climb. Nary a puffing breather surrendered the struggle. Proof once again that determination and precious pumpers can offset small size.

Upon finally reaching their objective, the feisty flyfolk gently lowered the ladfolk down onto the balcony. Then they touched solid themselves for a well-deserved rest.

Tiptin turned to Pint Little. "When Xebec and the winged monster flew from the courtyard, which way did they go?"

"Down there," she replied, pointing to the heavily forested glen at the seaside base of the plateau.

The ladfolk frowned. "That takes in a lot of area, Pint Little. Do you know exactly where down there?"

"Uh-uh. We chose to stay with our mission and find a way into the castle instead. Did we do wrong?"

"Oh no. Not at all," he assured her, granting her a broad smile. "In fact, you scouts did very well."

"We did?"

"Of course. It should be much easier to rescue our friends with the sorcerer gone, anyway."

"But I still don't understand why the sworcerer didn't take the staff?" The Sheebazz put in. "It is very strange."

"Very strange," Tiptin concurred. "Very strange, indeed."

"Sworcerer sure was riled right nasty," one of the weetykes injected.

"Oh, really?" Tiptin was curious.

"Mega mad," confirmed another. "Sworcerer kept cussing bad words and swinging his fists at the wind. Wind won fight, though."

An entire army gaffed into giggles.

"Shush! There may very well be bullybeasts about. Now collect your shields and prepare to move out. We don't have any more time to doddle."

"Yes, Sheebazz."

Tiptin new The Sheebazz was right, time did not favor them one bit. Yet he was still intrigued. "Pint, what exactly was Xebec cussing about?"

Pint Little shrugged. "I'm not too sure, really. The only words I could make out that I understood were dolt and Morgue. Everything else was kookoo jibberish." She wound a pointdigit about her hearer. "And I mean reeeeeal kookoo."

"Hmmmmm, interesting." Tiptin tightened his grip on the honeycombed hilt, and the fibered blade breathed ashimmer. "Anyway, The Sheebazz is right. We have virtually no more time to waste."

So, with his blade readied before him, Tiptin stepped through the archway and on into the tower. Then he froze in utter disbelief.

He had entered a napchamber unlike any other he had ever seen. A solitary mattress floated in limbo above a tangled heap of bedding. Two chests with short legs bearing hooves, and a lanky-limbed table, all trembled against the furthest wall, while a cheeky chair challenged the tall intruder by landing him a serious shin kicking!

"Ow!" Tiptin yelped, high stepping to escape the bruising blows. "Ow! Ow! Stop it! Hey, we don't – ouch!"

"**Charge!** *Stickem! Stickem! Stickem! Stickem!*"

An army of flyfolk set upon the woodlike attacker, jabbing at its seat and back. Yet the cheeky chair kept up its relentless assault, gradually backing its dancing victim into a corner.

"Look-ow! Look out, troops, I'm going to chop it! Ow!"

"Look out, he's going to chop it!"

"Aiyeee!" screamed the cheeky chair as Tiptin's first blow severed a leg. Angry flames shot forth from the fibered blade.

"YIKES!" shrieked the frightened furnishings huddled against the far wall. Then the table turned and bolted for the door.

"SMASH!!!!"

Splinters scattered as the terrified table bashed free of the chambers. It galloped to the end of a short corridor, before sliding and stumbling its way down a spiraled stairwell. Two shrieking chests quickclopped to catch it, while a charred chair hobbled along beneath a fleeing mattress, followed closely by wiggly blankets and a slithering quilt.

After all the clopchatter had faded into the distance, Tiptin warily poked his head out into the corridor.

"Coast clear?" The Sheebazz inquired, landing upon Tiptin's shoulder.

"Can't really say in this creepy place," he remarked with a shudder.

The Sheebazz smiled and brushed some long locks from her face. "Kinda freaky, huh?"

"Sure is." Tiptin soft-stepped into the corridor, and then paused briefly before sneaking over to the stairwell. He was quite aware of the dull drone at his back.

"Should I dispatch a scout?" The Sheebazz asked.

Tiptin nodded his approval.

The Sheebazz motioned to Mite Diver, and the obedient spy zipped off down the stairwell. Then The Sheebazz spoke in a soothing tone. "Don't fret, Tiptin, we've battled big bullybeasts plenty of times. One way or another, we'll save the others."

Tiptin was warmed by the courage of his tiny ally and her subjects, not a single one of which showed even the slightest trace of hesitation in the face of grave danger. He wished he could put their chest pumpers in the bodies of beings a thousand times their size. The very spectacle of these wee warriors in tipnut helmets, poised to tangle with an enormous enemy, nearly moved him to weep. And surely would have, had he not redirected his seers down the stairwell.

Only a few nods elapsed before Mite Diver zipped back around a corner and back up the stairwell. His seers were wided with worry and his voice was tangled in verbal vim.

The Sheebazz grabbed hold of his shoulders and shook him with much vigor. "Calm down and lower your voice, Mite Diver. And think of what you speak. Thus far, we have not understood a single sound from your lips."

Mite Diver touched down beside her and inhaled deeply to ease his excitement. "Sheebazz, I saw a whole batch of bullybeasts!"

"Whisper! Now where are they?"

"Whisper! Now where are they!" echoed the chorus.

"They're armswinging up a wiggly tunnel towards us."

"He means they're coming this way through a winding corridor," The Sheebazz translated for Tiptin.

"Does this – er – wiggly tunnel lead to this stairwell?" Tiptin inquired of the shaky spy.

Mite Diver shook his head and parted his arms to the max. "Uh-uh. A big hollow lies in between. Biggest hollow that I…"

"Shush!" The Sheebazz suddenly ordered. "I think I hear noise below?"

"Shush!" echoed the chorus.

It was true. Somewhere around the corner from the base of the stairwell, voices could be heard.

"Shmash beez more strong than ye, Belch!"

"Uh-uh!"

"Beez too!"

"Beez nod! Me zings things more far than ye, Shmash!"

"Tiptin?" whispered The Sheebazz.

"What?"

"Perhaps we should hide out on the balcony in case some bullybeasts come up here? If they find us, we might not be able to rescue the others."

Tiptin briefly pondered her suggestion while listening to the argument below boil over into near confrontation.

"Beez too!"

"Beez nod!"

"Beez too!"

"Nod!"

"Too!"

"Nod!"

"Too so!"

"Nod so!"

"Too! Too! Too!"

"Nod! Nod! Nod!"

"Too so! Too so! Too so!"

"Nod so! Nod so! Nod…"

Making his voice barely audible, Tiptin shared his thoughts with The Sheebazz. Then he put forth a strategy.

She returned him an agreeing nod, and then started using hand signals to relay instructions to her army.

Next, with his shimmering blade leading the way, the determined ladfolk started sneaking down the steps with Mite Diver, Pint Little and The Sheebazz perched upon his shoulders. A dark, droning mass hovered above. All were tense. But eager.

Now the heated argument did erupt into a direct challenge.

"Ye prooves it!"

"Me dooz! We zings things!"

"What things!"

"Um – uh – um – kay! We zings Taddler!"

"Dooz always zings me!"

"Cuzz ye always snitches!"

"Nod always."

"Yes, always. Ye snitched ole Schnozzy dooz peeks too Mastoor Xebec's webthings! Him beez schodes cuzz ye snitches!"

"And worze!"

"Me dooz snitches cuzz we nod spozed peeks in Mastoor Xebec's....huh?"

"Dooz ye see....huh?"

Every bullybeast dangled jowls in complete confusion as an army of thorn-wielding flyfolk poured into the enormous antechamber. The wee warriors split ranks and circled about to trap their hugely surprised foe. Then a lanky humanfolk came strutting across the floor towards them, wielding a shimmering blade and bearing a trio of tiny comrades.

"Stops!"

"What are you doing?" Tiptin calmly asked as some of the frightened bullybeasts finally unfroze and brandished their bats.

"Uh – we dooz fites?" replied one of their number in a most uncertain tone.

"But don't you bullybeasts know that fighting is dangerous?" Tiptin asked. "Somebody could get hurt."

The bullybeasts all exchanged uncertain glances.

"But we spozed fites," another one stated.

"We beez foze," added yet another.

"Yes," Tiptin concurred, "we are indeed foes. Which is why we've taken you prisoner."

"Nod fites yet?"

"Dooz cum we beez prizners, huh? Beez Mastoor Xebec's castle?"

Tiptin huffed heavily. Obviously these bullybeasts were the very quickest of the breed, so he knew he had his work really cut out for him this time. "Look, you bullybeasts, did we not see you first?"

Again the frightened bullybeasts exchanged uncertain glances, then shrugged and replied as one. "Dooz!"

"And do we not have you encircled?"

"Huh?"

"Dooz him sez?"

"I mean, don't we have you surrounded?"

All the bullybeasts looked about. "Dooz."

"So then, have we not in fact caught you?"

Every bullybeast was completely befuddled. Placing foredigits to lips, they tried hard to think. "????????????"

Sensing their confusion, Tiptin tactfully piled on the pressure. "And do we not have swords?"

"Dooz."

"And shields?"

"Dooz."

Plus we also have you greatly outnumbered, right?"

"????????????????????????"

"Okay, nix that question. But we are an army, are we not?"

"Um – dooz beez."

"So are you not surrounded by an army, then?"

Now the bullybeasts were well beyond lost. Each simply nodded and shrugged.

"Which means we've caught you, correct?"

A bunch of thick skulls nodded on cue.

"Now, if we've caught you, then doesn't that make you our prisoners?"

All nodded. "Dooz."

"Only prisoners are not supposed to carry bats, are they?"

The bullybeasts all hung and shook their heads.

"Then why are you prisoners' still carrying bats?"

"Nod spozed too," came a solitary reply.

"We pologize," offered another, dropping his bat. "Me dooz beddar prizner stuff."

"Me too," assured another bullybeast as his bat bonked to the floor.

Mumbling mixed with wood bonking upon stone as each and every bullybeast apologized profusely for his poor 'prizner' performance and promised to do 'beddar prizner stuff'. In no time flat, bats littered the floor.

"Alright," Tiptin continued. "Now put your hands on your thick skulls and interlock your digits."

"??????????????????????"

"Nix that. Just hold your hands up as high as you can reach. And I'm warning you prisoners right now, try any tricks and we'll untie your loincloths!"

"Huh?"

"Me thinks beez gacheez?"

"Uh – yes, I mean we'll untie your - er - gacheez."

"Yeah!" tenored the chorus, thrusting their thorns in a most menacing manner. "Then *stickem! Stickem! Stickem! Stickem!* Poke em in the nose, but be careful of the eyes! Jab em in the butt, and in between the thighs!"

The bullybeasts all shuddered and squeezed their knobby knees together. Only one of their numbers dared to speak up. "Gulp – we nod dooz trix. Pledges."

"Pledges," concurred the others, clunking 'skulz' to seal it.

"You there," Tiptin voiced with newfound authority. He pointed to the big bullybeast who had dared to speak up. "What is your name?"

"M-Me?" responded one very frightened bullybeast.

"Yes ye – er- I mean, you. What is your name?"

"M-Me beez Shmash."

"Shmash what?"

"??????"

"Nix that. Now, Shmash, I have some questions to ask you…"

"Counts questions?" the trembling bullybeast inquired with great concern. His skinny legs began to bend beneath his bulk.

"No, nothing to do with counting."

The shaky prisoner sighed heavy in relief.

"These are very simple questions. Only I'm warning you, Shmash, if you fib, The Sheebazz will command her entire army to start teasing all of you!"

"And we will," The Sheebazz concurred.

"I nod fibs!" Shmash surprisingly rebuked. It was readily apparent that he felt very insulted. "Me nod beez fibber!"

"Yeah!" reprimanded the other prisoners. "Shmash nod beez fibber! Taddler beez fibber!"

"Beez nod!"

"Beez too!"

"Nod! Nod! Nod!"

"Too! Too! Too!"

"Whoa!" Tiptin intervened. "Okay! Okay! I most humbly apologize to Shmash. I had no cause to question your – er – integrity?"

"Dooz ye sez?"

"That he trusts you," The Sheebazz explained with a smile.

Shmash returned the smile, then beamed proud and began bragging to his jealous brethren. "Ladfolk trusts me. Him sez."

"We heerd him, Mr. Stinks Feets."

"Me feets nod stinks!"

"Dooz!" all shouted, including the weetykes.

"Dooz nod!"

"Dooz!"

"Dooz nod!"

"Whooaa!!" Tiptin sensed he was quickly losing control of the situation. Frustration mounted on his face. "We really don't have any time to waste, so perhaps you bullybeasts might resume behaving like proper prisoners. Pleeeeeze."

“Ooopz. Dooz pologize.”

“We dooz beddar prizner stuff.”

Tiptin sucked wind and rolled his seers. “Okay, where were we? Hmmmmm? Now I forget!”

“Questions,” Pint Little reminded him.

“And do allow for their very short attention span,” The Sheebazz added in a whisper. “Do respect their minds, or you’ll lose yours.”

Turning back to Shmash, Tiptin continued asking questions in their most simplified form. “Why did Xebec fly off without the staff?”

“Mastoor Xebec seeks Braindolt,” Shmash replied, beaming at his brethren.

“And just who or what is a Braindolt?”

“Braindolt beez Mastoor Xebec’s best boob,” answered the bullybeast named Belch.

“Nod beez,” corrected the unusually thin bullybeast named Taddler. “Nod beez best boob cuzz Braindolt scoffed staff.”

It was becoming apparent that the other bullybeasts had no intention of letting Shmash snatch all the glory.

“Shmash shook his head in sympathy. “Braindolt beez schoded bad. And worze. Me nod see Mastoor Xebec so screems.”

All the other bullybeasts bit their upper lips and, with wided seers, nodded to support Shmash's claim.

The Sheebazz shared a puzzled stare with Tiptin before fluttering over to the 'prisoners'. Hovering in place before them, she took over the interrogation. "Shmash, are you saying that this Braindolt has taken the staff?"

Shmash nodded. "Uh-huh. Dooz scoffed it beez Mastoor Xebec snoozes in trance."

She gave Tiptin a glance before pressing on. "Do you know where the sworcerer keeps his Webscrolls?"

Feeling left out again, the other bullybeasts began joining in the interrogation.

"Mastoor Xebec keeps webscrozz always."

"Keeps in cloak cuzz ole Schnozzy peeks."

"We nod spozed touches. Nod ever," Taddler said with great emphasis.

All the other bullybeasts nodded their heads.

The Sheebazz was just about to inquire about Shoenia and the others, when suddenly two unsuspecting critters with long slurpy lickers and filthy fangs came romping into the antechamber. Both froze and gulped down large lumps of shock as they took in the situation. Then they grinned out an oops and tried slowly backing out into the corridor from whence they had just come.

They never made it. An alert unit of weetykes swooped down to block their exit. Brandishing their sharp thorns to show they meant business, the tiny flyfolk next shooed the lanky critters over to join the bullybeasts.

"Pleeeze nod hurts cridders," Shmash pleaded. "Cridders looks mean, but dooz beez big fradies."

"We don't want to hurt anyone," The Sheebazz assured the prisoners in soft, disarming syllables. "What we do want is for you to take us to our friends. Please."

"Ye budz beez too dungeon."

"We noze – er – we know that, Shmash," Tiptin cut in. "But we don't know how to get to the dungeon, so we want you to take us there."

The bullybeasts exchanged puzzled peeks.

"What's wrong?" The Sheebazz asked.

Shmash spoke up. "Dooz bullies spozed go to dungeon cuzz knuckles beez too sky?"

The Sheebazz smiled. "Oh, yes. Excellent observation, Shmash. Since you've all been such good prisoners, you may put your knuckles back down on the floor."

"We dooz?" Shmash inquired. "Dooz beez good prizners?"

"The very best prisoners ever," Mite Diver assured them.

After the elated bullybeasts had finally finished congratulating one another for actually being the best at something, they knuckled with purpose into the winding corridor. Each tried extra hard to be a model 'prizner', keeping chins up and armswinging in time. They certainly were a proud and delighted bunch. Even the cruel critters pranced with pride.

Tiptin and the weetykes escorted their pleasant prisoners through the long, winding corridor that gradually descended in stages. They were curious about its many scorched wall paintings, the point of which was known to none. Yet they need not ask which lunatic bore the blame.

Just prior to exiting into the burnt courtyard, they veered into a chilly corridor that eventually brought them to a narrow, winding stairwell. Smoke from wall torches stung into their seers as they coped with the slippery steps. A grimy wall, clothed in slime, bounded them on one side. The other side offered up a deep abyss.

Eventually the stairwell ended, and they paraded across a dirty floor until they reached an iron door.

"Beez keys, Taddler?" Shmash demanded.

"Keys beez heer, Shmash," squeaked the unusually thin bullybeast. He then produced a black ring loaded with keys and fumbled through them. Then he stuck one in the lock, but it would not turn. "Huh?"

"What's wrong?" Pint Little inquired.

Taddler gloated. "Ha! Door beez open! Shmash nod lock!"

"Ye got keys, ye spozed locks!" Shmash protested.

"Uh-uh. Ye clozed door, member? Ye spozed locks."

Shmash shook his head in his own defense. "Uh-uh."

Taddler nodded. "Uh-huh."

"Uh-uh."

"Uh-huh."

"Uh-uh."

"Uh-huh."

"Uh-uh."

"Uh-h…."

"Who cares!" Tiptin berated, wildly flailing his arms about. "Just open the dung door!"

"Nod plite sez bad woyds," Belch pointed out.

"Pleeeeeze," begged one very frustrated ladfolk. "We'll hold a trial later. For now, just open the door."

All the bullybeasts exchanged shrugs of confusion before Taddler finally opened the door.

"AAAAAAAAAAAAAARRRGH!!!!" An enormous green bulk lunged out and overwhelmed several bewildered bullybeasts with one timely tackle. They all landed together in a heap of thrashing limbs.

"Eeeeeeee!!" wailed a cruel critter as pointy biters chomped into its tail. Wriggling free of the grappling pile, it scurried to hide behind Mite Diver.

"Stop, ye green gooberschnozz!"

"Gitz off me, ye nubskulz!"

"Run Shoenia! I'll hold them off!"

"Uh, Thwack."

"Ouch! Stop squeeze face! Nod fare!"

"Keep going Shoenia! Don't fret about me! Save yourself!"

"Oh, Thwaaak. Yoo-hoo. Scrap the plan."

"I got this burly bunch – all – wrapped – up… Ahh….?" The giant flushed purple as he finally caught sight of his audience. "Gulp. Hee, hee. Hi ya, Tiptin. Hee, hee."

"Let go me feets, ye kooky Clopz!"

"Stop claws beez too heerer!"

"Oh, I am terribly sorry," apologized the abashed giant. "Hee, hee. Here, you may have your head back. So sorry about the gouges. Hee, hee."

"Gitz off me!"

"Certainly." Thwack released his victims and pressed astand. Still highly embarrassed, he blushed and parted his massive arms. "Whoops."

Tiptin warmly embraced Shoenia. Palm-cupping her cheeks, he stared into her emerald seers. "Are you well?"

Shoenia merely nodded, and then snuggled up tight against him. It was then that she realized that every single bullybeast was hanging his head in shame. Pulling free of Tiptin, she addressed the somber bunch. "Why all the long faces? You never wanted to put us in the dungeon. I know you didn't. And it was really sweet of you to hide fruit and quilts."

Shmash raised his head to expose trickles of weepwet blazing crooked trails down his puffy cheeks. "Nod wanna puts ye in dungeon, but Mastoor Xebec sez. Now ye scaped. Now Mastoor Xebec schodes bullies."

"An worze," Munch added.

"Yes, I know," Shoenia said. "But how worse?"

Munch rehung his head. "Him – Him…"

"He what?" Shoenia pressed. "What does that brute do to you?"

After some strong silence, Shmash finally solved the mystery. "Mastoor Xebec sez us names."

"He calls you names?"

Tiptin and Thwack exchanged puzzled looks, while the bullybeasts pouted and nodded their thick skulls.

"What types of names?" Shoenia wanted to know.

Now the bullybeasts really exchanged shameful glances.

"Well, what types of names?"

"Dense," one put out.

"Stoopid," added another.

"Sez we beez erpulsive."

"Sez bullies beez loozers."

"Oh, he does, does he?"

The burly bunch all nodded their thick skulls.

Thwack started to weep.

Shoenia was visibly irate. "Well, that's not very nice. Names can really hurt, even worse than bruises. However, we must always think of who is saying these mean things. Are they themselves miserable and insecure?"

The bullybeasts cocked their heads and scrunched brows in confusion.

Shoenia rephrased for them. "Is the name caller a doodoo dungskulz?"

"Uh-huh." All nodded that they now understood. Fully.

Shmash pouted behind wet seers. "But Mastoor Xebec nod fibs. We nod counts even."

'Ahhhhhhhhh…" sighed the chorus of weetykes.

A flood of compassion drowned Shoenia's ire. "But has anybody ever learned you to count?"

"Lerned?"

"Yes, weren't you taught counting at school?"

"Scooz?"

"Yes, you know, classes?"

"Huh?"

Warm drops of weepwet seeped past Shoenia's lids. "You're not dense."

"Bullies nod beez dense?" Shmash asked, exchanging befuddled looks with his brethren.

"No," Shoenia continued. "You've just never been learned, is all. No wonder you think so little of yourselves. Has anyone ever hugged you?"

"Hugz?"

"Yes. Or tickled you?"

"Taglez?"

Shoenia was hardly surprised that the bullybeasts knew naught of such things. "Why, I'll wager not a one of you has ever been kissed?"

"Mastoor Xebec cusses us always," Taddler objected,

"No, Taddler, not cussed. Kissed. Like this." Shoenia motioned for Shmash to bend down, and, stretching upon her tippydigits, she planted a peck firmly on his cheek.

Shmash bit his bottom lip and flushed deepest purple, while both cruel critters shrieked and fled.

The other bullybeasts moved to shy away.

"No need to be scared," she explained. "Hugs are even more fun."

"Hugz?"

"Yes, watch." Shoenia embraced the still flushing bullybeast.

Both smuzzles also hugged. The weetykes hugged. Even Thwack and Tiptin feigned a hug, then growl-muttered real macho like.

"Now," Shoenia directed of the intrigued bunch, "you bullybeasts try it with each other. Go on, give each other a nice, warm hug."

Although it required several attempts for the teetering bunch to successfully wrap arms around each other's bulky bodies, they nevertheless completed the task.

"Feels funny?" Shmash noted.

"Nod beddar beez noogies," Belch elaborated.

"Mmmmm. Dooz likes this," added another.

"We dooz hugz too sheebullies beez Ezu?" Taddler inquired of Shoenia while slyly wiggling his brows.

"Yes. Providing, of course, that they say it is okay first. Now, try it again. But this time say nice things to each other."

"Like this!" Tiptin exclaimed, suddenly eager to help out. He snatched the surprised galfolk up into his long arms. "I love you, Shoenia. I know this because every time I think of you, I feel all nice and warm inside. And I think of you a lot.

"And I figure you can be only one of two things. Either you are for real. Or you're just a dream passing by. And if you are a dream, then I don't ever want to unnap. But if you are for real, then you can only be a gift from Destiny. And nobody must ever mistreat any gift from Destiny.

"Shoenia, I would be so very proud to have you as my mate. Please unite with me. I do so love you."

Still somewhat stunned, Shoenia somehow managed a reply. "Yes, Tiptin, I'll unite with… mmmmmmmmmmmmmmmmmmmmm…"

"Dooz beez unite, huh?"

The Sheebazz intervened. "It's okay Belch, you bullybeasts can skip over that part for now."

Compliments now abounded throughout the dungeon as every bullybeast risked the hug part and started saying very nice things to one another.

"Ye schnozz nod beez so gross."

"Ye nod stinks gross always."

"Ye face nod beez so gross dooz cridders."

Thwack shrugged and sighted above. "Hey, it's a start."

"What beez taglez?"

"Tickles," Shoenia corrected, still blushing from Tiptin's kiss. "Well, tickles make beings tingle and laugh. See?"

She seized the unprepared ladfolk and began dipwiggling her digits about his torso. Then the weetykes, Thwack and the smuzzles all began tickling bullybeasts. Even the cruel critters, which peeked down from the stairwell, were coaxed into taking part.

Soon the entire dungeon roared with laughter, which kept on until the thoroughly drained lot slumped to the cold floor. Every bullybeast agreed that, 'Taglez beez near so fun dooz noogies!'. Although, of course, not quite.

Once all had reclaimed their wind, Shoenia addressed the burly bunch. “You know, you bullybeasts could help us unpower the staff.”

Most bullybeasts were visibly terror-stricken.

“But Mastoor Xebec…” Taddler began.

“Him beez dungskulz,” Belch interrupted. “We dooz secret huddle.”

“Me threez it!” Shmash exclaimed. “Me likes Shoenia.”

“Ooooooooo,” teased the other bullybeasts as they all bunched into a tight scrum, where Shmash promptly fell victim to a vigorous volley of razznoogies.

Thwack rolled his seer as the bunch loudly debated their course of action. Their loud arguing echoed throughout the entire dungeon.

“Relax,” Shoenia said to the big guy. “This is a very important discussion for them. Perhaps even the bravest choice that they shall ever make.”

“Okay. Okay. When they inform us of their decision, I’ll act reeeeal surprised.”

She patted his massive arm. “That’s our new and improved Thwack.”

“We chooses,” Belch finally announced after much heated debate. “Shmash counts cuzz him beez most smard.”

Shmash beamed proud at having been chosen the most 'smard'. "Sez ye nod dooz helps get stav?"

Only Taddler raised his arm.

"Um-um-nod beez one. Dooz sez helps get stav?"

Virtually every other bullybeast raised their arms, yet quite some time elapsed before Shmash finished tallying up the votes. "Dooz beez two! We dooz!"

"HOORRAY!!" The loud cheer was followed, of course, by the customary round of knuckle noogies. Then Belch broke the good news to their 'captors'.

"**WOW!**" Thwack yelled. "**What a stunning surprise!**"

Next the entire group all paraded back up the slippery steps, and hastened through the chilly corridor. After exiting the castle, they sped across the burnt courtyard. Next they started down a steep path, which led to the heavily forested glen at the seaside base of the plateau.

Upon reaching the glen itself, Shoenia noticed that one of the younger bullybeasts was grimacing. "What is the matter?" she inquired.

"Pixx got swiver," Belch explained.

The grimacing bullybeast extended a swollen pointdigit to show Shoenia the exposed shaft of a tiny splinter of wood.

"Is that from your bat?" she asked.

Pixx nodded that it was. "Me fites meeny buzzers cuzz dem bites butt."

Shoenia was somewhat puzzled. "So why don't you just pull it out?"

"Cuzz hurts," Pixx replied.

"Not if you pull it out fast."

"Huh? Pulls fast?"

"Sure, then it only hurts for a blink. Here, I'll do it for you."

As Shoenia pinched the minute object between her digit caps, the other bullybeasts all shuddered and turned away. None could bear to watch.

"Ahh-ahh-ahh…."

Shoenia frowned. "At least wait until I start tugging on it."

"Just praksin….**OW!**" Pixx yelped as the sliver was quickly removed.

"Now suck on it," Shoenia advised. "You must be more careful when you swing your bat. And do stop picking your nose, too. In case you bump into something and your digit gets stuck in it."

"Me dooz before."

"Then you should already know better."

Having tended to Pixx's battle wound, Shoenia hastened to rejoin Tiptin, Shmash and the smuzzles at the front of the column. The Sheebazz and her army hovered overhead, keeping watch for Xebec's flying monster. Thwack stole through the thick bush alongside the path, his pointy ears perked to snag sound.

The surrounding foliage was thick with stench. Rancid foulferns fell across the rugged path and sneaky roots surfaced to trip. Branches bearing stiff needles dipped to scratch skin. Twigs like crooked digits groped at hair and garments.

"I hear somebody sobbing," Thwack said, stepping towards Tiptin.

"Sure you do, Thwack."

"From which direction?" Shoenia inquired.

"From further on up the path, I think."

"Nice try…."

Shoenia's cross stare tangled Tiptin's licker. "Can you guess how far away?"

Thwack shrugged. "Not for certain. It's stopped now. I think…."

"Hey!" Shmash interrupted, pointing through the trees to a small clearing, where a lone bullybeast sat weeping upon the soil. "Dooz beez Braindolt?"

The lone bullybeast pressed to his knuckles and squinted to sight through badly swollen seers.

However, when the group broke out into the clearing, Braindolt panicked and moved to armswing away.

"Nod flee, Braindolt! Beez me, Shmash! See!" Shmash parted his arms and beamed a broad smile. "Ye broz dooz cum too!"

Belch emerged from the bush and swift-knuckled to join his 'broz'. "Braindolt, dooz hurts seers?"

Braindolt began to sob again. "H-Him got stav."

"Who?" Tiptin inquired. "Xebec?"

"Dooz beez him?" Braindolt asked, pointing at Tiptin.

Belch clued his broz in. "Him beez him."

"Oh." The sobbing bully shook his head. "Nod Mastoor Xebec got stav."

"Who has it then?" Shoenia pressed, already fearing the answer.

"Beez magic meeny got stav."

Shoenia's belly sank. "Braindolt, did this magic meeny have odd seers. I mean, were they two different colors?"

Braindolt nodded that they were. "Him trix me. Sez zitrus pupee beez beddar dooz dezzerts. Then him stings seers with joose."

"Braindolt, listen to me," Shoenia pressed, "which way did the magic meeny…?"

"Tiptin! Shoenia!" Mite Diver shouted as he swooped down from atop the foliage.

"What is it?" they inquired of the alarmed flyfolk.

"Over there!" he shouted, thrusting a tiny arm. "We spotted the funny folk on the seashore!"

"Did he have the staff?" both humanfolk shouted at once.

"Uh-huh."

Tiptin and Shoenia exchanged troubled looks.

"However shall we get it?" he asked.

"By trusting in Destiny and truly trying," she reminded him. "Mite Diver, lead us to where you last spotted the funny folk."

They followed the weetyke free from the path and in amongst the forest. Thwack took up the lead, stomping flat the bushy obstacles. As the group stumbled across the flattened foliage, their hearers soon snagged the crashing hush of wetrollers assaulting the shore.

"Dooz magic meeny beed!" Braindolt exclaimed, pointing at a boulder.

"Nod sez things," Belch whispered, pinching his broz lips shut.

A tiny army of flyfolk peeked out from behind leaves and stems at the extreme outer edge of the forest. None uttered so much as a peep as they scanned the nearby shore and sky, both of which were strangely void of squawkers.

The Sheebazz and her puny proxy swooped down and perched on Shoenia's shoulder.

"Where is he?" Shoenia inquired.

"Pint Little says he just vanished," replied The Sheebazz.

Both humanfolk looked to Pint Little. "Vanished?"

"Uh-huh," the puny proxy confirmed. "Some of us were following him, when he taked this bitty bottle from his robe and smashed with pink stick. Then, poof!"

"Poof?" Tiptin was confused.

"Bottle makes big puff like blue skysheep. Then, when skysheep drifts away, funny folk is gone? See where his stepmarks stop."

"Maybe he floated away, too?" suggested The Sheebazz.

Shoenia was skeptical as her seers traced the trail of fresh sandal dents across the sand. "Maybe?"

"Where are you going?" Tiptin inquired, clutching her arm.

She yanked free of his grip. "To follow those stepmarks."

"Shoenia, it's too dangerous," The Sheebazz noted with great concern.

"He might know we're here?" Pint Little pointed out.

Shoenia stared serious at her wee friends. "Destiny and Rimp would never have taken us this far to abandon us now. Either Destiny is with us, or it is not. So whatever must be will be. Besides, if Zebu does know we're about, I'm certainly no safer over here than over there. And neither are any of you."

Tiptin knew she was right. Destiny, as always, was any being's only hope for defeating Fear. Who else could have brought them all together and then protected them throughout so much? The ladfolk realized that he alone could never have done the things he had done to get this far. Something far superior was helping him. He examined the pulsing sword that he had been gifted from Spidey Smeals. Surely the arachnid had reason for trusting him with such a critical task?

Thwack likewise absorbed the meaning of Shoenia's words. He himself had often begged of Destiny to grant him just one friend, and the generous deity had instead delivered many of the very best. Who was he to turn his back on those who cared so much?

"I'm in!" Tiptin exclaimed.

Thwack brandished a fist big as a boulder. **"AAAAAAAAARRGH!!!"** Let's maul a magician!"

Both smuzzles nattered and traded punches with the breeze.

"**Yeah!** *Stickem! Stickem! Stickem! Stickem!*"

Now all seers settled on the bullybeasts, who trembled and looked away in shame.

"It's okay to be frightened," Shoenia assured them, herself stepping free of the foliage. "I still love you."

Tiptin, Thwack and the smuzzles all stepped from glen to beach, while an army of thorn-wielding flyfolk took to the sky.

"Dooz we spozed dooz?" one bullybeast inquired of Shmash.

"We dooz hides?" another asked of Belch.

Shmash and Belch exchanged confused looks, each expecting the other to take charge. Neither would.

However, a most unlikely bullybeast did. "Me nod dooz bad things no more! Me helps Shoenia fites magic meeny!"

All the other bullybeasts stared with swung jowls as one of their own snatched up a rock and knuckled out onto the sand. "Nod more snitches! Nod more fibs too! And ye nod more dooz zings me!"

"Taddler beez boink," remarked one of the bullybeasts.

"Too much hard hurts noogies," concluded another.

Most nodded in agreement, but not all.

"Me beez boink too!" Shmash announced, knuckling out after Taddler.

"Me too!" Belch declared, busting off a thick chunk of bough. "Me conks magic meeny kookoo cuzz him burns me broz butt!"

"Duh – hurts seers too!" Braindolt put in, also busting off a thick chunk of bough.

Next, all the bullybeasts began snatching up rocks or busting off boughs. Then they too knuckled out onto the sand.

"They're actually coming," Thwack remarked in total surprise.

Shoenia smiled. "I never doubted them for a..." she began as they neared the end of the stepmarks. But then a sense of movement beneath her feet chopped short her words.

Suddenly, the very beach shifted its plain, knocking all from feet and knuckles. In sheer panic, the sprawling bullybeasts groped at the wind. The frightened humanfolk clung together for balance, while the smuzzles bounced about like furry balls with seers. Thwack dropped to his knees and dug in his claws to keep from sliding into the sea.

"Shoenia!" Mite Diver screamed in horror, pointing with both hands. "Look!"

Shoenia had felt the gasping grip of uncertain fear during the initial tremors, but now the grip tightened into a grasp of sheer terror she'd known only once before. When bound by a root in The Fluorescent Forest.

A muddy form whirled free from the splitting surface and on up into the breeze. It spun sand from its garments, spraying the stinging particles into the seers of all who viewed it.

"You little fool!" Zebu berated, ceasing to spin. He glared directly at Shoenia and brandished the staff. "Did you really consider yourself to be any match for me?"

Shoenia desperately sought to recall Rimp's riddle, but her terrified mind thought forth blanks.

Settling himself down upon a beach slab, the magician simply nodded to end the quake. Then, with a gloating grin, he produced his wand and waved it at the charging cyclops.

"Tooooooooo much!" Thwack yelled as his huge form was lifted clear of the plain and rotated heels atop hearers. Then the cyclops began to agitate up and down, pounding his shiny dome repeatedly upon the sand. "S-S-t-t-o-o-o-p-p-I-I-t-t-t-t….."He pleaded to no avail.

"Stickem! Stickem! Stickem! Stickem!" tenored a dark mass as it bore down upon the funny folk.

Widening his evil gloatgrin, Zebu began sucking wind until his torso bulged near to burst. Then, with puckered lips, he blew forth an awesome gale that launched the wee warriors reeling from sight and scattered them amongst the distant trees.

"Dung!" Shoenia cussed. "I can't recall Rimp's riddle. Destiny, help me!"

"Destiny can't help you, you little fool! For it is I who wield the staff!"

"KAAPPOW!!" A blue beam shot forth from the weapon's tip. It blasted Tiptin's sword from his hand, searing his digits. He rolled and writhed and moaned in agony.

"Aha!" spat the magician, redirecting his weapon at the cowering smuzzles. "So, Shoenia of Ga, where was your trusty Destiny just now?"

"No!" Shoenia screamed, springing afoot and charging at Zebu with her fists balled to slug. Sparks spit from her enraged seers. "You demented traitor! I'll...."

"You'll meet Morgue!" he shrieked.

"KAAPPOW!!"

Upon impact, the beam of searing, blue light tore a gaping rift in the beach and sent its young victim hurling upon the breeze. She came down hard, sprawling for many strides across the gritty sand. Finally, her form slid to a halt in a still and silent lump.

Zebu was curious about the beam bending to strike the sand between her feet, for it had always shot straight before. But no matter, its purpose had been fulfilled. The little fool was silenced. And soon the increeping tides would dispose of her body forever!

Now the magician turned his attention to the bullybeasts, who cowed in a state like they'd never known. They huddled ashiver, with fur all afluff. Zebu noted their fear with great satisfaction as he launched into his tirade of new rules for the realm:

" I am the baddest brute there is,

The meanest there ever shall be,

If it's trouble you seek, ye dolts,

You'll do well by messin' with me,

"Now listen up, my servants new,

Because this is how it's gonna be!"

The bullybeasts all hung their heads as 'Mastoor Zebu' belted out his new rules. Each was overwhelmed with grief at the loss of the very first being who had ever shown them any real *'erspect'*. Wet flooded down their cheeks and seeped between their quivering lips.

".... no more having friends,

no more being nice,

no more desserts...."

"Shoenia?" Pint Little whispered, herself having eluded Zebu's gust by hiding behind Thwack. "Shoenia, please unnap. Shoenia?"

With wet seers, the puny weetyke struggled to revive the still galfolk. First, she raised each of Shoenia's lids, and then slapped her cold cheeks. Then she tried pleading and shaking and pummeling upon the brow. She prayed and begged of Destiny to unnap her friend; even promising to apologize to Mite Diver for the time she covered his slumbering form with bumblesweet and pink petals.

Yet all her efforts seemed in vain. Overcome with grief, the sad flyfolk curled up in her motionless friend's hair and wept.

Next, the smuzzles tried to revive the galfolk. They carefully pawed her still form, whimpering as they licked her cold cheeks. Likewise, to no avail.

Then the miracle Pint Little had begged for happened. Unseen voices whispered upon a warming wind. Destiny's breath had come to revive its chosen one. *"In the proper place, at the proper time, you shall know to do the proper thing.* Awaken, Shoenia of Ga."

"Uhhhh…" moaned the lump, parting its lips in breath.

"Shhhhh," Pint Little whispered directly into her friend's hearer. "Or Zebu shall discover you've escaped Morgue."

Both smuzzles licked her warm cheeks.

Nearby, the magic meeny kept adding to his list of rules:

"…. no more laughing,

no more singing,

no more fun...."

Shoenia blinked her seers and shook the blur from her mind. "Shhhh," she cautioned as she sighted on Zebu. His back was to her!

".... no more swimming,

no more playing games..."

Shoenia's mind became strangely cleared and she recalled Rimp's riddle.

"WHEN NEXT YOU MEET UPON A SHORE,

HOW SHALL FLAMES LICK CLOTH NO MORE?"

Kissing a pointdigit to stress quiet, Shoenia smiled. At last, she understood what Rimp's words meant.

".... no more being happy,

no more joy,

and absolutely no more knuckle noogies!"

Most of the bullybeasts wailed aloud upon hearing the final rule. But not Shmash. Having noticed Shoenia crawling towards the unsuspecting magician, the smartest bullybeast's mind struggled for a way to keep the unwary 'dungskulz' from noticing her. "Pzzzzzzzt"

"Huh?" Belch turned towards Shmash, who used his seers to motion behind Zebu.

"We got helps Shoenia," Shmash whispered.

Belch nodded and began waving his arms to draw Zebu's attention onto himself.

"You there!" growled the irate magician, sighting upon the flailing bullybeast. "Why are you acting weird? Well, speak up!"

"Uh-uh-uh…?"

Thinking quickly, Shmash tactfully jumped in. "We gots questions."

"Questions? Questions! I think the situation is perfectly clear! I'm now your new master and you are all still dirt!"

"Ah – buts we beez dense dirt," Taddler injected, also noticing Shoenia. "We needs things sez much so get."

"Dooz," Braindolt 'threed' it. "Cuzz we beez dense dirt!"

Zebu rolled his odd seers. "Alright, I'll say it all just one more time! Now listen!"

By now, every single bullybeast had clued in to what was really going on. So each nodded and hung his licker out to look extra dense in order to help out.

Even the cruel critters played along. They wrapped their lickers about their own snouts, and crossed their yellow peepers.

"Okay – no more having friends,

no more being nice,

no more desserts …."

Sneaking within easy reach of her babbling target, Shoenia carefully retrieved the flint and striker from her skirt pouch. Both hands trembled and her pumper pounded, yet she knew that Destiny was within her. Its warm energy cooled her fright.

She fumbled with both items, trying to strike the flint gently to negate sound. Yet not enough spark was produced. Panic crept into her mind. If she struck any harder, Zebu would surely hear her. What to do?

Destiny errors not in its choices, however, and Thwack, too, still had his role to play in this drama. One for which the big guy was most suited.

"HARR!! HARR!! HARR!! HARR!!" roared the downside-up cyclops, who by now had poundpacked the sand so that his dome no longer touched. He winked at Shoenia. "Hey, Zebubblebrain – is that a pointy cap, or did ya just paint yer head? **HARR!! HARR!! HARR!! HARR!!"**

Zebu was flabbergasted. "How dare you address me like that!"

"HARR!! HARR!! HARR!! HARR!! Hey, spearhead! What do you call that scent you're wearing – Essence of Swamp? **HARR!! HARR!! HARR!! HARR!!"**

Now the bullybeasts launched into laughter.

"Hey, where'd ya get them crazy seers? Did the fiendish finners have a parts sale? **HARR!! HARR!! HARR!! HARR!!"**

Hysterics ruled the beach. Even Shoenia almost lost it.

"And catch a whiff of those feet! Whew. Should be more careful where ya step! Mooooo! **HARR!! HARR!! HARR!! HARR!! HARR!!"**

"Why you!" The beyond livid magician pointed his weapon to blast. "I'll burn you into dust, you insolent…? Huh? What's that awful smell? Snff. Snff. Something's burning…HEY!!"

Zebu began frantically slapping at the flames, which eagerly licked all about the hem of his robe. But the breeze from his swats merely fed the famished flames to grow and climb higher, until the panicking magician was left with only one option.

"Yeeeeeooowww!!" he screamed as he sprinted headlong for the drink.

"HARR!! HARR!! HARR!! Are those streamers, or did yer skull sprout roots! **"HARR!! HARR!! HARR!! HARR!! HARR!! HARR!!"**

Holding the staff high atop his head, Zebu waded in up to his chest. Next, having doused the scorching orange spears, he turned and fisted vengeance at all.

Then suddenly, directed by Destiny's breath, a monster wetroller reached up from the deep and curled him under.

Frantically, the drowning magician foolishly fought to keep hold of his precious staff while struggling for the surface; and for breath. But before the submerged 'fool' could recover, the retreating surf sucked him out into the sea's chilly depths, where a waiting black spouter with mean, red seers swallowed him whole. And the staff became unpowered.

"HOORRAY!!!" the bullybeasts all cheered and granted each other congratulatory blissnoogies, as well as 'hugz' and 'taglez'. One unusually skinny bullybeast even offered out kisses.

Thwack tumbled to the sand, and the smuzzles waltzed and whirled about the beach. Pint Little blushed as Shoenia and Tiptin locked lips for a major 'smoocheroozy'. Plus the rest of the weetykes, now regrouped and rearmed, swarmbombed to boogie!

Then, without warning, the solemn whooping of metallic wings ended the fun. All seers stared up in shock as a gold and silver beast descended upon them. Aboard its back rode a glumdreary lunatic.

Xebec gripped tight the Webscrolls as he leapt from his mount, already shouting commands at the bullybeasts. "Seize them all! NOW!!"

Every single bullybeast glanced about in confusion, entirely uncertain of what to do next.

Burning crimson with delirium and rage, the dim sorcerer began scolding his boobs. And worse. "I said seize them, you boneskulls! Now, you moronic losers! What are you waiting for! Move your lazy butts, you boobs! I said now, dungit!"

"Remember who is saying the mean names!" an irate galfolk reminded her bulky friends. "And you don't have to be anybody's boobs anymore!"

"*Stickem! Stickem! Stickem! Stickem!* Reeeeeeeeeeallly *Stickem!!*"

The psycho sorcerer swatted and cussed at the tiny pests who stuck sharp thorns in his flesh. While performing a vibrant version of the 'Ouchow Hop', he failed to note the burly mob knuckling across the beach towards him. Until it was simply 'tooooooooo' late!

"Stop it!" Xebec commanded, as hordes of hairy hands clutched hold of his robe. Then they whisked his frail frame clear off the ground, shaking the Webscrolls free from his grip. "Put me down! I said, put me down!"

"Dooz him hard hurts noogies!" shouted a voice from the bunch.

"HARD HURTS NOOGIES!! HARD HURTS NOOGIES!! HARD HURTS NOOGIES!!" chanted the others. **"Noogie! Noogie! Noogie! Noogie! Noogie!"**

"Griffin!" Xebec screamed, in both fear and anger. "GRIFFIN!!"

Baring its sharp talons, the metallic beast flapped aloft. Next, with its jagged beak parted to rip, it descended upon its creator's burly tormentors.

"Oh no you don't!" Tiptin shouted, snatching his mangled sword from the sand. Spinning his body around to increase the force, the ladfolk hurled the fibered weapon with all his might.

"EEEEEEEEEEEEEEE!!!" squealed the great griffin as the shimmering blade burned through its armor. It immediately crashed down upon the beach, where it quickly molted into a messy mound of metal mush.

The fibered blade, its final task completed, shimmered beyond bright as it breathed its final farewell. Then its shine was snuffed, and it wilted to meet Morgue.

"Farewell," Tiptin acknowledged, offering his parting friend a wave.

"Dooz nasty knocks noogies!"

"NASTY KNOCKS NOOGIES!! NASTY KNOCKS NOOGIES!! NASTY KNOCKS....."

"NOOOOOOOOOOOOOOOOOOOOOOOOOOOOO000 00..............."

"Noogie! Noogie! Noogie! Noogie!" chanted the hairy mob while they knuckled Xebec's skull a deep blue. **"Noogie! Noogie! Noogie! Noogie! Noogie!"**

"Dooz zings in sea!" Shmash suggested.

"Zings in sea! Zings in sea! Zings in sea!"

Shmash and Belch tore the screaming sorcerer away from the others, and then started swinging him to and fro.

"We zings beez five!" Shmash instructed.

Belch nodded. "Zings beez five!"

"One – uh – four- seven- uh - ??? Dooz beez next?"

"Nod cares!" Taddler piped up with enthusiasm. "Dooz zings anyways!"

"We zings on zings!"

Now every bullybeast helped out with the count. **"Swingz! Swingz! Swingz! ZINGS!!"**

"NOOOOOOOOOOOOOOOOOOOOOOOooooo……… ………" A frail figure flailed frantically as it flew through the sky, before eventually plunging deep beneath the giant wetrollers.

Cheers resounded all across the shore as the joyous bullybeasts rewarded themselves with some super-serious knuckle noogies. Then the entire bunch called a secret huddle.

Finally, after reaching some sort of agreement, they knuckled across the sand and lined up before Shoenia.

Shmash explained. "We dooz makes ye 'fishal' bullybeast budz."

Shoenia was choked with emotion. "I'm – I'm honored to be an official bullybeast 'budz'. You know, you're really all kinda cute."

The bullybeasts all blushed. "Nod beez."

"No, really Pixx. And The Sheebazz has kindly offered to let some of her weetykes remain here awhile to learn you how to read and write."

"Dooz lern counts too?" one bullybeast inquired with pleading seers.

"And counting too," Shoenia assured him.

"Dancing too? Bullies lern dancing?"

Shoenia smiled. Sure, and dancing too."

Belch bore moist cheeks. "Dooz cum sees bullies, Shoenia. Ye stop us beez schoded. An worze."

"Pleeeeeeeeeeeze!" begged the others.

Then the dam burst and the overwhelmed galfolk began to weep openly. "I would like that, except I dwell very far from here. But I shall always carry a part of you bullybeasts right here inside of me." She palmed her chest.

First, the bullybeasts hung their heads in sorrow. Then, one by one, they filed past their only ever 'fishal' bullybeast budz. Each bid her goodbye with a tender luvs noogie, that didn't bruise her skull one bit.

"See!" Taddler suddenly shouted, pointing slightly past the shore. "Xebec dooz swims to beech!"

Tucking Spidey's Webscrolls under one arm, Tiptin smiled and warmly embraced Shoenia with the other. "First we must return these Webscrolls to Spidey Smeals. After that, I go wherever you go – me 'fishal' best budz."

"I love you, Tiptin," she replied, removing his arm. She studied his burnt digits. "Too bad I am without the stalkhollow. Titanroot sap would sooth the pain."

"Seeing your face soothes my pain," he remarked, drawing her form tight against his and sealing her lips with his own.

"HARR!!" Thwack interrupted, pointing past them. "HARR!! HARR!! HARR!! HARR!! HARR!!"

Both turned about and giggled as they witnessed a sopping sorcerer sprinting along the shore, mere strides ahead of a herd of huge, hairy beasts. Each of which armswung upon extremely hard knuckles, and shouted, **"NOOGIE!! NOOGIE!! NOOGIE!! NOOGIE!! NOOGIE!! NOOGIE!!"**

DOOZ BEEZ END!!!!

Taleteller's Farewell

"Hi! Hi! Hi! Hize! Beez me! Dooz so! Ha! Doncha just love them bullybeasts? Dem beez so plite. And believe you me; they're even more lovable in the hairy flesh.

"You know, they've really come a long way throughout the eons. I understand that some of Shmash's scions recently obtained degrees from The Ezu School of Higher Learning. In physics! Of course, if you buy that, then perhaps I could interest you in purchasing one slightly abused planet? Has a few holes in its ozone, but nothing that can't be repaired in time after its current inhabitants are all fried. Lots and lots and lots and lots of time.

"What? You already have one? So sorry. I shan't burden you with another then. Or should I say, I shant burden another with you. Uh-uh. Noper. No way. Not a chance. Not with such a big mess of your own making to clean up. After all, whoever makes a mess should clean it up. Should too. Should so. For certain. For sure. You betcha.

"OOOps! I am straying off topic. Where was I? Oh, yes. Yes, yes, yes, yes. So now the bullybeasts are off to school. Gee, this should be interesting? Talk about your teacher burnout.

Count to ten in twelve easy grades. Whew. Scary stuff. But one thing's for sure. I'd trust any tot into the care of any bullybeast long before I'd put them into the care of some of your so-called 'intellectuals'. That burly bunch sure 'lerned' me a few things about 'erspect'. And manners, too.

"Plus, they ignited their intellect when it mattered most. Did so. Did too. For certain. For sure. Even if the magic 'meeny' has survived, would you fear any magician who'd been duped by a bunch of bullybeasts? Ha! Bet ole Zebu wouldn't be bragging about that at too many Wizard Musters. And imagine being swallowed whole by a black spouter? Gulp. Gulp. Gulp. Gulp. BURP! Geeeeross!

"The Sheebazz and her army actually became quite fond of their eager students, even teaching the burly bunch how to sort-of-dance. Knucklebopping at its beast! Ha! Hmmmmm? While Hoot and Hweet Beaker just carried on being themselves.

"Soon the bullybeasts became most welcome wherever they went; even in Cycity and Folkton. 'Not overly bright,' other beings would note, 'but most polite and kind, especially to the little ones.' They were always eager to share of their nice nohurts noogies, and sometimes even hugz and taglez.

"Then we have the glumdreary sorcerer. Completely washed up. Ha! A looney without a bin! Ha! But with many headaches. Many, many headaches. And we're talkin' screamin' skullbangers, here! Ha! Ha! Hee. Hee. Ho! Ho! HA! Hee. HO!!

"Nix the staff. Scratch the griffin. Kiss the Webscrolls goodbye. Castle torched. Zero friends. No boobs to do his bidding. Sub-zilch 'erspect'. Not a single possession. Gone completely 'round the twist'. All in all, not a very happy 'loozer'.

"Thwack – well, what can I tell ya! **HARR!!** The big guy finally did meet that special cygal, then discovered that whatever we give, in time we shall get. Yep, when they first met, Hoaxy sure tripped him off his feet. Literally. Yes, we're talking one faaaaaaaaar out gal here! **"HONK!! HONK!! HONK!! HONK!!"**

"Lastly, Tiptin, Shoenia and the smuzzles did eventually make it back to The Divided Continent, to discover that the war was still raging – as wars are prone to do. Yet, eventually, the senseless slaughter did end. I'd say thank Destiny. But if you mortals would be content to walk with Destiny in the first place, then there wouldn't be wars that need to end in the first place.

"So the young lovers managed to stay together until their time to meet Morgue. And although neither ever made it back to the Land Of Ranidae, they forever carried a warm feeling for all their friends, both huge and tiny, deep within the pulp of their precious pumpers.

"Anyway - I gotta go, do too, do so,

It's time to leave, I gotta blow,

On to where, I do not know?

Yet time has come for me to go,

"Got things to see, places to be,

New adventures beckon me,

So now I'm off, I'm on my way,

But to where, I cannot say,

"So, until we meet again, if ever,

May Destiny feed and shelter you,

And keep you safe,

And bless you with a precious pumper.

"Fare ye most well, my special Earthkind friend –

"FAREWELLLL.......................*"

Deron Rennick

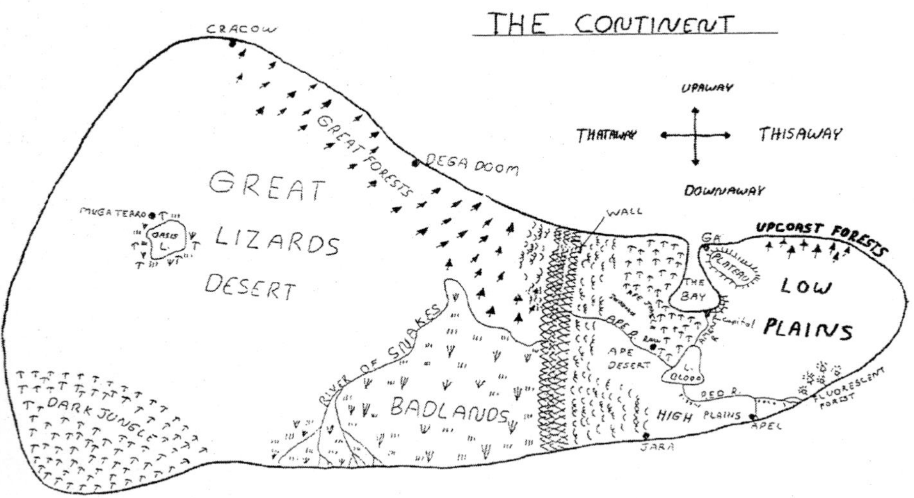

UPAWAY

THATAWAY THISAWAY

DOWNAWAY

– THE CONTINENT (DIVIDED)

ORANGE ISLAND

SALINE SEA

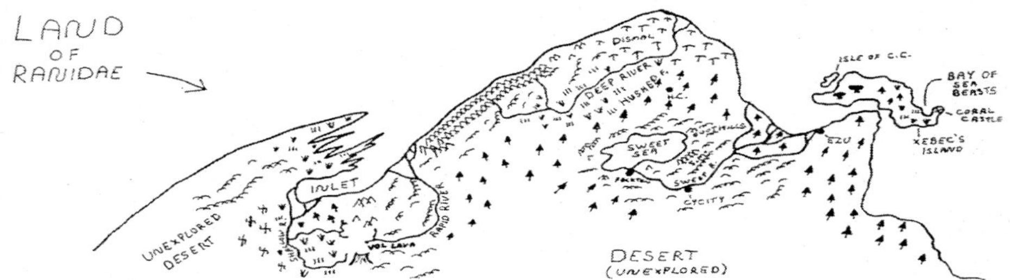